Readers love
JOHN INMAN

The Hike

"*The Hike* is one of my favorite stories of the year so far."
—Joyfully Jay

"John Inman might just be at the top of my 'must read' list of authors."
—Love Bytes

Love Wanted

"This book simply blew me away. The writing and storytelling were outstanding, and I couldn't take my eyes off it once I started."
—OptimuMM

"*Love Wanted* is a superbly written story and left me happy and smiling, wishing for more. Always a good sign of a book worth reading."
—The Novel Approach

My Dragon, My Knight

"If you're a fan of well-written suspense, don't mind a bit of bloodshed and love a heart stopping, edge of your seat climax where you're cheering for the villain to get what's coming, this is one book you'll want to pick up."
—Sinfully: Gay Romance Book Reviews

"It was definitely a very emotional book but so very good at the same time."
—Gay Book Reviews

By JOHN INMAN

Acting Up
Chasing the Swallows
A Hard Winter Rain
Head-on
The Hike
Hobbled
Jasper's Mountain
Laugh Cry Repeat
Love Wanted
Loving Hector
My Busboy
My Dragon, My Knight
Paulie
Payback
The Poodle Apocalypse
Scrudge & Barley, Inc.
Shy
Spirit
Sunset Lake
Two Pet Dicks

THE BELLADONNA ARMS
Serenading Stanley
Work in Progress
Coming Back
Ben and Shiloh

Published by DREAMSPINNER PRESS
www.dreamspinnerpress.com

LAUGH CRY *Repeat*

JOHN INMAN

DREAMSPINNER PRESS

Published by
Dreamspinner Press

5032 Capital Circle SW, Suite 2, PMB# 279, Tallahassee, FL 32305-7886 USA
www.dreamspinnerpress.com

Laugh Cry Repeat
© 2017 John Inman.

Cover Art
© 2017 Reese Dante.
http://www.reesedante.com
Cover content is for illustrative purposes only and any person depicted on the cover is a model.

ISBN: 978-1-63533-633-7
Digital ISBN: 978-1-63533-634-4
Library of Congress Control Number: 2017910299
Published December 2017
v. 1.0

Printed in the United States of America

This paper meets the requirements of
ANSI/NISO Z39.48-1992 (Permanence of Paper).

CHAPTER ONE

WYETH BECKER peeled his nose off the computer screen and faced a lady of indeterminate age and questionable fashion skills. She wore flowered pajamas under a pink overcoat and had bright red galoshes on her feet. It was ninety degrees and sunny outside. Her blue-and-pink hair lay severely bobby-pinned in tight little pin curls beneath a clear plastic shower cap. The top of her head looked like a bowl of Froot Loops covered with Saran wrap.

Wyeth blinked. "May I help you, ma'am?"

"François Rabelais. Where is he?"

"Entombed in Paris, I'm afraid."

"Oh, he's dead, then."

"Well, *he* preferred to call death the Great Perhaps."

"But his books. Where can I find his books? I hear he tells a bawdy tale."

Wyeth finally smiled. He loved readers. Even the weird ones. "He does indeed. You'll find him in the Renaissance section, second floor, east end of aisle three just past the water fountain."

"Thank you." The woman hesitated for a moment while scratching her head, which made the plastic shower cap crinkle loudly, drawing everyone's attention within a thirty-foot radius. "I say, are you *sure* he's dead?"

"He's been encased in marble for five hundred years. If he wasn't dead when he went in, he most certainly is now."

"Poor man. I suppose you're right."

"Yes, indeedy."

"Well, thank you, honey."

"You're quite welcome, ma'am."

Wyeth was still smiling when the old lady shuffled off across the library floor, her oversized galoshes flapping, the little metal buckles tinkling merrily, craning her neck left and right looking for the stairs. He noticed one of her pin curls had sprung loose at the back of her head and leaked out of the shower cap. It spiraled down across her back, bouncing around like one of those trick snakes that fly out of a can when you open it.

Wyeth gave his head a teeny shake of wonder and reapplied his nose to the computer screen.

He was in the process of inventorying self-helps and how-tos. The San Diego Public Library had recently moved into new quarters—a gorgeous rotunda with a courtyard cafe, a vast auditorium, a gymnasium-sized reading room, a charter high school tucked safely on the premises, and over one million books available for public consumption. At least 999,000 of those books were how-tos, or so it seemed. Wyeth had never been so bored in his life. For a librarian, that's saying a lot.

He checked his wristwatch for the hundredth time that morning and finally breathed a sigh of relief when he saw that both the hour and minute hands had finally crawled their way up to twelve and bumped heads. Thank God. Wyeth logged off the computer, saving his data first, and then struck out across the library floor toward the employees' lounge in the back. There he opened his locker, removed his tie and dress shirt, and hung them neatly inside. After donning a dry-wiking T-shirt and spreading a layer of sun block over his freckled arms, neck, and face, he toed his way out of his dress shoes and slipped his feet into a pair of Asics walking shoes, taking extra precautions to lace them neatly and securely. He pulled a copy of the latest Dan Brown thriller off the little shelf above his head, stuffed an energy bar in his back pocket, reclosed the locker door, and carefully twirled the combination lock that secured his belongings inside. Waving shyly to the handful of coworkers sipping coffee and gossiping in the employees' lounge, he headed out the back door and into the scorching San Diego heat. By the time he stood outside, he was already engrossed in the book.

Not really watching where he was going—he did, after all, walk these streets every single day of his life—he took a left at the next corner and, still reading, strode a few blocks farther on. Ducking into the air-conditioned lobby of a four-story apartment building at the corner of Ninth and Island, he finally closed the book while waiting for the elevator to take him up to his third-floor apartment.

From the other side of the door marked 3C came a scratching and clamoring, and when Wyeth unlocked the door, out sprang Chaucer, his black-and-white, wiry-haired mutt. Wyeth called him his mutt because that's what he was. A mutt, rescued from the Humane Society two years prior. It was without a doubt the best thing Wyeth had ever done for himself—*or* the dog. It had been love at first sight when they spotted each other through the chain-link fence in the Society's display room, and their love had only grown during the time they had spent together since. While Wyeth had been unable to teach Chaucer a single trick—*not one*—neither dog nor man minded much. Everybody can't be a genius. And to prove it, right now Chaucer was dancing around Wyeth's feet with his leash in his mouth, tangling the leash around all six of their ankles, hobbling them both. Neither dog nor man minded that much either, since Chaucer did the same thing almost every single day.

Since Chaucer knew the lunchtime drill as well as his master did, he occupied his time licking Wyeth's face while Wyeth knelt down to free the tangled leash from around their ankles. Eventually Wyeth managed to clip the leash to Chaucer's collar, where it belonged. Without further ado, he relocked his apartment door and hustled back to the still-open elevator, this time with Chaucer romping happily at his side. A moment later, they threw themselves through the apartment building's front door and flung themselves onto the street outside. When the air hit them, it was so hot it was like opening the oven door to check on a Thanksgiving turkey.

Trying to ignore the heat, both man and dog, knowing they were free, at least for an hour, took off with eager strides, heading for the bayfront less than half a mile away. As they strolled side by side, Wyeth kept his nose in his book while Chaucer sniffed excitedly at every human leg, dog's ass, parking meter, and mysterious pile of disgusting crap he could find along the way.

At intervals, Wyeth took his nose out of the book long enough to dodge a speeding city bus or avoid being flattened by a marauding garbage truck. He also caught occasional glimpses of himself in passing storefront windows. What he saw neither pleased or displeased him. He was who he was. A somber, twenty-nine-year-old, red-haired librarian, slight of frame, pale-skinned, lightly freckled, with good teeth and blue eyes. Those eyes were only partially hidden by the black-framed glasses he had been wearing since his freshman year in high school. His ears were small and nicely tucked in, and his arms and the back of his hands were brushed with blond hair. His red locks were, at the moment, in dire need of a cut and waving all over his head in the breeze coming in off the bay. Wyeth's waist was a twenty-nine-incher and he wore size nine shoes.

He was also gay. Not that it made much of a difference in his life, for Wyeth was also a loner. He enjoyed his books, his dog, the library where he worked, and silence. In truth, what librarian *doesn't* like silence?

While it was true that Wyeth was a little shy, or perhaps *reserved* is a better word, it should never be assumed he hadn't partaken of a few affairs of the heart in his day. Well, not affairs of the heart, perhaps, but most certainly affairs of the *flesh*. He did, after all, enjoy sex as much as the next man. It's just that he probably didn't partake of it as *often* as the next man, in which his shy, quiet, *reserved* lifestyle most certainly played a part. After all, it's not like he was ugly or anything. Just *quiet*. He wasn't born *without* a slut gene exactly, and it certainly wasn't *recessive*. He just didn't drag it out and put it to work as often as some.

At the time of our story, Wyeth had been without a love—or even a *sex*—interest for three or four months, thanks to the last man he had grown close to having turned out to be a real dick—and not in the good sense of the word. The truth was, the man had broken Wyeth's heart, or if not broken it, at least bent it into new and painful shapes. The last thing Wyeth wanted was to go through that again. Not for a while anyway. No, his heart and libido were on hiatus, and he intended to keep them that way for a while.

This was not the first hiatus Wyeth had inflicted upon himself. It was, however, the first time he had noticed a crusty shell growing around himself while he was on one. He was not as kind as he used to be, he noticed now and then, and that troubled him a bit. But still, one has to protect oneself. If withdrawing into oneself like a turtle was the only way to accomplish that, then so be it. He would worry about turning into a cranky old man later. For the moment, he just didn't want to be hurt anymore, and not letting anyone in was the easiest way to make that happen.

So he focused on his work, his dog, his little apartment. He stayed detached from the world around him. And one day he would maybe rejoin the human race. But to paraphrase Viggo Mortensen, the hunky Aragorn in *Lord of the Rings*, "it would not be this day."

Or so Wyeth thought.

He stopped at the last traffic light before crossing the busy intersection into Seaport Village, a cobblestoned hive of touristy high-end shops and restaurants with a beautiful antique carousel twirling out front. Seaport Village was perched on the very brink of the San Diego Bay and being situated directly on the water, was Wyeth's best shot at catching a cool breeze on this humid summer day.

While he waited for the light to change, Chaucer humped Wyeth's leg. Chaucer's slut gene wasn't recessive either.

The light finally flipped from red to green, and man and dog set off in search of a shady spot by the water's edge where they could watch the ships thrum in and out of the harbor. There, Wyeth could enjoy his power bar and maybe read a little more, and Chaucer could exercise his humping skills on any passing dog who might be similarly inclined. They found an empty bench beneath a flowing pepper tree in front of a tiny fake lagoon with ducks and koi swimming around.

Together Wyeth and Chaucer settled in to while away their lunch hour in peace and seclusion, just the way they liked it.

Neither man nor dog had the vaguest notion their lives were about to change. But then we never really do, do we?

DARRYL ZACHARY Long, or Deeze as he preferred to be called, raced past the top-hatted doorman in front of the US Grant Hotel on Broadway and Fourth. He smiled to himself when he saw the doorman stare at him as if he couldn't believe anyone would be dumb enough to run in this heat unless he had snatched a purse or something. Clearly, for the doorman, even his own top hat was a trial to put up with on a day such as this, since beads of sweat were rolling down either side of the poor man's face, and he had that bug-eyed look of numbed surprise a lobster gets when it's tossed into a pan of boiling water.

Deeze pitied the poor doorman immensely, standing there with his pot belly and clearly sedentary lifestyle, a pack of cigarettes peeking out of his vest pocket and his arteries probably clogged up from a poor diet and little exercise. Deeze was tempted, in fact, to tell the unfortunate doorman to pull that silly hat off his head and run around the block a couple of times, but of course he didn't. Even Deeze knew that nobody hates an exercise fanatic more than the guy who sits on his ass all day eating Cheetos.

What Deeze also knew, and so many others didn't, was that running, even in ninety-degree heat, produced a refreshing breeze flowing over your body. Not only that, but running on a hot day also produced sweat, and sweat cooled the skin. The faster he ran, the harder the wind whipped past, the more he perspired, and the cooler he got. Elementary, really. Until, of course, one keeled over from a heat stroke. A good runner simply has to know when to pull the plug before the heat stroke kicks in.

The echoing clap of his running shoes smacking the sidewalk and ricocheting off the surrounding high-rises was a familiar sound to Deeze. He lived downtown, after all. This was where he did most of his running. He knew every curb, every loose sewer grate, every uneven sidewalk, and every pothole that could trip up a runner. He even knew which traffic lights to avoid, since some were so much longer than others. Nothing is worse than being really in the groove—every muscle finely tuned and perfectly calibrated for forward momentum, the synapses firing, the body exquisitely limber, the lungs and heart efficiently pumping and pounding like a bellows—and then finding oneself suddenly forced to dawdle at a street corner, waiting for a stupid traffic light to piddle around for three excruciating minutes before finally turning green. While one waited, of course, one's muscles froze up, one lost his rhythm, a cramp started in a hamstring, one looked down to see that one's shoe was untied, and one suddenly needed to pee.

Deeze Long was a month and a half into his thirty-first year on the planet. He taught preschool at a Catholic elementary school—St. Luke's to be exact, a mile or so up Fifth Avenue from downtown. He also attended night school three evenings a week at City College, working toward an associate's degree in exercise science, hoping one day to augment his day job by becoming either a part-time fitness specialist or a sports injury therapist. He wasn't sure which.

At the moment, while he was clomping along Kettner Boulevard, headed for Seaport Village and trying to sip from his water bottle at the same time without knocking his front teeth out—it really was a hot day!—Deeze was quizzing himself on kinesiology. He had a quiz coming up in a couple of days that would account for 10 percent of his final grade.

Deeze wore his dark hair in an explosion of curls, which managed to look both trendy and unkempt, and incidentally showed off his high cheekbones and the clean, crisp lines of a Dick Tracy jawline. He stood six feet tall, had large expressive hands, size twelve feet, and biceps that rolled around at the top of his arms like croquet balls. His eyes were brown, his eyelashes curly, his skin tone olive, his well-muscled legs hairy and long in his little mauve running shorts, and at the top of his running shirt, a sprinkling of dark chest hair could be spotted at the base of his throat, peeking out into the noontime sun. To say Deeze was handsome would have been understating the facts considerably.

Deeze Long was not only handsome, he was damn near perfect. The only one who didn't know it was Deeze. Which, of course, made him *more* handsome.

As any frustrated woman in the world would be apt to tell you, a specimen as perfect as Deeze would almost have to be gay. And she would be right. He was indeed gay. Just her luck.

Deeze had been seeing someone for a couple of months, but it wasn't working out. Not for Deeze at any rate. The guy was so clearly enamored of Deeze's body that Deeze was pretty sure he didn't care about Deeze's mind at all. For a one-nighter, that wouldn't be a problem. For an extended dating experience, it was not to Deeze's liking at all. Plus the guy wasn't a runner. It was shallow, he knew, but Deeze didn't completely trust anyone, man or woman, who wasn't a runner or at least didn't hit the gym on a regular basis. Barring old age or quadriplegia, he simply could not understand how anyone could spend their days sitting on their ass. The final nail in the coffin of Deeze's latest relationship was that the guy clearly wasn't fond of kids, while Deeze thought kids were the greatest thing since peanut butter and jelly sandwiches.

But back to running.

To Deeze, movement was life. As long as he could run, he was happy. He didn't mind going home to an empty apartment. He didn't mind sleeping in a queen-size bed that was cool and empty on one side while he lolled around all alone on the other. He didn't miss romance at all. He had his job, his night school, his running. That was all he needed. All he cared about.

Or so he continually told himself. Even today. Even as he jogged past the harbor tour boats packed with laughing sunburned tourists, even while he breathed in the oceany scent of the fishy waters of San Diego Bay and listened to the mellow sound of gentle waves lapping at his feet as he ran past. This was what made him happy. The freedom to run. If it was such an ordeal for love to find its way to him, then he would simply be content doing without.

Yeah, right.

Deeze Long was about to run that thought through his head one more time, maybe to see if he could wring a little truth out of it, when a black-and-white mutt that clearly saw him coming and didn't give a shit stepped purposely into his path.

Deeze had just enough time to yell something nonsensical as his feet left the cobblestones and he flew through the air, somersaulting in midflight, ass over teakettle. The dog yelped beneath him. (Oh, like *now* it saw him coming!) A young redheaded guy with a horrified expression on his face reached out from a park bench to block Deeze's fall, but it was clearly too late for intervention, and both parties knew it.

Deeze had a moment to take in a few details while he was airborne: 1. The guy had freckles and glasses; 2. When the guy tried to catch him in midfall, his book went flying and landed in the lagoon with a splash, startling a duck, which was actually pretty funny; and 3. The guy was tethered to the stupid black-and-white dog that had caused the whole mess to begin with. Consequently, that made the redheaded guy Public Enemy #1 as far as Deeze was concerned.

He was about to say so when he completed his somersault and the back of his head hit the cobblestones with a brain-rattling *thud*. Right at the redhead's feet.

"Ouch," he wheezed with what breath was left in his lungs, which wasn't much. He squinted straight up into the noonday sun and waited for his eyeballs to stop twirling from the impact. As soon as they ceased spinning like cherries in a slot machine, he tilted his head a little to the left to take in the redhead staring down at him with a worried expression.

"Freckles," Deeze muttered, and his eyes rolled up into his head one last time. His brain took that opportunity to shut down completely, and Deeze's thought processes went black.

Suddenly, Wyeth wasn't the only one out to lunch.

WYETH KNELT in front of the park bench while the startled duck continued to squawk behind him and his poor book settled to the bottom of the lagoon, getting fatter and fatter as it soaked up more and more water. The noonday sun banged down on the back of his neck as Wyeth squatted there like an idiot, staring down at the unconscious guy sprawled out in front of him.

"You killed him," he said to Chaucer.

Chaucer wagged his tail and pranced proudly about as if to say, "Thanks. I do what I can."

There were several people milling past on the cobblestoned path, but they turned away from the drama unfolding before them—the modern-day version of being polite, Wyeth assumed. If a person wants to break his neck in a public place, the least he should be granted is the right to do it without a bunch of strangers staring and making droll comments. Consequently, no one gave the guy lying flat on his back in the middle of Seaport Village a second glance.

No one but Wyeth. Wyeth, in fact, gave the guy several long and appreciative glances. His eyes made several trips back and forth from the guy's battered running shoes to the crown of his curly-black-haired noggin, lingering at several points of interest in between, of which there were many.

He turned to Chaucer again. "The least you could have done was kill somebody ugly."

Chaucer turned away and hacked up what looked like a burrito wrapper.

Wyeth mumbled, "Lovely. Thanks for the input," and centered his attention back on the unconscious guy. He reached out and gave the man a tentative poke in the chest. No response. He laid a hand to the man's cheek and received a surprise rush of endorphins galloping up his arm at the delectable feel of the man's blue-black five-o'clock shadow (and here it was only noon; how butch was that?). He lifted one of the guy's eyelids and saw nothing but the snowy white of an extremely healthy eyeball—no colored iris, no recognition, no sign of life, nothing.

"This can't be good," Wyeth blabbered to himself, giving the guy another nudge with his finger. Wyeth was starting to get a little desperate here. Maybe Chaucer really *had* killed the dude.

Wyeth was about to reach for his cellphone and dial 9-1-1, already rehearsing inside his head the spiel he would give the EMT's. "Yes, sir. I don't know what happened. The guy came out of nowhere and keeled over like a tree. It had nothing to do with my dog, you understand. The man just collapsed right there in front of me. *Wham*. He should have known better, of course. Who in their right mind would be jogging on a hot day like this anyway, I ask you? It must be 110 in the shade. *Tsk, tsk*. He's clearly insane, sir. Clearly." And then maybe he'd throw in a couple more *tsk*s for good measure.

Yes, Wyeth decided, that sounded pretty good. Nicely absolved him of all blame and laid it clearly on the handsome moron's very own shoulders.

At that moment, the handsome moron opened his eyes and said, "What happened?"

He appeared to stare up at the sky in considerable surprise before blinking a couple of times to get his bearings. Then twisting his head to the side, he took in the redheaded guy leaning over him.

"You fell," Wyeth blurted out, sliding his glasses up his nose with his index finger. "My dog had nothing to do with it."

DEEZE BLINKED again. It was all coming back to him now. Jogging, the waves lapping at his feet, the stupid dog stepping out in front of him, the collision, the uncontrolled flight, the crash landing.

And eventually—the pain. Damn, his head hurt.

"Liar," he rasped through a voice box that wasn't quite up to snuff yet for casual conversation. Complete sentences were still out of his grasp, so he added, "Dog. Yours. Cujo."

The redhead in front of him opened his eyes wide and tried to look innocent. "Dog? Dog? What dog? I don't have a dog."

"But you just said—"

"You're hallucinating. I didn't say anything."

Deeze lowered his eyes to the guy's hand, which happened to still be resting on Deeze's chest. Around the man's wrist a leash was wrapped, and at the end of the leash, down around Deeze's feet, was a dog. The dog was sitting on its ass and eating what looked like a burrito wrapper. Judging by the condition of the burrito wrapper, it wasn't the first time it had been eaten.

It was clearly the dog that had sabotaged his run—black and white, scruffy, none too bright, just tall enough to spectacularly trip over. It was the same dog, all right. He'd know it anywhere.

Refocusing his eyes on the redhead, he said again, "Liar."

This time the guy staring down at him had the good grace to blush and look guilty. His fingers spread wide across Deeze's chest, and for some reason, Deeze really enjoyed feeling them there.

"You're right," the redhead said. "It's my dog. And I'm sorry. But it really was an accident. Here, let me help you up."

Clutching the redhead's arm, Deeze pulled himself to a sitting position, but not without a few creaks and groans. His first instinct was to pat the back of his head, then gaze wonderingly at his fingertips to check for a smear of blood or a chunk or two of gray matter. There were none. Clearly all neurological damage was contained within. Great. That should simplify any future exploratory surgeries needed to unscramble his brains.

Deeze once again focused on the man at his side. The redhead had a nice, gentle smile on his face, although his blue eyes still looked a little worried behind those godawful black-framed glasses he wore.

"Nothing's broken, right?" the redhead asked. "Can I get you anything? A Coke, a cold pack?" With a little smile, he added, "An ambulance?"

Deeze narrowed his eyes. "I can't believe you're smiling. Nice teeth, though. Very white."

"Uh, thanks." The man immediately molded his face into a more acceptable expression of solicitude. But his eyes appeared to be studying Deeze's bare legs and the bulge in the front of his running shorts. What was that about?

"I really am sorry," the redhead finally said, wrenching his eyes back to Deeze's face.

This time he looked like he meant it, so Deeze decided to forgive him. "I like your hair," he said.

A flush crept into the man's cheeks. "Uh, thanks," he muttered again, this time clearly embarrassed. As if he couldn't think of what else to say, he added, "It's red."

For the first time, Deeze smiled. When he did, he noticed no teeth fell out and no jawbones snapped apart, so he was encouraged to smile a little wider. "It certainly is," he said softly.

The redhead stood and offered a hand. "Let me help you up. Maybe you'd better sit on the bench for a minute until you pull yourself together."

"I'm together. I need to finish my run," Deeze said.

The redhead put a finger to his lips and said, "Shush. Let's just get you on your feet first."

"You shush like a librarian," Deeze said.

The redhead looked startled, then impressed. "How incredibly prescient of you. As a matter of fact, I *am* a librarian. Maybe when you landed on your head, it made you psychic."

Deeze grinned. "Wouldn't that be cool?"

"Yeah well, I wouldn't get my hopes up."

Deeze finally accepted the proffered hand and snapped, crackled, and popped his way to his feet. A groan leaked out when he lowered himself to the park bench.

"What hurts?" the redhead asked.

"Butt, right shoulder blade, left heel, thumb—no, wait, *both* thumbs, a couple of metatarsal ligaments, third vertebra, index finger, little toe, brain stem, ego. Everything really," Deeze answered. Then he decided he probably sounded like a whiner, so he recanted. "Just kidding. It's not like I haven't fallen before. I really will be all right."

He reached out and petted the dog.

"That's Chaucer," the redhead said.

Deeze cast a squinty-eyed leer at the animal, who still had half a burrito wrapper hanging out of his mouth. "Hello, fucker." Then he turned to the guy. "And *you* are?"

He was blessed with another very attractive blush. This one crawled up the dog owner's neck and reddened everything from his chin to his hairline, ears included.

"I'm Wyeth," the guy said.

"Deeze," Deeze answered. "As in DZ. Short for Darryl Zachary. Are you really a librarian?"

"Yeah."

"At the downtown library?"

"Yeah."

"Do you work Monday through Friday?"

"Uh, yeah. Are you working your way up to making a point? Got a book overdue? Need your library card renewed?"

It was Deeze's turn to blush. "Nope. Just chatting." He let his eyes graze over Wyeth. The dry-wiking shirt, the Asics, the…. "Say, do you always exercise in dress pants?"

"I'm not exercising. I'm walking my dog on my lunch hour and reading a book, which is now lying at the bottom of the lagoon with a fish nibbling on it." He looked sadly at the lagoon. "Make that two fish."

Deeze didn't care about the book. "Do you ever run?"

"Not unless I'm being chased by a velociraptor."

"So that would be never."

"Pretty much."

Deeze sadly watched while the redhead—while *Wyeth*—checked his watch and looked immediately uneasy.

"You have to get back to work," Deeze said. He had no idea why that thought depressed him so.

He was even more depressed when Wyeth said, "Yes. Are you sure you'll be all right?"

Deeze grinned. "What if I said no?"

Wyeth lowered his chin and gave Deeze a look of weary impatience, rather like a schoolteacher who's had a tack put in her chair one too many times by the rottenest kid in class. His voice dropped an octave. "I asked if you'd be okay."

Deeze still had his hand on Chaucer's head, scratching the mongrel's ears. "Yes," he said softly. "I'll be okay. If you have to get back to work, just run along. I can limp home on my own. Shouldn't take me more than one or two excruciating hours. Don't fret yourself. Have a nice day. Life. Whatever."

"You're not going to make this easy, are you? Where do you live?"

Deeze smiled brightly. "Not far."

Two minutes later, they were walking side by side along the waterfront. Chaucer bounced along behind, sniffing at everything they passed. Wyeth's hand cradled Deeze's elbow, and Deeze purposely staggered a little bit every couple of minutes so the guy wouldn't remove it. He wasn't born yesterday.

"I LIKE redheads," Deeze said out of the blue. "I'm gay, by the way. Are *you* gay? I'm single too. Are *you* single?"

They were walking in front of the Hyatt Regency. Wyeth could smell the lunch menu wafting out across the patio and circling his head. Smelled like something fishy.

He tried not to smile. "My single status is none of your business. Are you sure you're really hurt?"

Deeze dragged him to a stop. "We forgot to scoop your reading material out of the lake."

"It was a lagoon. And don't worry about it."

"Did you check it out of the library? Will they bill you for it?"

"I'll cook the books. Won't be the first time."

"Then you're a *dishonest* librarian. *That's* a relief. So. Was that the first time you ever dropped a book in a lake while walking your homicidal dog through Seaport Village prior to tripping an innocent jogger and feeding pilfered reading material to city-owned salmon?"

"Lagoon. And they were koi, not salmon. And you are hardly innocent. Nor is Chaucer homicidal. He's just—oh, never mind. It's none of your business."

"Which part is none of my business?"

"*All* of it."

Now Deeze *was* smiling. He gave another intentional reel sideways, not quite going so far as to slap the back of his hand to his forehead like a swooning Aunt Pittypat in *Gone with the Wind*. He pointed toward a table outside a bayfront cafe, making sure he made his finger tremble a little while he did it. Great acting requires attention to detail, after all. "I think I'd better sit down for a minute. Woozy."

Wyeth wasn't falling for that. "We'll have to order something, you know. You can't just sit anywhere you want around here."

"Then let's have lunch. You treat. I don't have my wallet."

"How convenient. And I already had lunch. Keep walking and stop pretending to stagger. The Academy Awards are over. Let's get you home so I can get back to work and you can resume your life of annoying people and trying to cadge free meals from total strangers."

Deeze pouted. "I thought we were *friends*."

"You're hallucinating again."

"You're a hard man."

"Only under the right circumstances," Wyeth said.

He stumbled to a stop, dragging Deeze to a stop beside him. His face got the reddest it had been so far. His entire head looked like a giant strawberry. "I didn't mean that the way it sounded."

Deeze chewed on his lower lip, flashing a dimple momentarily. "I think you did."

"I'm not sure I like you very much."

Deeze chewed a little harder. "You'd be surprised how many times I hear that in the course of an average day."

Again, Wyeth tried not to grin. "Oddly enough, no, I don't think I would."

"Oh look!" Deeze said, pointing up ahead. "There's my apartment building."

"Holy shit," Wyeth said. "You live right across the street from me."

"Really?"

"Yes. Can this day get any blacker?"

Deeze gave him a gentle elbow in the ribs. "You're such a kidder. The word of the day on my Word of the Day calendar this morning was 'serendipitous.' Can you beat that?"

"Mine was 'horseshit,'" Wyeth responded.

"Your Word of the Day calendar sounds more interesting than mine."

They stopped in front of the street door leading into Deeze's building. The moment they stopped, and just before Wyeth could say, "Here you go. Sorry about your fall. Seeya," Chaucer rose up on his back feet and started humping Deeze's leg.

Deeze stared down at him. "I hope he's using protection."

Wyeth was mortified. Well, even more than he was already. "Chaucer, come away from there!"

Chaucer humped all the harder, tongue hanging out, eyes crossed, his little doggie butt flying up and down. If he kept it up, he'd probably barf up the burrito wrapper again.

Deeze was sort of bouncing around due to Chaucer's energetic humping, but he managed to say, "C-come up for t-tea."

Wyeth rolled his eyes. "I'd rather set myself on fire. Chaucer, *stop* it!"

"Then I hope I see you at the library," Deeze said through a 300-watt smile.

"Seems unlikely," Wyeth snorted. "I don't imagine you read much."

"Do Bazooka gum wrappers count? The ones with the little cartoons inside?"

"No."

"Well, that's just not fair. Elitism in literature really pisses me off. You as a librarian should be offended by it too."

"You're impossible. I've gotta run."

"You said you don't run."

"I meant I've got to *go*."

"No, you don't."

"Yes, I do."

"Okay. Toodles."

That caught Wyeth off guard. "Oh. Well, g-goodbye then," he stammered, and spinning on his heels, he hustled off in what was clearly a hasty retreat, dragging a still-humping Chaucer along behind him, straining at his leash. The dog was clearly not a fan of coitus interruptus.

Deeze watched until the redhead disappeared around a corner.

Only then did Deeze dab gentle fingertips over the bump on the back of his head. With his other hand, he patted his heart.

"Ouch," he said again, this time with a grin.

CHAPTER TWO

TWO DAYS later, Susie, the young volunteer who roamed through the library gathering up all the books ignorant people left lying around because they were too lazy to put them back on the shelves where they belonged, waved to Wyeth from across the stacks and hustled toward him with a manila envelope tucked beneath her arm.

Blushing prettily, she handed it over. "Somebody dropped this down the book return slot outside. Since you're the only redheaded librarian on the premises named Wyeth, it must be for you."

Wyeth stared at the envelope. "Huh?"

He took it from her hands, ignoring the flirty wink she cast in his direction, said, "Thank you," and walked away while Susie sighed and watched him go.

Wyeth ducked behind a bookshelf marked Romance A to D and plopped himself down at his own private desk before checking out the envelope in his hand. Sure enough, right there on the front of it, in a rather ungraceful hand with what looked like a fourth-grader's clunky penmanship, in orange crayon, no less, was printed the words For Wyeth—The Redheaded Librarian.

Subtle.

Wyeth weighed the envelope in his hands. It was fat and bulky. Curious, he peeled it open and gave the envelope a shake. Two items slipped out. One wafted gently onto his lap, the other landed with a thump on his desk. The one on his desk was the book he'd dropped in the lagoon when the gorgeous but annoying jogger tripped over his dog. The book was dry but swollen to three times its normal size, the pages brittle and crackly and fluffed up like they'd been force-fed growth hormones. Several of the pages had come loose and were crookedly taped back into place. Most of the back cover was missing, and several other pages appeared to have had their corners nibbled off. Possibly by hungry koi.

Wyeth shifted his attention to the paper in his lap, which turned out to be a note in the same clunky penmanship in the same orange crayon.

> *Dear Wyeth,*
> *It was lovely running into you and Chaucer the*
> *other day. My rehab is coming along nicely, thank you*
> *for asking. They tell me I should be able to walk without*
> *blubbering in pain within a year or two. As soon as I*
> *became mobile, I wheeled myself back to the lagoon and*
> *retrieved your book. With the assistance of my microwave*
> *oven, a neighbor's blow dryer, a box of kitchen matches,*
> *and two quarts of medicinal gin, I succeeded in drying*
> *the fucker out. It's a little poofier than it used to be, but I*
> *trust it's still legible. Give my regards to your four-legged*
> *friend. Tell him I hope his mange is getting better. Or not.*
> *Deeze*
> *P.S. Sorry about the crayon. I couldn't find a pen.*

Wyeth stared at the note, then picked up the book. He stared at it for about a minute and a half before spitting up a laugh. He studied the note again, and while he studied the note, he remembered everything about the man who wrote it. The way he looked. The way he smiled. The way he could annoy the tread off a car tire.

The way he looked.

Wyeth gave his head a shake, grumbled something less than kind, and dropped the book into a wastebasket. He started to drop the note in with it, but at the last moment changed his mind and stuffed the little piece of paper into his trouser pocket instead.

That evening when five o'clock rolled around, he stepped through the library's front door, breathed in the stagnant ninety-degree heat that hadn't let up one little bit in over a week, and gazed across the street to see Deeze leaning against a tree, watching him.

"Oh God," Wyeth muttered to himself. "Not this guy again."

"GET ANY interesting mail lately?" Deeze asked. He wasn't dressed in running shorts this time. He was decked out in faded jeans and a simple white dress shirt neatly tucked in. His sleeves were rolled up, which set off his olive skin and hairy forearms perfectly. Wyeth wondered if that thought had crossed Deeze's mind while he dressed, then decided that was an unworthy and uncharitable idea that… was probably true. Deeze wore Birkenstock sandals over bare tanned feet and a simple braided gay pride bracelet on his left wrist. He was also holding a bouquet of yellow daisies interspersed with purple heather, which he had clearly just purchased from the flower stand on the corner. The bracelet and the flowers were the only splashes of color on him.

Wyeth gazed uneasily at the flowers. "I don't want those," he said.

Deeze smiled brightly. "That's fortuitous. They're not *for* you."

"Oh."

"And in case you've forgotten, my name is Deeze."

"I know. Short for Doogie Zamboni."

"Darryl Zachary, actually."

"I was close."

Deeze continued to lean against the tree. He didn't stick out a hand to shake hello. He didn't ask how Wyeth's day was going. He just stood there, shoulder digging into the bark, ankles crossed, smiling and holding the flowers in front of his chest.

The silence was getting a little awkward, so Wyeth asked, "How did you get the book dry?"

"Oh, so you *did* get my package and note."

Wyeth sighed. "Yes."

"No thank you?"

"Umm, thank you."

"You're welcome. Were you surprised by the orange crayon?"

"Strangely, no. And the book?"

"I stood over it with a blow dryer, like I said. Took *hours*. Ponderous task. I hope you appreciate the effort. Next time read Winnie the Pooh. Fewer pages. Less absorption capabilities for soaking up pond water. I'm sorry, did you say you *did* appreciate the effort?"

"I was deeply touched."

"You're lying."

"Yes, I am."

"Just so you know, Wyeth, I'm lying too."

"About what?"

He thrust the flowers in Wyeth's face. "These," he said. "They really are for you. I thought maybe I could follow you home where you can stick them in water to preserve their virginal freshness, not unlike your own, then me, you, and Cujo could go for a walk together before dinner. I'd like to get to know you better."

Wyeth thought it best to ignore the "virginal freshness" remark. "What on earth do you want to get to know *me* for?"

Deeze smirked and fluttered his eyelashes. He must have figured that was answer enough.

"Good grief, Deeze. What are you, twelve? And tell me the truth. Why do you have crayons?"

"I teach preschool. I not only have crayons, I have paste at home too. Gallons of it. And construction paper. Reams and reams of construction paper. All colors. Wait till you see the hand-crafted Christmas card I'll send you come December. Sparkles, little gold stars, tinsel. You'll be charmed right out of your socks."

"Holy shit, you're serious."

"Thank you. If your interests run to a more hands-on approach to dating, I also have a paddle with holes drilled in it for the really rotten kids. We might drag that out one evening just for shits and giggles. I could bend you naked over my lap and pound the living—"

"You beat your students? Preschoolers? You spank *preschoolers*?"

"A mere jest. A whimsical flight of fancy. I don't really have a paddle. Well, I do, but it's not for—"

"Did you say 'dating'?"

"Yes. Dating. Me. You. The dog. Dating."

Wyeth just stood there. Dumbfounded. It was the oddest thing, but for the space of about ten seconds, he lost the capacity to speak. Finally, he coughed up some rudimentary noises. A couple of grunts, a snort, a sort of wheezy gagging sound that was a little off-putting, even for him. By stringing those noises together, he managed to create a reasonably coherent sentence. It wasn't the mention of dating that threw Wyeth for a loop. Or even the paddle. It was the other thing. The truly incomprehensible thing.

"Wait a minute. Are you telling me you're a *teacher*?"

Deeze narrowed his eyes. "You didn't benefit from preschool as a child, did you? If you had, you would clearly be more adept at comprehension. Yes. I'm a teacher. And I'm asking you for a date. A normal person would have figured that out by the flowers alone. You really are quite slow, aren't you? I mean, for a librarian."

"I don't want the flowers."

"Yes, you do."

"I don't want to date you."

"Yes, you do. Let me buy you dinner."

"Oh, you have your wallet this time?"

Deeze smiled. "Yes. Wallet. Credit card. Protection. And by protection," he hastily added, apparently seeing Wyeth about to snap his head off, "I mean long pants in case your dog starts humping me again."

"Where did you go to college?" Wyeth asked, one eyebrow climbing up into his hairline, still clearly unconvinced Deeze was telling the truth.

"University of San Francisco. How about you?"

"San Diego State."

"When did you graduate?"

Wyeth counted on his fingers. "Five years ago. You?"

"Six."

"How do you like teaching?"

"I love it. How do you like librarian-ing?"

"It's called library science, and I love it."

Deeze's face softened. He was still holding the flowers under Wyeth's nose. He gave them a little shake, rustling the blossoms, and said softly, "Look how much we have in common. Look how easily we communicate. We're practically on a date already, and you don't even know it. Take the flowers. Please. I want to see them in your hand."

"Why?"

"Just fer cause."

Hesitantly, Wyeth slipped his fingers around the bouquet and brought them to his nose, lightly inhaling their fragrance. "They smell nice," he said quietly. "Thank you. But I really can't—"

"Yes, you can," Deeze smiled. "You know you can. In fact, you already did."

Wyeth swiveled to look behind him at the library entrance, wondering if any fellow employees were watching him being wooed in broad daylight by a guy wearing a gay pride bracelet. Not that he much cared. About the bracelet, at any rate. Or witnesses either.

He turned back to Deeze. He stared deep into the man's eager brown eyes. There was kindness there, he suddenly noticed. Kindness mixed with mischief. Deeze was clearly a menace. He was also clearly waiting with bated breath to see what Wyeth's answer would be. And if the truth were known, so was Wyeth.

He honestly didn't know what words were coming until he opened his mouth and spit them out. "We have to walk Chaucer first. Maybe if we eat at an outside cafe somewhere, we can take him with us. He's been alone all day. He's used to company. He tends to get destructive when he has too much time to himself."

"You mean like ambushing joggers and humping strangers?"

"No, I mean like eating throw rugs and hiding the knobs off the kitchen stove."

"Pets are *such* a blessing."

"You have no idea."

"So you *are* coming to dinner?"

"I guess I have to eat sometime."

"Your enthusiasm makes me all tingly."

Deeze offered Wyeth a wide, handsome smile. Wyeth was surprised to see a very sweet and very honest thank-you in that smile. Deeze patted his chest like his heart had gone all fluttery for a second, and blushing, Wyeth whapped Deeze upside the head with the flowers, telling him to stop being such a twit.

"Ouch," Deeze said, picking a petal out of his hair. "Glad I didn't buy anything with thorns."

"Serves you right. You really are the most annoying man I've ever met."

"At least I'm the most at *something*. Pinnacles are good, don't you think? Why slog up the hill at all if you can't claim the summit?"

"So says the guy who suffered through four years of college to teach toddlers how to finger paint."

Deeze appeared mortally offended. "Hey, finger painting's tough!"

Shaking his head, Wyeth sniffed the flowers once again and peered across their colorful heads to the man opposite him. The man under the tree. The man who didn't seem to know how to give up. The man who was totally unconcerned (maybe) by how good he looked in that white shirt.

Wyeth breathed in a long, shuddering breath. "Well, come on, then. Let's go get Cujo. I mean, Chaucer." Mumbling to himself, he added softly, "I'm going to regret this. I know I am."

Deeze bumped him with his hip. "It's just dinner. No reason to get all weird about it."

Wyeth nodded. "You're right. Sorry."

"You're a little high-strung. You know, they have medication for that."

"*I'm* high-strung? You're calling *me* high-strung?"

"Yes. If you could only admit that, it would make it so much easier for you to cope with your plethora of psychoses."

"My plethora of psychoses? Did you say plethora of psychoses?"

"Yeah. That's what I said. Fear of friendship. Avoidance of restaurants. Inability to train your dog. Unreasonable aversion to exercise. Tendency to employ daisies as weaponry." The longer Deeze talked, the broader he smiled.

Wyeth rolled his eyes so far up into his head he could see his hair follicles dangling down. Deciding eye-rolling was a little too cavalier, especially under the circumstances—after all he was about to cop a free meal—he offered a commiserating grunt instead.

Deeze slipped his arm through Wyeth's and steered him up the street. Clearing his throat, he leaned in close and whispered, "I'm glad you're finally accepting the truth about yourself. Now then, about that paddle…."

DEEZE STOOD at Wyeth's living room window, staring out at the window directly across the street. *His* window. He could see the familiar pictures on his walls, the colorful afghan thrown across the arm of his favorite chair, the efficiency kitchen at the back of the living room with its microwave oven on the countertop next to a dish drainer by the sink with his coffee cup still sitting there from this morning. He could even make out the door leading into his bedroom. Hell, he could see everything.

"I guess I should stop running around naked when I'm home."

His voice was fluttery because he was being jarred continuously from behind. Chaucer was humping his leg again, and he was really going to town. Apparently Deeze was the best lay he'd had in years.

"I had no idea you lived so close!" Wyeth called out from the bathroom. "Just so you know, I'm not a Peeping Tom. Like I care what you do. If you want to run around naked, run around naked!" He stuck his head out the bathroom door. "I mean, after you get home, not here." He ducked back inside. "Just close your stupid drapes so you don't inflict it on the rest of the world."

"I feel I should take offense at that remark," Deeze said, his breath fogging the window.

"I'll be out in a minute!" Wyeth yelled over the sound of flushing water. "I'm going to brush my teeth before we go! You and Chaucer get to know each other."

Deeze gazed down at the dog still clamped around his leg, his sharp little toenails digging into Deeze's tender flesh while the mutt humped away for all he was worth. "Your dog and I know each other well enough already, thanks!" he called back. "I'm starting to feel like a slut!"

"I'm sure that's not a new experience for you," Wyeth mumbled, probably not quite as softly as he intended.

Deeze turned from the window and glowered across the room. "I heard that."

The flowers he had bought were standing in a drinking glass on the coffee table. Deeze still couldn't believe it, but Wyeth didn't own a vase. What sort of self-respecting homosexual didn't own a vase? Deeze turned from the window and gravitated toward a bookcase along the wall, dragging a still-humping Chaucer along with him like a ball and chain.

Wyeth seemed to have a wide range of novels from a wide range of writers, although most appeared to be thrillers. Deeze wasn't in the least surprised to see the books were neatly sorted in alphabetical order by authors' names. The guy hacking up toothpaste in the other room was, after all, a librarian. He plucked one book out at random—a Stephen King—and flipped to the inside of the back cover looking for a time card to see if it had been stolen from the library. Disappointingly, it hadn't.

"No," Wyeth said from the doorway behind him. "They're not stolen from the library, if that's what you're wondering. I buy my books just like you do, only mine aren't full of pictures, and I don't get them from Geppetto's Baby Boutique."

Deeze slipped the book back on the shelf. "I'm sure I don't know *what* you're talking about," he said with a grin.

Wyeth moved to the window. "Which apartment is yours? Just so I'll know where not to look." He turned back briefly to glance down at Chaucer, who was still happily humping away with his tongue hanging out of his mouth. Wyeth opened his mouth as if to yell at the beast for his incessant humping, but at the last moment, he clapped his mouth shut and turned back to the window as if admitting he knew a lost cause when he saw one. Some weird sixth sense must have told Chaucer that the two humans in the room were both thinking about him, because he suddenly released Deeze's leg. Deeze was afraid to look at the back of his jeans for fear of seeing a doggy semen stain there. He looked down at the mutt, who was still doing some fragmented humping in midair while his engine idled down.

"Was that good for you?" Deeze asked.

Chaucer turned and walked away.

"Typical," Deeze sniffed. "You give of yourself, you offer it all—"

"Oh, do be quiet."

"Sure, boss." Deeze stepped up to the window beside Wyeth. "There," he said, pointing. "My apartment is the one with the red curtains."

"Good lord," Wyeth said. "You really are right across the street from me. Your apartment looks nice. It looks like you actually keep it clean. I'm surprised."

"There's a mean streak in you. Did you know?"

"Wait a minute!" Wyeth barked, leaning close enough to the window to rattle his eyeglasses against the pane. "You've got a cat!"

Deeze rested a hand on Wyeth's shoulder, wondering if he'd have his arm ripped out by the root. Oddly enough, Wyeth didn't seem to notice. He was too engrossed in the cat across the way. Following Wyeth's gaze, Deeze stared through the window. Sure enough, a cat sat on the back of Deeze's couch, licking its butt.

"That's Napoleon," Deeze said, wondering why cats always lick their butts at the most inopportune times. Of course socially speaking, he supposed, it was never an opportune time for *anybody* to lick their butts.

"He's a Maine coon cat," Wyeth said, clearly impressed.

Deeze nodded, impressed that Wyeth was impressed. "Yes, he is."

"He's beautiful."

"Yes. And he knows it."

Deeze still had his hand on Wyeth's shoulder. He enjoyed the sensation of strong bones and lean musculature moving beneath his palm. He could feel Wyeth's heat, and that was enjoyable too. So he sidled a little closer.

Standing so close, Deeze realized he was about half a head taller than the redheaded man beside him. When Wyeth almost caught him staring, Deeze pivoted his head to peer through the window again.

"You're awfully close," Wyeth said softly.

Deeze nodded. "You smell minty."

"Toothpaste."

"I know."

At that moment, Wyeth stepped back. He was blushing again.

"I guess we'd better go to dinner before Chaucer pees on the door."

They both looked at the dog. Sure enough, Chaucer was standing at the door with his leash in his mouth, looking eagerly expectant.

"I always have to pee after sex too," Deeze stated.

"Way more than I needed to know," Wyeth muttered, and sliding out from beneath Deeze's hand, he headed for the door. "Coming?"

Smiling, Deeze followed along behind.

Outside in the hall, they passed a stairwell, and Deeze said, "Oh. We're not walking down?"

"Why would we walk down when there's a perfectly good elevator?"

"It's healthier?"

"It's insane."

"But, but—"

"Hush," Wyeth said.

"Wow. You hush people at the drop of a hat. You really *are* a librarian."

They took the elevator down.

THEY STEPPED out onto the street from the lobby of Wyeth's apartment building, and suddenly the unresolved logistics of the evening were back in play.

"Where are we eating?" Deeze asked.

Wyeth shook his head. "I don't know, but if we take a car, we'll take mine. You could be a serial killer for all I know."

"Why should we take a car at all?" Deeze asked, ignoring the insult. "There must be 150 restaurants within a six-block radius. Let's just walk the hump monster and see what catches our eye."

"Fine," Wyeth snapped. "And his name is Chaucer." After a beat of consideration, he asked, "Why did you name your cat Napoleon?"

"Because he's short and he thinks he owns the world. You know, you have beautiful eyes."

Wyeth stood there. Blinking. Deeze grinned. Wyeth started getting mad, then Chaucer broke the tension by peeing on a parking meter while a lady was putting coins in it.

Her scream snapped Deeze and Wyeth out of their reverie. Two seconds later they were hurrying down the street, tugging a dribbling

Chaucer along in their wake while the lady stared down at her urine-spattered pumps and fumed. Screamed epitaphs pummeled Deeze and Wyeth like pigeon droppings while they made their escape, giggling. Chaucer didn't giggle, though. He strutted. It wasn't often he got to nail a pair of satin heels. Usually he had to pee on bushes and trees and other inanimate objects, which of course limited the excitement factor considerably.

"I'm starting to like your dog," Deeze said, grinning, when they finally stopped running.

"Yeah, he gets under your skin after a while."

"You mean, like scabies?"

"Scabies, ringworm, venereal warts. You name it. He's quite a dog."

Deeze stared warily down at the mutt. "Yes, indeedy." He bent and with a certain amount of trepidation, scratched the back of his leg where he'd been humped by said dog. Twice.

"I was kidding," Wyeth drawled, shaking his head. "He doesn't have venereal warts."

"Oh. Thank God."

Wyeth waited until they had strolled a couple of blocks farther from the screaming woman before asking, "Why did you want to become a preschool teacher?"

"Simple. I love kids. Why did you want to become a librarian?"

Wyeth hated himself for it, but he had to smile. "Simple. Because I love books."

"Thought so. Life is pretty simple all around when you analyze motives. For instance, Wyeth, my man, let's take you and me. I asked you out to dinner because I wanted to get to know you. You accepted my invitation to dinner because—"

Wyeth saw his cue and took it before Deeze could complete his sentence. "Because you're clearly insane, and I knew you'd never leave me alone if I didn't."

"Precisely! Cause and effect! Although I like to think my sparkling conversation, my romantic overture with the flowers, and my fawning sycophancy in relation to your clearly deranged dog might have had something to do with it."

"Yeah, keep thinking that." Then Wyeth laughed. "Jesus, you really are nuts."

Since it was summer, it was still broad daylight at six in the evening. They walked toward the bay, squinting against the sun hanging low in the sky. Occasionally, their shoulders brushed, and after about the fifth time, Wyeth stopped freaking out about it.

"Do you really love kids?" he asked.

They waited while Chaucer sniffed lackadaisically at a fire hydrant. "I do," Deeze said. "At the preschool age, before life gets its claws into them and screws them up beyond redemption, they are sweet and good and innocent and kind. Well, most of them. There are a few clunkers, of course, even at that age, but on the whole, children under six are moldably pure."

"Moldably pure?"

"Yeah. They're teachable. They absorb knowledge like that book of yours sucked up water in the lagoon. It's my job to make sure the knowledge they suck up is what they need for their particular stage of development."

"Eating paste and coloring inside the lines?"

Deeze frowned. "There's more to it than that. There's teaching them to interact with others. There's teaching them to respect opposing points of views. There's teaching them to obey, to accept, to understand, to care. And there's teaching them how to have fun."

"Aren't they already having fun?" Wyeth asked. "They're kids, aren't they? Kids have fun. That's what they do."

Deeze stared off into the distance while still waiting for Chaucer to get bored with the stupid fire hydrant. Wyeth studied his face, waiting for his response. Was he imagining it, or was Deeze enjoying knowing Wyeth was waiting for his response?

"No," Deeze said quietly, turning to hit Wyeth with a gaze of his own. "Some kids need to be taught how to have fun, believe it or not. Some kids, in fact, never learn the secret to fun at all."

"There's a secret?" Wyeth asked, his own voice hushed now, so rapt was he in the conversation, so lost was he in Deeze's warm brown eyes. "I thought fun was just fun."

Deeze gave him a studied gaze. "The secret to having fun is to share it back. Fun doesn't just flow in, it has to flow out too. If a child is selfish, or doesn't connect well with others, or is afraid to laugh, he'll never understand fun. He has to give of himself, give of his toys, give of his *laughter*, for fun to be real."

Wyeth blinked. "Some kids are afraid to laugh?"

"Sadly, yes. Did you ever watch a string of preschoolers being led through your library on their way to Reading Time? Did you ever notice among all those smiling young faces, one child who isn't smiling at all?"

"M-maybe."

Deeze nodded. "See? That's the child I concentrate on. That's the child I teach to laugh."

They were walking on now. Wyeth suddenly realized they were standing in front of the antique carousel at Seaport Village, not a hundred feet from where they had first met.

With a mischievous glint in his eyes, Deeze wrested the leash from Wyeth's hand and tied it to a light pole. Digging in his pocket for money with one hand while tugging Wyeth along behind him with the other, he leaned into the ticket booth window and purchased two tickets for the ride.

Wyeth tried to pull away. "No, Deeze, this is embarrassing. Come on, let's just go eat somewhere and—"

"Hush!" Deeze grinned. "See? You're not the only one who knows how to shush." He handed over a ticket stub and pulled Wyeth up onto the floor of the merry-go-round. Deeze continued to tug him along, slipping between carousel horses and emus and dragons and fairies while the calliope music blared in the background and a bunch of screaming kids scampered around claiming the mounts they preferred.

Just as the carousel jerked into motion and began to spin, Deeze pulled Wyeth between the upsurged wings of a huge white swan and practically shoved him into the double seat there, claiming the space beside Wyeth at the same time.

As the carousel sped up, twirling faster and faster, and the music swelled even louder, Deeze slipped his fingers though Wyeth's as the city glided past around them. Wyeth tried to gently pull his hand away, but Deeze's grip tightened until Wyeth stopped struggling.

After that, the music of the spinning machine and the great cradling wings of the snow-white swan carried them away to unimagined heights. Wyeth stopped being embarrassed and found his lips turning up into a gentle grin. He glanced at Deeze in time to see Deeze's own smile erupt full force. Deeze leaned in and whispered in Wyeth's ear, just loud enough to be heard above the blaring pipe organ's music. "Now you're having fun," he said around a laugh.

When Wyeth turned to look at him, Deeze carpe diemed the shit out of the moment and stole a kiss. Just a little one, but a kiss. Smack on the mouth.

Wyeth was so surprised, he didn't even fight back, and Deeze stole another.

For one brief moment, just a mere flash of time, Wyeth's eyes slipped closed when their lips met for the second time, and he tightened his fingers around Deeze's.

Then both men pulled back, studying each other. While the carousel slowed and the music softened, their eyes unlocked and they saw Chaucer's head slip by time and time again as he watched them slide past, slower and slower with every revolution as the carousel spun down to silent stillness.

After the merry-go-round bumped to a stop, Wyeth pulled his hand away and stood.

"Let's have dinner now," Deeze said, and Wyeth nodded, a little breathless. Wyeth licked the last kiss from his lips, and as he watched, Deeze did the same. Deeze wasn't surprised at all to realize Wyeth's kiss was delicious.

He *was* surprised when Wyeth said, "Thank you. That was fun."

Deeze didn't know if he meant the kissing or the carousel, and he didn't much care. Just hearing the beautiful redhead say the words was reward enough for him.

Both men laughed when Chaucer greeted them as if they'd been gone for a month. They ordered takeout food from a seafood restaurant, plus a couple of fritters for Chaucer, and claimed a picnic table looking out over the bay. From there they stared out at the fishing boats bobbing on the water, their masts swaying this way and that while fat white sea gulls swooped overhead, screaming raucously like a bunch of angry old women.

Once, while they ate, Deeze's hand brushed Wyeth's as if by accident, and his heart quickened. He wondered if Wyeth's had as well.

They spoke quietly of nothing really. Enjoying the food. Enjoying the company. Enjoying the view. At one point during their meal, Wyeth stuck his hand in his pocket, looked confused for a second, then pulled out the crayoned note and gazed at it oddly, as if he didn't remember saving it. Deeze smiled but didn't say anything. He smiled even wider when Wyeth slipped the note *back* in his pocket.

LATER, DEEZE walked Wyeth home in the rosy glow of a summer sunset and didn't even *try* to kiss him at the door of his apartment building. Wyeth watched in surprise when the dark-haired man simply tipped him a salute and walked away without saying a word. At the last minute, before turning the corner, Deeze turned and waved, a wicked little grin on his face. Wyeth haltingly waved back. Both men returned to their separate apartments alone.

Later that night, Wyeth stood in his living room and stared out at the window directly across the street. Deeze's apartment was dark, the red curtains drawn. A huge sheet of yellow construction paper was taped to the glass. On it, in orange crayon, were printed the words Thank You.

Wyeth stared at it for the longest time. Finally, he knelt at the base of the window and Chaucer walked into his arms. Wyeth buried his face in Chaucer's wiry coat, and for the first time in months, he felt alone.

He lay in bed that night holding Deeze's note in his hand. Somehow the waxy feel of the crayoned words against his fingertips gave him peace.

Hours later, while he slept, he dreamed of swans.

In the morning, the Thank You sign across the street was gone. Replacing it was a sign on red construction paper, printed out in green crayon this time, that read Let's Do It Again.

Wyeth stood at the window for long minutes, lost in thought, unnerved by that casual—yet *not* so casual—note aimed at him from across the street. *Be careful*, a tiny voice warned inside his head. *Be careful.*

Finally, his mind made up, he yanked the curtains closed, taking a moment to arrange the fabric so that every sliver of light flowing in from outside was blocked. Once again sealed into his own little cocoon of safety, he stepped away from the window and, eyes downcast, made his way to the bathroom to shower for work.

Once he was dressed and ready to go, he felt a little better. The last thing he did before leaving the apartment was make his bed. He found Deeze's crayoned note among the tangled sheets and slipped it into a desk drawer for safekeeping. If he had asked himself why he did such a thing, he wouldn't have been able to come up with an answer. So he didn't ask. There was a font of regret welling up inside him too, but he didn't dare try to analyze that either.

On his way out the door, he kissed Chaucer between the eyes and ordered him not to eat the couch while he was gone. As usual, Chaucer didn't make any promises.

Three floors down, Wyeth forced a smile to his face as he stepped out onto the street. There was no happiness in the smile. It was camouflage, nothing else.

For some reason, Wyeth needed camouflage this morning.

CHAPTER THREE

WYETH'S NEIGHBORS were as nosy as the Sunday school God he remembered from childhood—always watching, always prying, always judging. Never looking away to give you a moment's privacy, forever *tsk tsk*ing inside your head when you least expected it.

Agnes Mulroney, who lived next door in 3B, proved it the second Wyeth stepped outside his door. Since the deciphering of Agnes Mulroney's true age might require carbon dating, Wyeth didn't even try to figure it out. He just knew she was o-l-d and left it at that. She used a walker that squeaked, rarely wore matching shoes, and was known to steal newspapers from neighboring doormats. When caught red-handed, she placed the blame solely on her meager Social Security check and suggested if people wanted to keep their papers to themselves, they should contact the government and file a complaint with the SSA.

"Mr. Becker!" she cried out as he was locking his door. "I see you stopped taking the paper."

Wyeth narrowed his eyes and snorted an ungenerous laugh. "Yes. They kept disappearing."

"How odd," Agnes said, moving closer. She was in her housecoat, her hair in rollers, and she had her teeth out. She was eating a peeled orange like an apple, without sectioning it first. Orange pulp was dribbling down her arm. Her toothless gums were smacking happily while she chewed and slurped and talked at the same time. Occasionally she would spit a seed into her housecoat pocket.

"I saw you with that nice young man who lives across the way. Striking up a new friendship, are we?"

Wyeth stood rooted, staring at her. "Where were *you*?" he asked. "Hiding in a tree?"

She guffawed and slapped his arm with a sticky hand, leaving a smear of orange juice on his nice clean shirtsleeve. "Oh, don't be silly. I was at my window with binoculars. I saw the two of you and that strange dog of yours, walking along the street. I assume you saw the sign he left in his window for you this morning."

"How do you know he didn't leave it for you?" Wyeth asked, and before she could slap him again, he stepped back out of reach.

"Oh pooh," Agnes cackled. "That note was for you and you know it."

"I have to go to work now," Wyeth droned. "Have a nice day."

"Call him," she said. "You need more friends."

"And you need to stop snooping, Mrs. Mulroney."

"Oh pooh," she said again. "I don't snoop. I *observe*."

Since Wyeth seemed incapable of just shutting up and diving for the elevator, he turned and said, "If you must know, I'm not calling the man again because he isn't normal. He actually made me ride on a merry-go-round yesterday."

"How lovely!"

Wyeth growled. "It wasn't lovely at all. It was ridiculous. Two grown men spinning around on that ridiculous contraption with a bunch of screaming kids."

"If I was eighty years younger and had the proper body parts to entice him, I'd go after that man myself."

Wyeth didn't want to ask. He had no intention of asking. Then he asked anyway because he couldn't seem to stop himself. "What do you mean, proper body parts?"

Again, she guffawed. Toothlessly, with orange juice dribbling off her chin. "Oh, don't be naïve. He's gay. You're gay. What's the problem? I have a friend in Cincinnati who's gay. He married a sweet man more than two years ago, and they are *so* happy. That could be you and him. He likes you, you know."

Wyeth exhaled a tankful of air and resisted the urge to toss the old lady down the elevator shaft. "I think you should go take your Alzheimer meds. You're hallucinating. And I may be gay, but the last thing I need is a boyfriend. They are too annoying, too time-consuming, and just plain too much trouble."

The last of the orange disappeared down Mrs. Mulroney's pie hole. She dragged a handkerchief out of her sleeve and wiped herself down, all the while shooting sad little darts of pity Wyeth's way.

"You'll never be truly happy alone," she said quietly and began plucking rollers from her hair. Most of her gray locks, he noticed, stuck to her sticky fingers. One by one, she dropped the rollers in the pocket with the orange seeds.

"That's what you think, ma'am. I'm perfectly happy the way I am."
Seeing the disbelief in her eyes, he reiterated, "I *am*, dammit!"

Mrs. Mulroney looked supremely unconvinced.

"Oh, I don't have time for this," Wyeth grumbled, and with that, he ducked into the elevator and waited impatiently for the door to close behind him, praying to God it would close before Mrs. Mulroney could swoop in like a vulture to pester him some more.

Just before it slammed shut, he heard her cry out, "Call him! He's a fine boy!"

"He's nuts!" Wyeth yelled back. "*You* call him!"

Finally the door dinged shut and the elevator jerked and grumbled its way to life, dragging him down, down, down toward another day at the library, another day of his life—his blessedly uncomplicated, uneventful, unromantically plagued life.

What Wyeth didn't expect was that once he was there, toiling away inside the library, he would think of Agnes through most of the morning and Deeze through most of the afternoon. That pissed him off. He had to put up with the old lady because she lived next door. But Deeze? Why should he be thinking about Deeze at all? It was confusing.

To make matters worse, he kept hoping Susie, the flirty library volunteer who couldn't quite wrap her head around the fact that the redheaded librarian she had such a crush on was gay, would stop by with another crayon-addressed envelope with another strange surprise inside. When she didn't, he grew even surlier, although he couldn't quite understand why.

By the time five o'clock rolled around and Wyeth was heading home, sweltering once again under the broiling summer sun, loosening his tie even as he walked down the street, he was totally depressed at the idea of eating dinner alone in front of the TV. This was confusing too. He had never been depressed about eating dinner alone before. Why the hell did it bother him now?

And yes, for a smart guy, Wyeth Becker was really that dumb.

If there were any new crayon-painted signs taped to Deeze's window across the way, Wyeth didn't know it, because he refused to look. He spent his Friday night the way he always did. He walked Chaucer—heading off in the opposite direction from where he usually went because he didn't want to pass Deeze's building. They had a quiet dinner alone, he and the dog, and then about 10:00 p.m., Wyeth slipped on a ratty pair of Bermuda shorts, grabbed a wrinkled shirt from the dresser drawer, and set off for the final stroll of the evening so Chaucer could drain his pipes one last time before turning in for the night.

In front of the all-night deli on Eighth Avenue, where Wyeth had stopped to purchase a bag of bagels for breakfast, he ran head-on into Deeze. Literally. They crashed into each other while Wyeth was digging through his bag of bagels and two little packages of cream cheese to make sure he had everything and Deeze was jogging full-tilt down the sidewalk gazing at the Garmin strapped to his wrist.

Their collision was spectacular. The only one who wasn't knocked on his ass this time was Chaucer, who took the opportunity while both humans were flat on their backs on the sidewalk, to stand on Deeze's chest and give his old friend a thorough tongue bath.

Deeze spit his way out from under Chaucer's kisses and sat up with a groan to stare at Wyeth, who at that moment was mumbling curses and crawling around the sidewalk gathering up his scattered bagels.

"I like your shorts," Deeze said.

Wyeth stopped gathering bagels and turned to stare while Deeze mumbled his way to his feet and dusted himself off as if he did this sort of thing twenty times a day, which Wyeth wasn't so sure he didn't. While Deeze did all that, he still found time to ruffle Chaucer's coat and return the dog's happy greeting.

"Chaucer! Come away from there," Wyeth snapped. Then he snapped at Deeze. "What the hell is wrong with you? Why don't you look where you're going? When you jog, you're a menace. You know that? Every time we bump into each other, one or both of us ends up flat on his back!"

A sexy grin lit up Deeze's face. His eyes smoldered merrily. "I like the way you put that," he said with a leer.

"Oh for Christ's sake," Wyeth growled. "Grow up!"

"It must be karma," Deeze said. "It's the only way to explain it."

Wyeth stopped fiddling with his fucking bagels and just stared. "*What* must be karma? It's the only way to explain *what*?"

Deeze's grin widened. "Me. You. Us. The way we perpetually plow into each other."

"We don't plow into each other. You plow into *me*!"

Wyeth sucked in a deep breath and made a concerted effort to calm down. He stared at the man in front of him. His eyes traveled from Deeze's brown eyes, across the blue-black shadow on his unshaven cheeks, to his broad bare shoulders poking out of the muscle shirt he wore, which was the same shirt he had worn the day they collided by the lagoon. Deeze was also wearing the same tiny running shorts he had worn that day too. And he still had the same beautiful legs.

Wyeth swallowed hard, staring down at himself. Why in the world had he worn his stupid gaudyass Bermuda shorts and a wrinkled polo shirt that was so old the little polo player had fallen off. He was all too aware of his pale, hairy legs in comparison to Deeze's fuzzy, olive-colored ones. So when Deeze spoke again, he spoke words Wyeth never expected to hear in a million years.

"My God, you're beautiful," Deeze said.

Wyeth's jaw dropped. His ears turned red. He scrunched up the paper bag holding his stupid bagels and simply glared.

"I don't care what you think of me, Deeze! Everybody can't look like you, you know. Everybody isn't muscle-bound and tanned."

Deeze's face fell. He stood there blinking, such a look of hurt crossing his face that Wyeth began to wonder what the hell he had said to deflate the guy so quickly. Then he remembered what Deeze had said and got mad all over again.

"I am who I am! You have no right to comment on my appearance at all!"

Deeze's face fell even more. "I-I'm sorry." He stepped closer and laid his hand on Wyeth's arm. "Did you think I was making fun of the way you look?" he asked quietly.

"Yes!" Wyeth brayed. "And you're an asshole for doing it!" Wyeth tried to shake off Deeze's hand, but Deeze wouldn't let him. He clamped his fingers around Wyeth's wrist instead.

"Stop trying to pull away and listen to me, Wyeth Becker, you insufferable jackass. I *do* happen to think you're beautiful. If you *don't*, that's your problem, not mine. You should learn to take the occasional compliment without going nuclear. If you did, you might get a few more now and then."

"I don't want compliments, Deeze! I just want to be left alone."

"No, you don't," Deeze quietly answered.

Wyeth's ears burned even redder. He tried again to wrestle his wrist from Deeze's grip. When Deeze refused to release him, Wyeth said, more softly this time, "You're hurting me. Let go."

So Deeze did. He released Wyeth's wrist and took a step back. Then he spoke in an almost inaudible whisper while late-night pedestrians paraded past and a brittle spray of palm fronds rattled in the night breeze above their heads.

"I still think you're beautiful," Deeze said.

Wyeth squeezed his eyes shut and tightened his grip on Chaucer's leash. "Are you finished?" he asked. "Can I go now?"

Deeze stepped closer. Again, he wrapped his fingers around Wyeth's wrist, but he did it gently this time.

"I'll let you go if you promise to spend the day with me tomorrow."

Wyeth couldn't believe it. This guy never gave up. He wore you down with sheer, obstinate doggedness. No matter what you said, he just kept blathering on. Then he made you feel guilty when you fought back.

"Sorry. It's my day off. I have things to do."

A small grin twisted Deeze's lips. "Like what?"

Wyeth stammered out the first thing he could think of, knowing while he did that he was sounding like a twit. "I have to wash the dog."

Deeze's tiny grin morphed into a full-blown smile of incredulous proportions. "That's it? You have to wash the dog?" He stared down at Chaucer. "You want a bath, boy?"

Chaucer ducked his head and tried to make himself invisible. A tiny whimper erupted from his throat while his tail shot between his legs. Suddenly he was the poster boy for abused, overwashed dogs everywhere.

Deeze turned back to Wyeth. "Well, there you have it. The dog doesn't want a bath. So spend the day with me and give the poor filthy mongrel a break."

"No."

"Yes."

"I don't want to spend the day with you. You're annoying."

"No, I'm not. I'm charming."

"You're an ass."

"I know. That's part of my charm."

"You're not going to give up, are you?"

"Nope."

"Oh fuck it, then. All right."

Deeze went through the motions of digging a pound of wax out of his ear and smearing it down the side of the palm tree next to them. "Did you say 'all right'? Is that what I heard? Did you honestly agree to spend the day with me tomorrow? Saturday? *This* Saturday? I mean like—*tomorrow*? In *this* lifetime?"

Wyeth was not amused, merely resigned. "What else am I supposed to do? You won't shut up. You won't take no for an answer. You won't leave me alone. And my neighbor said you're a nice guy. Of course, she's older than God and makes about as much sense as you do."

"You must mean Agnes."

"I should have known you two would be friends."

Deeze laughed. "I'll have to give her a gift for bringing us together."

"She didn't bring us together. We aren't together. And if we are together, it's only because you never watch where you're going and keep running into me. But if you must buy the old witch a gift, give her a subscription to the newspaper so she'll stop stealing everyone else's."

Deeze beamed. "Good idea! I'll do just that."

"The rest of my building will love you forever."

Deeze shuffled forward a little closer. "Tell me, Wyeth Becker, will you love me forever too?" he asked quietly.

Wyeth tried to turn away, but Deeze still held his wrist. "You're hopeless," he mumbled.

Deeze batted his eyelashes. "No, I'm persistent."

Wyeth felt a sudden urge to step closer too, to walk directly into Deeze's arms and let Deeze scoop him into an embrace, and wouldn't *that* startle the shit out of the guy. Then Wyeth quickly realized *he* was the one who was startled. Startled to even *think* of doing such a thing. In fact, that sudden urge to walk into Deeze's arms frightened Wyeth more than anything that had happened.

That Wyeth was drawn to Deeze was inescapable. But the possibility that Deeze might be drawn right back scared the bejesus out of him. A heartache waiting to happen, that's what this was. He just knew it. There wasn't a hope in hell that two men so different in looks and personality could find anything but disappointment together. Wyeth had endured these situations before. The handsome one always bailed, and Wyeth was never ever the handsome one. He was inevitably the dumpee, not the dump*er*, and he really didn't have the stamina to go through it again. He tried one last time to weasel his way out of tomorrow.

"You could do way better than me," he said, with more than a trace of hurt lacing his words. "You should look for someone in your own pay grade to spend the day with."

At that, Deeze frowned, and this time it looked like an honest one. "Please tell me you don't believe that," he said, all the while stepping closer, clutching both of Wyeth's pale wrists now, his fiery brown eyes burning a path straight into Wyeth's brain. That soulful, heartfelt stare frightened Wyeth even more than the words the man used. There was no humor in Deeze's face anymore. He was no longer joking.

Somehow, Deeze's crystal clear certainty of Wyeth's worth made Wyeth ashamed of what he'd just said. "I didn't mean that, Deeze. I'm sorry. I'm just—rattled. You rattle me. I-I promise I'll try not to be so paranoid in the future."

Deeze's gaze softened. He almost smiled but didn't quite. "Good. I'm going to hold you to that promise." Lowering his voice even more, he said, "And by 'the future' I assume you still mean tomorrow. I'll be at your door at eight in the morning. I'll stop in for a bagel—" He lifted the hand Wyeth was holding the paper bag in and shook it in his face. "—and then we'll go. And yes, you can bring the dog."

"Where are we going?"

"I don't know. I haven't figured it out yet."

"Do I really have to wear shorts? My legs are so pale."

"Does that bother you?" Deeze asked.

Wyeth blushed. "I usually only wear shorts at night. Like now. When I walk Chaucer."

"We'll change all that."

For some reason, Wyeth couldn't think of a reason to disbelieve him. "Will we?"

Deeze's teeth shone white in the glare of the streetlight. "We will." He stepped back. "Can I walk you home?"

"Why would you want to—" Wyeth forced himself to shut the hell up. He took a deep breath and said, "Yes, if it means that much to you, you can walk me the fuck home."

Deeze laughed. "You're learning," he said happily. He took Wyeth's arm, and the three of them headed off down the street.

"I like that I rattle you, you know," Deeze said while they waited for a light to change.

Wyeth had to bite back a smile. "I suspected you might."

At the front door to Wyeth's apartment building, Deeze once again faced Wyeth and gently grasped his wrists. "Thank you," Deeze whispered. He leaned in for a brief kiss without asking permission, and while their lips were still together, he muttered, "Thank you," again. Wyeth closed his eyes in the middle of the kiss and only opened them again when Deeze broke the kiss, said, "Good night," and walked away, whistling, before Wyeth had a chance to say anything.

Wyeth watched him go until he couldn't see him anymore. This time Deeze didn't turn and wave at the corner. As soon as he knew he was really and truly alone, Wyeth's legs went weak. He collapsed to his ass on the front step while Chaucer wiggled his way between his knees and tried to stick his nose in the bagel bag.

Wyeth yanked the bag away, scratched Chaucer's ears, and thought of the kiss. Ten minutes later, he hauled himself to his feet and made his way home.

Once again, the apartment seemed strangely empty. He stood at the living room window, staring out. He was still watching when the lights in the apartment across the way blinked on, but Deeze's red curtains never moved.

Not sure if he was relieved or disappointed, Wyeth finally gave up and went to bed.

CHAPTER FOUR

"THIS IS the first time we've come face-to-face without somebody getting knocked on his ass," Wyeth said.

He had just answered the rap at his door. It wasn't quite eight in the morning yet, but he was such a nervous wreck he didn't care that Deeze was early. He had been up for hours anyway. He had needed all that time to decide what to wear. What he finally chose was a pair of khaki cargo shorts with tennies and white socks and a white T-shirt with a picture of Shakespeare on the back. The shirt was baggy and untucked and one white sock hung lower on his ankle than the other, but by then it was too late to change. Wyatt kept tugging nervously on the errant sock, which made it even worse.

The moment Deeze saw him, he roared his approval. "You look *great*! You're not an insufferable stuffed shirt after all! You can actually be *casual*! I *love* it!"

Wyeth went through the motions of trying to close the door in Deeze's face, but Deeze just grinned and barged his way inside, mumbling, "What a kidder."

Deeze wore cargo shorts as well, and another muscle shirt, exposing broad shoulders and lovely plump biceps. This shirt was bright yellow and complimented Deeze's skin tone to perfection. Wyeth supposed if he had Deeze's olive skin and Deeze's shoulders and Deeze's *everything*, he'd wear that muscle shirt too. Instead of tennis shoes, Deeze had slipped into a pair of sandals. Once again, he had the braided gay pride bracelet on his wrist, and a San Diego Pride baseball cap perched cutely on his head.

"I guess we're not trying to pass for straight, then," Wyeth sniped. "Should I wear a feather boa and heels?"

"You're bordering on mean again," Deeze said around a grin.

"Who, me?"

The minute Deeze passed through the door, Chaucer headed up the welcoming committee by sticking his nose in Deeze's crotch, causing Deeze to go "Whoop!" in surprise.

"Now that's what I call a hello!" he laughed. He dropped to his knees and gave the dog a hug. While he was down there, he took the opportunity to gaze up at Wyeth in his shorts and baggy shirt. He took an extra moment to study Wyeth's legs, much to Wyeth's chagrin. Not only was Wyeth self-conscious about how pale they were, he was uncomfortably aware of the scab on one knee, which Deeze had apparently just noticed. Deeze reached out and tapped the scab gently with his fingertip, causing Wyeth to jump. "Did I do that last night when I ran into you in front of the deli?"

"Don't worry about it," Wyeth said. "I expect more extensive injuries than that before the day is over." *Full body cast. PTSD. Broken heart.* He squeezed his eyes shut to block those thoughts. "Just don't worry about it," he said again.

Deeze still knelt at his feet, looking up. His eyes were serious, and he spoke haltingly. "Why would you say something like that? Boy, you really don't like me, do you?"

At that, Wyeth blushed. "I'm sorry, but I really don't think this is a good idea. And why are you still on your knees? Get up. Please."

Deeze slipped the fingers of one hand around the back of Wyeth's knee to pull himself up. Wyeth gave a tiny gasp at the touch.

By the time he was on his feet, Deeze was once again standing inches from Wyeth's face. He stared into Wyeth's blue eyes and spoke in measured tones. "I'm going to pretend you like me."

Wyeth could feel his pulse pounding in his temple. It had been a long time since he was this nervous. "You're too close."

"I'm also going to pretend you're not afraid of me."

"I'm not afraid of you. And I said you're too close."

"I heard you. But to do what I'm about to do, I have to be close."

"What are you about to—?"

Before Wyeth could finish, Deeze slid light fingertips down the length of Wyeth's arms and stepped even closer. Wyeth expected a kiss, so he was surprised when Deeze simply laid his cheek to Wyeth's and whispered in his ear, "If this is going to work, you have to trust me."

Wyeth smelled Ivory soap, mouthwash, and the clean, cinnamony scent of a freshly showered man. It was all he could do not to sniff at Deeze like a wine connoisseur breathing in the heavenly scent of a vintage Bordeaux. It had been a while since the smell of a man had affected him so. Before he could stop himself, he reached around and laid a hand to the small of Deeze's back, for the first time accepting him into his space rather than pushing him away.

The motion clearly wasn't lost on Deeze. He leaned back just far enough to study Wyeth's eyes. "That's better," he said. "Thank you, Wy."

"It's Wyeth."

"My mistake. Wyeth." Deeze took a step back, still smiling, and said, "Now then, about that bagel. I hope you have cream cheese."

Wyeth looked offended. "What sort of moron would serve bagels without cream cheese?"

Deeze laughed. "Oh goody. A man after my own heart."

"Don't get ahead of yourself. I can still barely tolerate you standing in the same room," Wyeth said, but he said it jokingly. At least he was pretty sure he did.

Happily, Deeze seemed to think so too. "And the librarian can not only dress casually, but he has a sense of humor too. Will wonders never cease!"

Wyeth pointed to the kitchen table. "Sit down, shut up, and eat your fucking bagel. And yes, there was an Oxford comma in that sentence."

Deeze was in the process of decorating his bagel with cream cheese. He arched one eyebrow high and left his knife to hover in midair long enough to say, "I assumed there was. I'm a teacher, you know. I did go to college. I know what an Oxford comma is. I'm actually quite well-read, believe it or not. Just because I'm a kindergarten teacher, don't think my literary credentials apply only to *See Spot Run* and *Dick and Jane Go to Happy Town*. By the way, there's also a very good word for people who try to cast an illiterate pall over their friends when they aren't looking."

"And what word might that be?" Wyeth asked, beginning to enjoy himself, but leery nevertheless.

"Asshole," Deeze answered with an evil glint in his eye. "The word is asshole."

Wyeth barked out a laugh. It was the first honest laugh he had ever shared with Deeze, and Deeze looked properly astounded by it. Astounded and intrigued.

Chaucer ran around in circles, clearly enjoying the humans' banter, while Deeze bit into his bagel and said, "Eat up. We have a nine o'clock appointment."

"We *do*? For *what*?" Wyeth asked, surprised.

Deeze wiggled his eyebrows and said mysteriously, "You'll see."

THEY STOOD on the street corner six blocks over from Wyeth's apartment building. All three heads, Wyeth's, Deeze's, and Chaucer's, stared up at the sign over the business's front door. Wyeth and Deeze were actually reading the sign. Chaucer was only gawking at it because the other two were. Chaucer truly was illiterate, and no amount of spin anyone tried to put on it would ever change that fact.

The sign read the Tan Banana.

"*Spray tans*? I'm not going in there," Wyeth announced, clearly appalled.

"Yes, you are," Deeze replied, giving him a gentle bump with his hip to get him moving.

"Huh-uh. No way in hell am I going in there."

Still unflappable, Deeze reached out and pulled open the door. "They've opened early just for us. So yes, you are. We're here. We have an appointment. It's already paid for. You're going. I hope you wore underwear."

"Well, of course I wore underwear! And what do you mean, it's already paid for?"

"Just what I said. It's already paid for."

"I'll reimburse you the money. Let's just leave."

"Go through the fucking door, Wy."

"My name is Wyeth. Stop calling me Wy."

"But why, Wy?" Deeze simpered. Then he tossed a grin over the comment to show he was being a wiseass. A young woman stood inside the shop, back among the shadows, watching the two morons waging a battle of wills at her front door. The woman was built like a refrigerator and wore bib overalls like she was about to harness up the team and head out to the fields to plow the south forty.

"In or out," she called. "Air-conditioning ain't cheap, you know."

Wyeth whispered, "She's not even using proper English. I'm not going in there. How do I know it's sanitary? How do I know I won't be blinded or end up with orange hair or suntanned teeth?"

Deeze laughed out loud and pushed him through the door, dragging a startled Chaucer along behind.

The young woman gave a friendly wave to Deeze, then turned her attention to the redhead he had just shoved through her door.

"So this must be him," she said. "You were right. He *is* cute, in a reluctant sort of way." Before Wyeth could take offense at that, she stepped forward and lifted the hair off his forehead to study the skin underneath. Then she lifted the tail of Wyeth's T-shirt without asking permission and checked out his pale chest.

"Ooh," Deeze said, peering over the woman's shoulder. "Nice torso. A little meager on the six-pack, but nice and trim nevertheless. Quite yummy actually."

The young woman agreed with a mumbled, "Yes, indeed," then added a wistful, "What I wouldn't give for that waistline." Wyeth stood there opening and closing his mouth like a guppy, evidently too shocked to speak.

The woman was smiling now, oblivious to Wyeth's scowl. "You're right, Deeze. It *is* lovely. With a tan it'll be even lovelier."

Deeze leaned in closer. He reached out a hand and brushed his fingertips through the strawberry blond hair circling Wyeth's belly button. "I sort of like it the way it is."

The young woman got huffy. "Well, this was your idea."

"I know, dammit," Deeze whined, still dragging his fingers through Wyeth's treasure trail.

Wyeth slapped his hand away and yanked his shirt down. "You people are crazy."

"Yes, well," the clerk said, "that's a matter of opinion." She turned to Deeze. "Are we doing full body, or should we leave a tan line?"

"Tan line, I think," Deeze said, turning away to study several full-length photos of freshly spray-tanned individuals plastered across the walls. He pointed to one young man wearing a teeny tiny tan line and little else. "Ooh, I like this one." He whirled back around and tapped Wyeth on the shoulder. "What sort of undies are you wearing, Wy? Boxers, trunks, teeny tiny briefs, like I should be so lucky?"

"B-b-briefs. And you can forget about being lucky. And they aren't that teeny tiny," he finished with a snarl.

Deeze blinked. "Wow. Cranky."

"Tempus fuji," the clerk said, tugging at Wyeth's shirtsleeve and dragging him toward the back of the shop.

"Your Latin sucks worse than your English," Wyeth said conversationally enough, shuffling along in the woman's wake because he really didn't have much choice in the matter. The woman was strong as an ox.

The clerk ignored him while she aimed a finger back at Deeze and the dog. "You two stay here."

"I DON'T think I want to do this," Wyeth wheedled, even while the clerk dragged him into the recesses of the building.

"Pshaw! You're gonna love it. Ain't nothing like a paleface getting his first tan. It's a life-changing experience. You'll see if it ain't."

"Ain't isn't a word" was all Wyeth could think to say. "No matter how many times you use it, it will never *be* a word."

"If it's in the dictionary, it's a word."

"Well, that's not strictly...."

Fifteen feet down a long corridor, she made a right turn and dragged Wyeth through a door with a big metal *A* screwed into the wood at about eye level. In the room were what appeared to be a dressing screen in one corner and a shower stall in the other. The lights were dim. Wyeth could barely see anything at all.

The clerk handed him a pair of paper panties. "These will give you the proper tan line without staining the briefs you're wearing. Go behind the screen, take everything off, and put them on."

"I don't want to take everything off."

"Do it anyway."

"I don't want a tan."

"Yes, you do. You look like Casper next to your boyfriend."

"He-he's not my boyfriend."

"Well, he *should* be," she said. "He's gorgeous."

Wyeth stopped what he was doing, the paper underpants almost forgotten in his hand, and stared back at the door he'd just come through. "Yes," he said, rather breathlessly, "he is, isn't he?"

Apparently not big on romance, the clerk shoved him none too gently toward the screen and snapped, "Get naked and put those on. We'll be done before you know it."

"How long will it take to dry?"

"Less than five minutes."

"How long will I look orange?"

"You won't look orange. You'll look tanned. And it lasts two weeks."

"Will I be spotty when it fades?"

"No."

"If I like it, can I come back?"

The clerk smiled her first smile of the morning. When she did, she looked far less like a refrigerator and more like a fairly attractive young woman with perhaps a wee bit of a weight problem. "See how smart your boyfriend is? He *knew* you wanted this, even when *you* thought you *didn't*."

Wyeth sighed. "He's not my boyfriend."

The clerk shot him a wink. "Well, after you get your tan, maybe you should work on that next."

"I don't want to work on that next."

"Yes, you do. He told me all about you in class."

"What class? Are you in preschool? Are you the one he buys all the crayons for?"

The clerk laughed and slapped Wyeth on the back so hard, he almost flew across the room. "In kinesiology, silly. We attend night classes together at City College."

"Night classes? I didn't know."

She stuffed a fist on her hip and glared. "If you don't start undressing, I'll rip your clothes off myself. Or get Deeze in here to do it for me."

Wyeth quickly ducked behind the screen. "Sheesh! All right. I'm undressing already."

While he did that, he listened to her fiddling with the spraying stall, getting things ready.

Through the screen, Wyeth asked, "Why are the two of you taking night classes?"

"We're studying to become personal trainers, or at least I am. I think Deeze hasn't decided yet. He may go for physical therapist in relation to sports injuries."

"Doesn't he like teaching kids?"

"He *loves* teaching kids. He just wants to do this too." She rapped her knuckles on the screen, causing Wyeth to jump because by this time he was stark naked and had only one leg poked through the paper panties, which in his opinion seemed really, really flimsy. "For someone who's going out with Deeze, you'd think you would know all this stuff."

"We're not going out."

"Yeah, right. He's springing for your spray-on tan because you're his charity of the month."

"I'm *nobody's* charity!"

"He *said* you were touchy."

By the time Wyeth stepped out from behind the screen, feeling more exposed in the stupid paper panties than he would have starkass naked, he was fuming. "Let's just get this over with. And Deeze and I are not going out, so's you know. Nor is he my boyfriend. *And I'm not touchy!*"

The clerk pointed him into the shower stall, mumbling, "Oh no, not touchy at all. You're a fucking tranquilizer, you are."

The door to the hallway opened, and Deeze stuck his head in. His eyes immediately focused on Wyeth in the open tanning stall in nothing but the tiny paper panties that left little or nothing to the imagination.

He whistled softly, causing Wyeth to slam the stall door shut and scream, "Get the fuck out of here!"

"Your boyfriend's shy," the clerk said.

"I know," Deeze stage-whispered back.

All of which prompted Wyeth to scream, "I'm not your fucking boyfriend! And I'm not fucking shy. And I'm *still* not fucking touchy."

Through the stall door and his own agitated breathing, Wyeth heard Deeze say, "I'd best go before his dog shits in your waiting room."

"Please do," the woman snarled.

Still not sure how things had come to this, two minutes later, Wyeth, practically naked and strangely turned on, was holding his breath and being sprayed down with a blast of suntan juice like a used car at Earl Schieb's.

OUT ON the street, Wyeth stopped in front of yet *another* store window and stared at his reflection. Truth be told, he was also staring at the handsome man standing next to him. Deeze. The man whom, against all better judgment, he was beginning to find considerably less annoying than he once had.

"So I'm guessing you like the look," Deeze commented, arms crossed, head cocked, cupping his chin like an art connoisseur studying a Monet he'd never seen before. Not only did he appear to be amused and happy to see Wyeth appreciating his new tan, but he had also been promoted to handling Chaucer's leash. He appeared to be amused and happy about that too.

Wyeth gazed into the storefront window. He eyed the reflection of his newly bronzed legs, then he held both arms out in front of him and looked at those. Ignoring the shoppers inside staring out at the man admiring himself, he pulled up his shirttail to stare at his tanned belly.

He didn't want to sound like an egotistical twit, but he honestly couldn't believe what a difference it made. "I've never been tanned in my life."

Deeze grinned. "Well, you are now."

"I look healthy."

"You *are* healthy. You always *were* healthy. And you *always* looked it."

"I've been pale my whole life."

"Pale and handsome. Now you're simply *tanned* and handsome."

Wyeth turned from the window and stared at Deeze, standing there in front of him with Chaucer at his feet. He slowly shook his head. "I've never deluded myself into thinking I was handsome. I'm not." When Deeze smiled at his words, clearly disbelieving, Wyeth sighed. And finally, he smiled back. "You are the handsome one, Deeze. I-I think you're the most handsome man I've ever met."

Deeze didn't blush. Deeze merely stared back. "I'm glad you think so. It doesn't seem fair, though, that I should have to believe you when you won't believe me."

"I don't care what you believe. I know the truth."

Wyeth turned back to the window for a final glimpse of his newly tanned image. "Thank you for this. If nothing else, it's a lot of fun to be something I'm not for a while."

"Do me a favor, then," Deeze said. "Be something else you're not. Do something you wouldn't ordinarily do."

Wyeth looked wary. He hadn't known Deeze very long, but he knew him well enough to know he had to be on his guard around the guy. He was sneaky.

"And what exactly might that be?" Wyeth carefully asked.

"Hold my hand. While we walk."

Wyeth shuffled his feet, suddenly nervous, suddenly uncomfortable. "Why?" he asked.

Deeze didn't hesitate. "Because I want to touch you. I want to connect. I want to feel you while we stroll down the street to the train station."

"We're strolling down the street to the train station?"

"Yes. It's your next surprise."

"You've spent enough money already."

Now, oddly enough, Deeze blushed. "I haven't spent a nickel yet."

"But… the *tan*."

"Laurie's my cousin. Your tan was a freebie."

"She's your *cousin*? She said you guys went to night school together."

"Yeah. We do that too. So will you hold my hand?"

"I still don't under—"

Deeze gave an exasperated huff. "Jeez, Wyeth. Just hold my stupid hand. I'm not asking for a kidney here. Just a little physical connection. A smattering of human bonding. It's not gonna kill you."

It might kill me, Wyeth thought. *It just might.*

But instead of speaking those words and spending the rest of the day trying to explain them, he resignedly reached out and took Deeze's hand. "There," he said. "Happy?"

Deeze wove his fingers through Wyeth's, tightening his grip. Their hands were warm, even a little sweaty—the day was getting hot already—but Deeze obviously didn't mind.

With a gentle tug, he steered Wyeth along the street toward the Santa Fe Depot down by the bay, maybe eight or nine blocks away. It was there the silver Amtrak trains, with their red, white, and blue stripes along the side, splintered their way out of the city, heading for parts unknown.

They walked quietly for a couple of blocks. Then Wyeth broke the silence. "You won't believe this, but I've never ridden a train."

Deeze nudged him with a shoulder but didn't break stride. He did, however, bear a wide grin on his face. "Then it's time my baby did," he said.

"I'm not your baby, Deeze," Wyeth softly said. He was not smiling when he said it.

CHAPTER FIVE

THE LOCAL Coaster train shuttled locals back and forth along the California coast. Thus its name. Unlike the silver Amtrak trains, the Coaster cars were green and blue. Modern and air-conditioned, the Coasters slid along the rails in a gentle hush of whispery sound. Wyeth sat in the window seat because Deeze had insisted he should. They had ensconced themselves on the left side of the northbound train, also at Deeze's insistence, and because of that savvy decision, Wyeth now stared out at the grand Pacific Ocean gliding past, not a hundred feet from the rails. The view from the other side of the car would have been far less appealing.

Down at their feet, Chaucer lay sound asleep, drooling on Wyeth's sneaker. He had never been on a train before, either, but it didn't seem to impress him much. The same could not be said for his master.

"This is wonderful," Wyeth said. He tore his eyes away from the window and stared down at Deeze's bare knee brushing up against his newly tanned one. His own legs looked like someone else's now, and he realized for the first time that with a little color they didn't look half-bad. Of course, they were nowhere near as beautiful as Deeze's. He noticed suddenly that Deeze's hairy forearm was brushing against his too. He suspected that, from those two small points of bare-skinned contact alone, he could close his eyes and imagine the two of them sitting there naked. That was such a monumental thought, and such a stunningly terrifying one, he didn't dare try it out.

"Unless the ticket guy back at the station was a cousin of yours and this is another family freebie, I'll pay you back for the train fare," Wyeth said.

"No, you won't," Deeze said. "This day is on me. And train tickets are cheap. Don't worry about it."

Wyeth sighed. The guy was impossible. "At least tell me where we're going."

"No. You'll find out when we get there."

"Supercilious much?" Wyeth mumbled to himself, making Deeze erupt in a snort of laughter.

There was nothing else he could do, so Wyeth settled back in the seat and stared once more out the train window. At that moment, the Coaster car was passing a string of weathered beach cottages. Out past the cottages, Wyeth spotted wetsuit-clad surfers hunched over their boards, paddling like crazy, waiting, watching, eyeing the swells for that perfect wave.

Quietly, barely over the hum of the rails, Deeze leaned in and said, "Do you surf?"

Startled, Wyeth stared at him. "I was just thinking about that. No," he said. "I-I don't even swim. It's something I've never learned."

"A Californian who doesn't swim is like a hooker who doesn't screw."

Wyeth narrowed his eyes. "What a profoundly philosophical thing to say."

"Thanks. Would you like to?"

"Would I like to what? Swim or screw?"

"I think if I try to answer that the way I'd *like* to answer it, I'll be in a whole lot of trouble. Although I should point out that if you choose screwing, you'll have far less chance of drowning."

Wyeth laughed. "Or being ravaged by a shark."

Deeze eyed him shrewdly. "Oh, you'd be ravaged, all right."

Wyeth's ears burned. Just joking about sex with Deeze was enough to rattle him. But it was a rattling he kind of enjoyed. And that rattled him too.

He was sifting through his head for something noncommittal to say when Deeze beat him to it. "You didn't grow up here, did you? Unless I'm mistaken, there's a Midwestern twang in your voice. I think I'd peg you for being from somewhere around the Corn Belt. Iowa? Kansas?"

"Indiana," Wyeth said. "And you get one of your kiddygarden gold stars. I thought my accent had disappeared."

"Not quite, and that's a good thing because I like it. What brought you out here?"

"An overly religious family. Growing into a lifestyle I knew they would never accept. A brother who outed me when I was sixteen. An allergy to corn pollen. Take your pick. Those are the true reasons. If you'd like to hear the reason I *usually* use when impertinent strangers ask me, it's because I wanted to go to college here, which isn't a lie. It just isn't the whole truth."

Deeze slipped his fingers over Wyeth's on the armrest. "I'm sorry. I mean because of the reasons you're here, not because I'm impertinent."

"I get the impression your impertinence is beyond even your control."

Deeze clucked his tongue. "Pretty much."

"I thought so," Wyeth said around a grin. Then he shrugged. "Anyway. I'm better off here than I ever would have been there." He brightened, if only for a second. "I'm *happy* here. I can be myself. Well, usually."

"What does that mean?"

Wyeth refused to answer. He merely shook his head, avoiding the question completely. Using a gambit he was pretty adept at after long practice, he turned the conversation back to Deeze.

"I get the impression you were born here, right?"

"Yeah."

"I suppose you surf and swim."

Deeze nodded. A twinkle lit his eye. "And screw. Yeah."

Wyeth decided it would be safer to ignore that remark. He turned his eyes away to stare through the window for a moment, then twisted back around to study Deeze's face. "Why are you doing all this?"

"All what?" Deeze asked, although he was clearly hedging. He knew what the question meant as well as Wyeth did.

"All *this*. Everything you're doing for me. The tan, the train ride, the secrets. The sweetness."

Deeze pointed to the window on the opposite side of the car. "Look," he said. "The Del Mar Racetrack!" He glanced at his watch. "The horses will be running later."

Wyeth stared out across a small expanse of chaparral to the two perfectly groomed ovals of the racetracks in the distance, one inside the other, one green, one dun. Grass and dirt. The grandstands were empty at the moment, but he could imagine the screaming crowds that would fill them later. He had seen snippets on the news. The Del Mar racing season was a big deal in San Diego. "I've never bet on a horse in my life," Wyeth said, somewhat wistfully.

Deeze didn't seem surprised by that revelation, but he refused to comment on it. He clearly still had other things on his mind. As the train trundled on past the racetrack, and later through the colorful seaside city of Del Mar, his eyes softened as he watched Wyeth's face. "Am I being sweet? Is that what you said?"

Wyeth's eyes skittered away from the window, and he turned to Deeze, exasperated and rebellious. "You know you are. It's unnerving."

"My being sweet is unnerving to you?"

"Yes."

Deeze slipped around in his seat to face Wyeth head-on. Even as he did so, he never released Wyeth's hand. Wyeth was hypnotized by the feel of Deeze's leg hair scraping through his own as Deeze wiggled around for a better vantage point.

"I like you is all," Deeze said, his face somber. There was no laughter in his eyes. "I want you to like me back."

"But *why*?"

Softly, Deeze answered, "That question says more about you than you want me to know, I think. Why is it so wrong for me to want you to like me?"

Wyeth tried to free his fingers from Deeze's grip then, but Deeze wouldn't let them go. Even when a woman came down the aisle, glanced down at them, and smiled, Deeze wouldn't release Wyeth's hand.

"Sorry I asked," Wyeth said, shaking his head and hating the feeling of his ears getting hot.

"Are you really sorry?" Deeze asked. "Or are you just too embarrassed to pursue it? I'll tell you, you know. I'll tell you anything you want to know."

Wyeth tore his eyes from Deeze's and stared out the window. The light faded and the train grew suddenly shadowed as it slipped through a tunnel of trees enveloping the tracks. Wyeth closed his eyes, happy for the dimness to shield him from Deeze's gaze, even if it was only for a moment. Too quickly, the train shot out of the leafy tunnel, and the light flowed back in, baring all.

"That's what scares me about you," Wyeth said, keeping his voice down so no one else in the car could overhear. "Your lack of boundaries. Your unhesitating openness."

To Wyeth's surprise, Deeze lifted his hand to stroke Wyeth's cheek. "I refuse to back off because you're afraid of honesty, Wy."

"Wyeth. You're supposed to call me Wyeth. And stop that."

Deeze just smiled and continued to stroke his cheek. "Wy works just fine. Stop being so picky. I have other battles to wage."

"What battles might those be?" Wyeth asked, but he was immediately sorry he did.

"You," Deeze answered, pulling his hand from Wyeth's face and laying it back on the armrest, reclaiming Wyeth's in a gentle grip. "You're the battle. Getting *you* to open up. Getting you to like *me*."

"I'm… I'm not a battle, Deeze. I'm just me."

"Okay, my mistake. You're not a battle. But neither am I, Wy. I just want to be friends. It's no biggie. Honest. There's nothing underhanded about it. Friendship is a pretty basic human condition."

Wyeth blinked. "I'm not good with friends. I never have been. I'm better with books."

Deeze gave an uncharitable chuckle. "Yeah, I was beginning to get that impression. So you can practice your humanity skills on me."

The train began to slow. Before Wyeth could argue any more, Deeze pointed to a sign outside the window. Solana Beach.

"Our stop," Deeze said.

"Why? What's in Solana Beach?"

"The best Mexican food this side of Puerta Vallarta. Please tell me you like Mexican food."

For some reason, Wyeth felt himself blushing. "I do," he said. "I *love* Mexican food."

"Then good. Grab the dog."

Still gripping Wyeth's fingers, Deeze tugged him from his seat. Two minutes later they were standing outside the rustic Solana Beach depot while the other departing passengers scurried off this way and that. Deeze pointed north.

"We're going that way."

Still a little stunned by the way the day was turning out, Wyeth worked his fingers a little more tightly between Deeze's and followed him from the station.

On the way out, Chaucer tried to hump an ATM machine.

THEY LUNCHED on steaming bowls of albondigas soup on a terraced cafe overlooking the beach off Cedros Avenue, the main Solana Beach thoroughfare. Afterward they strolled through a farmers' market and picked up fresh peaches, which they ate while ambling along the sandy shore barefoot, their shoes and sandals tied together and draped over their shoulders to free up their hands. From this vantage point, Wyeth could not only see the surfers much closer than he had from the train, but he could also hear them happily calling out to each other as they bobbed among the swells, paddling this way and that, occasionally catching a wave just right and rising up to balance gracefully on their boards and skim along the foaming crests of surf with gleeful whoops and bellows.

Wyeth laughed and pointed at their antics, while Deeze had eyes only for the redheaded man beside him. Peaches eaten, they rinsed their hands in the surf and sat in the sand, gazing seaward. It was high noon, and the sun was hot on their skin, but the cool breeze flowing in from the water made it bearable. Unlike San Diego Harbor, with its reek of fish and the raucous cries of sea gulls screaming overhead, here the ocean smelled clean and crisp, and the air was alive with the sigh of surf pulsing against the shore like the gentle breath of a sleeping beast.

Deeze wiggled his toes in the sand and smiled to himself when Wyeth did the same beside him.

"You have pretty feet," Deeze said.

Wyeth blushed. "Oh, shut the hell up." Then he relented. "Thanks for bringing me here. It's lovely."

"You're welcome," Deeze said, fighting back a smile once again at Wyeth's formalities. "With your new tan, you look like any other Southern California beach rat, sunning himself to toast. You belong here."

Wyeth wedged a hand across his brow to shield his eyes from the sun's glare while he stared out once again at the surfers in the distance. "A fake tan doesn't make me suddenly belong, Deeze. It might make me less noticeable than I would be as a paleface, but belonging has to come from inside. I'm not much of a belonger, if you want to know the truth. I never quite feel like I'm in the right place at the right time no matter where I am. Instead of fitting in, I always seem to—*intrude*."

Deeze shifted around in the sand to better face Wyeth, folding his legs beneath him and reaching out to lay a hand on Wyeth's knee. He slid his fingers through the hair there and studied Wyeth's blue eyes when they dropped to watch Deeze's hand on his skin. When Wyeth didn't pull away, Deeze felt as if he had scored a victory. Still, Wyeth's words bothered him.

"I guess it's hard when you're shy," he said.

Wyeth's eyes slid from the hand on his knee and focused on Deeze's face. There was a look of quizzical uncertainty in their depths. "Is that what I am? Shy? Or am I just the polar opposite of you, Deeze? You seem to fit in everywhere you go. Nothing intimidates you. You're never an outsider. You own every situation you're in. I envy you that. But it isn't me. It never will be. I'm just not as social as you are." A weird little smile twisted his mouth. "Actually, Deeze, without a little pharmacological help, I don't think many people are."

Deeze ignored the jibe and continued to study Wyeth's face. "I don't believe that. Being social is just a matter of practice. The secret is to not let yourself care what people think."

"Yes," Wyeth said, his smile still in place, but his overall expression resigned. "And that's a concept a few of us struggle with every day."

Deeze's fingers had never stopped moving over the hair on Wyeth's knee. Sliding a little closer across the sand, he cupped Wyeth's calf muscle in his hand and was surprised by the bulge of it. There was substantial muscle there. And the skin felt like heated satin against Deeze's palm.

This time when he moved his hand, caressing the back of Wyeth's leg, Wyeth blushed. "Don't," he said quietly. "There are people around."

Deeze shook his head. "I don't care."

"What if I care?"

Not only did Deeze not remove his hand from Wyeth's leg, but he placed his other hand there as well, all but claiming full ownership. He slid both thumbs across the now-golden skin, and he thought he saw Wyeth reacting to the touch, whether he wanted to or not. His expression mellowed. He no longer gazed at the other people on the beach. Instead, he focused his eyes solely on Deeze's face. The innocence in those azure eyes with their long, pale lashes made Deeze suddenly aware of his own softly thundering heart. He was enchanted to see that in the short time they had been in the sun, it had already brought out a spray of freckles across Wyeth's nose and cheeks. Even his eyes looked bluer.

"The sun agrees with you," Deeze said.

At that moment, a little boy ran past. A few paces farther on, the child skidded to a stop, kicking up a cloud of sand, then turned and walked hesitantly back toward them. He couldn't have been more than five. He had a shaggy mop of brown hair, dried into ropy tendrils, clearly styled by the sun and wind after a dip in the surf. He was coated with sand and smeared with mud, and he wore a baggy pair of swim trunks that were perilously close to sliding off his slim little hips. He stared slack-jawed at Deeze's face.

"Mr. Long?" the boy squeaked. "What are you doing here?"

Only then did Deeze turn toward the boy.

"Jake?" Deeze asked with a broad smile. "Is that you? And how did you get so dirty? You look like you just crawled out of the primordial soup."

"Whatever *that* means," the kid said around a goofy grin. He shuffled from one foot to the other for a moment, then apparently made up his mind, and hurled himself into Deeze's arms. Deeze caught him with a bray of laughter while Wyeth looked on, amazed.

While man and boy hugged each other, Deeze saw Wyeth watching and shot him a wink, which confused Wyeth even more. Deeze finally gripped the kid under the armpits and stood him back on his feet in the sand in front of them.

"You here with your folks?" Deeze asked.

The boy ducked his head in shame, like someone caught up in circumstances far beyond his control or liking. "Yeah," he grumped, clearly not happy about it. "They're over there sitting under that stupid umbrella."

Both Deeze and Wyeth looked in the direction Jake pointed, and saw a young man and woman sitting on tenterhooks after apparently witnessing their five-year-old son throw himself into the arms of a total stranger.

Then Wyeth saw the two relax and exchange words. They obviously had recognized Deeze. The mother waved and called out, "Hello, Mr. Long!" To her son, she bellowed, "Jake, give the poor man his privacy. He's stuck with you five days a week. That's more than enough for any human being."

Jake rolled his eyes. "Mom thinks she's funny." His little chin suddenly puckered up like a sieve as he pointed to his knee. "Lookit." He sighed forlornly. "I fell down."

And sure enough the kid had scraped his knee. It wasn't oozing blood, but it did look kind of nasty.

Deeze offered him a sympathetic pout in return and started fishing around in his shorts pocket. "Let me fix that," he said, hauling out a Band-Aid. While Jake smiled and Wyeth stared in amazement, Deeze tore the wrapper off the Band-Aid, removed the sticky covering on both ends, and after carefully blowing the sand from Jake's knee, slipped it over the scratch. When he was finished, he gave the knee a gentle pat and asked, "Better?"

Jake beamed, admiring his bandage. Jake and Wyeth obviously both noticed the Band-Aid had little rocket ships on it. In unison, man and boy said, "Cool."

Jake turned to stare at Wyeth for the first time.

Deeze leaped in to make introductions. "Wyeth, this is Jake. One of my students. He has a bad habit of throwing spit balls, so don't turn your back on him. He also has an inexplicable knack for falling down every time he stands up. I've never seen anything like it."

The boy grinned, and two deep dimples bored holes in his cheeks. He tugged at his cowlick, looking thoughtful, and said, "I think maybe if the world was flat I wouldn't fall down so much."

"From the mouths of babes," said Deeze.

Jake had discovered the dog by this time. He squatted in the sand with his face buried in Chaucer's fuzzy belly and giggled, "I'm not a babe. My mom's a babe. That's what Daddy said, although I don't think I was supposed to hear it." Without looking and with his face still smothered in dog hair, he extended his hand to Wyeth, who accepted it in a shake. Wyeth smiled as the itty-bitty hand, gritty with sand, burrowed inside his own.

"Jake!" his mother screamed out, startling various people up and down the beach and possibly a few whales at sea. "Get back here! Leave those poor men alone! Toodles, Mr. Long! Have a nice day. Jake, get over here *now*!"

Deeze waved back while Jake peeked out of Chaucer's coat to stare at Wyeth. "Nice to meetcha," the boy said shyly, and Wyeth returned the sentiment. Jake suddenly pointed to Wyeth's scabbed knee and said, "Did you fall down too?"

"Yeah," Wyeth said. "I'm clumsy."

Jake nodded as if he understood completely. "Yeah. Me too. So how come you didn't get a Band-Aid?"

"I don't know," Wyeth said, casting Deeze a theatrical pout.

Deeze laughed, and a moment later he pulled another Band-Aid out of his shorts pocket. He tore it out of its wrapper, and both Wyeth and Jake watched with rapt attention as Deeze carefully placed it over Wyeth's skinned knee.

"Better?" Deeze asked when he was finished, and both patients grinned.

A moment later, the kid was running back toward his parents, sand flying, little swim trunks riding low on his tiny butt.

Deeze laughed watching him go.

Wyeth grinned. "You're his teacher and he actually likes you. Isn't that a little unheard of? He's not another cousin, is he?"

Deeze laughed. "No. Just a student. And for your information, *all* my students like me. I'm a likable guy. Besides, I get them before they are turned into hateful little troglodytes by their peers and the world at large. They don't begin dickhead training until they reach first grade. I catch them while they're still in the purity stage."

Wyeth laughed. "Lucky you."

WYETH SLID his eyes from Deeze's still-smiling face and gazed along the beach to where he saw Jake's mother now smearing sun block over the squirming boy while Jake proudly showed her the bandage on his knee. The woman glanced up while Wyeth was looking and shot him a friendly wave. Surprised, Wyeth waved back, then pointed to his own knee, showing the woman he had a new bandage too. The woman gave him a hesitant thumbs-up, like maybe she was suddenly wondering if Mr. Long's friend was running on all cylinders.

Turning away, Wyeth let his eyes roam back to Deeze. With no little amount of wonder in his voice, he said, "I think you must be a very good teacher."

Deeze snorted a laugh. "Why would you assume that?"

But Wyeth didn't answer. He just shrugged and filed away the whole interlude with the kid on the beach, placing it on a shelf in the back of his mind to be dragged out and dissected later. He knew already, however, that the odd chance meeting he had witnessed on the beach had changed the way he thought of Deeze Long. It had, in fact, taken everything he thought he knew about the man and flipped it on its head.

When Deeze finally turned away from the family up the beach and reclaimed Wyeth's leg in both his strong hands, Wyeth didn't object. And suddenly, he didn't care what people on the beach might think about it either.

He had almost closed his eyes to better savor the feel of Deeze's fingers on his skin, when Deeze said, "We'd better go, or we'll miss the train." He released Wyeth's leg with a final pat to the Band-Aid on Wyeth's knee, then slipped his feet in his sandals and stood to dust the sand off his shorts.

Wyeth quickly pulled on his sneakers and let Deeze haul him to his feet. He didn't even try to disguise his disappointment when he said, "Are we going home, then?"

If Deeze heard the regret in Wyeth's voice, he didn't let on.

"Nope," he said. "We're not going home. Not yet anyway. We have to scratch another item from your bucket list of unfulfilled experiences."

"I don't have a bucket list of unfulfilled experiences."

But Deeze wasn't listening. He was already running up the beach, dragging a scampering Chaucer along behind him. Wyeth didn't have much choice but to race to catch up.

By the time they got back to the train station, puffing and panting, Wyeth's shoes were full of sand and he was laughing like a loon. His hair was sticking straight up, his cheeks were flushed, and he stood in front of a depot window, laughing at his own reflection and trying to make himself look a little more presentable.

"Now *that's* what I like to see," Deeze panted, dropping onto a bench by the tracks. "A happy librarian. You should smile all the time."

Wyeth had heard that line before. He had hated it then, and he hated it now. Still he didn't let it wipe the smile away. He turned from the window, giving his hair a final pat, which really didn't help it much. "If I smiled all the time I'd look like a fool." As if to prove he was a serious-minded fellow, he tugged his glasses off and cleaned them on the tail of his shirt.

"Fine," Deeze answered teasingly. "*Don't* smile all the time. Just try to look a little less homicidal now and then."

Wyeth slipped his glasses back on. "I'll do my best."

Deeze patted the bench beside him, and, already laughing again, Wyeth dropped onto it. He immediately pulled off his shoes and shook the sand out. In the distance, he heard a train whistle.

"So you've never been to the horse races, huh?" Deeze asked through a sneaky leer.

Chapter Six

WYETH STOOD at his dresser counting out the money for the fifth time. Yep. Three hundred and thirty dollars. He still couldn't believe it, but his horse had won. Good old Bookish Betty. At forty-to-one odds. Deeze had kidded him for betting on a long shot just because the animal had the word "book" in its name, going into long detail on the best way to gamble at Del Mar by sticking with more favored horses and not falling for cutesy monikers. He himself had placed a sizable sum on the favorite of the day who, much to Deeze's embarrassment, stumbled in the backstretch and had to be removed from the track in a horsey ambulance. Poor thing. Wyeth's horse, on the other hand, plodded on, eventually claiming the race by a length and a half to the astonishment of about thirty thousand people, including Wyeth.

When Wyeth screamed and jumped up and down at his good luck, Deeze jumped up and down with him. Still leaping in the bleachers, they had found themselves falling into each other's arms and laughing like fools while Chaucer wagged his tail and sniffed around looking for something to hump. Even now, even after all the excitement was over, Wyeth remembered the feel of Deeze in his arms as they stood there in the midst of that sweating throng of cheering people, not caring one little bit what *any* of them thought about the two guys jumping up and down and hugging each other in Grandstand C, Aisle 12, seats F and G.

It had been a hell of a day.

Wyeth laid the money aside and stripped out of his clothes. Standing in front of the dresser mirror, he studied his newly tanned body naked for the first time. Aside from a sunburn here and there at various points in his life, this was the first time he could look at himself and see an honest-to-God tan line. That pale strip of flesh across his hips, surrounded by golden skin, was such a new experience for him, he turned to see what his ass looked like. His ass was still snow white, he noticed, but somehow when it was framed by a golden back and golden legs, it didn't look quite so anemic.

He turned back to stare at his front, and suddenly the memory of Deeze in his arms at the racetrack sent a surge of blood rushing into his cock. His burgeoning erection rose from its nest of ginger pubic hair and, in a matter of moments, stood straight up, pointing due north like a compass.

Wyeth snorted a laugh at himself and headed for the shower. Deeze was picking him up for the final portion of their day together—dinner—which Deeze said Wyeth would be springing for since he was the one who made a killing at the track. Wyeth had laughed, but he hadn't complained. It seemed only fair.

He was glad his time with Deeze wasn't over yet. Something had happened during the course of this remarkable day that Wyeth had not expected to occur. He found himself fending off emotions that hadn't touched him for a very long time. They still frightened him, those emotions, but he had also during his many hours with Deeze realized he had begun to trust the man. Maybe not with his heart. It was far too early for that. But with his time.

With the beginning, perhaps, of friendship.

To resurrect a highlight of the day, he only had to recall Deeze digging through his shorts pocket on the beach and pulling out a Band-Aid for the boy's scraped knee. He recalled the trust that Jake had put in Deeze to let him treat his wound. And how Deeze had gone so self-assuredly and so caringly through the motions. Tender, competent, gentle.

Wyeth smiled under the shower spray, remembering how Deeze had bandaged *his* scraped knee as well. He reached down now and pulled the Band-Aid free, taking a moment to stare at the little rockets on it before wadding it up and setting it aside. Ignoring his erection as best he could, he finished showering and quickly toweled off. He blasted his red hair with a blow dryer, admiring the way it looked so much lighter now against his newly tanned face. He brushed his teeth, gargled, dug around in his ears with a Q-tip, and gave himself a final going-over, before heading into the bedroom to dress.

Once that chore was accomplished, he put his good watch on his wrist, slipped the race winnings in his wallet, and hurried into the kitchen, where he pulled out a fistful of dog biscuits to keep Chaucer occupied while he stole out the front door.

He was meeting Deeze on the corner in exactly three minutes. When Wyeth hurried through the main entrance of his apartment building to find the sun-slathered day had finally morphed into cooling dusk, he spotted Deeze under a tree, steps from the front door, waiting for him.

They laughed, because they were wearing almost the exact same clothes. Pressed jeans, dress shirts, sleeves rolled up, collars open, both now exposing a wedge of tanned chest—Wyeth's smooth and golden and lean, Deeze's brown and hairy and far better muscled.

Standing speechless for a moment as pedestrians slipped past and around them, they stared at each other. It was at that moment when Wyeth first knew it was real, that feeling he had been fending off all day. The feeling that had finally hit him full force that afternoon when Deeze gently plastered that Band-Aid over his stupid knee.

Wyeth now knew he liked this man. He liked him a lot.

That sudden blast of awareness hit him like a ton of bricks. *I'm not afraid*, Wyeth said to himself. *Whatever happens, happens. Let it come. I'm not afraid. I just want to spend a little time with this guy. Now. Today. Tonight.*

With a smile, Deeze reached out and took Wyeth's hand. Compliant for once in his life, Wyeth allowed him to do so, causing Deeze's face to light up.

"You're letting me hold your hand without an argument?" Deeze asked. "How come?"

Wyeth refused to blush. At least he *told* himself he did. "Why? Do I need a reason?"

Deeze's face softened as he edged a little closer. "No. You don't need a reason for anything."

At a casual pace, Deeze led them up Broadway. As the sun slid past the horizon, the air cooled even more while the silken darkness of a summer evening gathered around them. Streetlights blinked on. Gradually, the headlights of passing cars came to life, and in their passing flashes, Wyeth caught teeny glimpses of Deeze's smile, Deeze's eyes, Deeze's white teeth gleaming in the shadows, his dark curly hair shifting in the evening breeze. Deeze's expression seemed to change every second, and Wyeth never tired of watching it. Once, when Deeze's eyes landed on *him*, Wyeth sucked in a tiny breath as if he had been impaled by the look.

To cover his surprise, Wyeth scrambled for something mundane to say. "We haven't touched our cars all weekend."

The statement brought a broader smile to Deeze's handsome face. "I know! I *love* living downtown."

"Why do you?" Wyeth asked. "I mean, where is your school? Is it close?"

"We'll pass it in a few minutes. It's a Jesuit school next to the cathedral on Lincoln Boulevard."

"Are you Catholic?"

Deeze frowned, then grinned, then frowned again, as if he couldn't quite decide what mood would best answer the question. "I'm not much of anything, as far as religion goes. Happily, proof of faith wasn't required for the job. Just the proper teaching credentials."

"How many students do you have?"

"Currently there are twenty-four in my class. The number fluctuates on how many I have to toss out the window during any given week."

Wyeth laughed. "If they are all like Jake, they can't be that bad."

Deeze nodded. "You're right. They aren't. I love them to death, every one of them. Someday I'll have you stop by and give a short lecture. You can explain to their young minds everything you know about the workings of the San Diego Library."

Wyeth wasn't buying it. "I imagine they're a little young for that. I'd bore them back to diapers."

Deeze gave him a long, piercing stare. "Don't underestimate the little buggers. You'd be surprised by what they find interesting. And as you damn well know, it's never too early to learn about books. Although I'm sure they'll be more enthralled by how sexy their guest lecturer is. I know I will."

Wyeth reddened, already losing his battle not to blush. "Oh brother…," he mumbled, causing Deeze to laugh.

They approached a tall, ornate church, rendered in limestone, with towering rococo spires and bulging buttresses scattered here and there. High arched windows were footed with decorative balustrades carved in pink marble. The marquee on the lawn proclaimed the compound St. Luke's Parish and Church School. A stained glass window rising high above the cathedral's front steps and framed by Gothic stanchions depicted the good man himself, St. Luke, gazing down with welcoming arms spread wide, beckoning his flock inside.

To the left of the majestic stone church, a flagstone pathway led around back. There, in an atrium tucked neatly inside a cool grove of pepper trees, Deeze pointed to a line of three prefab classrooms that had been erected at the edge of a playground. The first classroom, Deeze explained, was for the nursery, the second classroom housed four-year-olds in transitional kindergarten. The last classroom, for five-year-olds, which Deeze and Wyeth now stood in front of, was reserved for the true kindergarten, which prepared students for grade school. Grades one through eight were taught on the main campus at the opposite side of the cathedral grounds.

Pulling a key from his pocket, Deeze unlocked his classroom door, and after he flicked a light switch, the interior came to life. With a proud gleam in his eyes, Deeze waved Wyeth inside.

Deeze's classroom was laid out like every classroom Wyeth had ever seen. Wooden desks, much smaller than any Wyeth remembered from his own years at school, sat in less than even rows. An oval play area dominated one side of the room, carpeted in interlocking blocks of rubber flooring. Rows and rows of hand-drawn pictures graced the walls. And Deeze's own desk stood at the front of the room before a blackboard badly in need of a wash. The room was colorful and merry and breezy and chaotic, all at the same time. Wyeth thought it fit Deeze's personality perfectly.

"It's wonderful," he breathed, reaching out to trace his fingers over a crayoned rendering of what appeared to be either a griffin or a deformed chicken. The creature was perched atop what looked like a dumpster that had been welded together by a dyslexic psychopath.

Deeze laughed. "Funny you should pick that picture to admire. The artist is none other than little Jakey Armbrewster."

Wyeth grinned. "Jake from the beach?"

Deeze nodded, and the two men stood for a moment admiring the ill-conceived beast, whose head was far too big for its body, and who for some strange reason bore three wings instead of two. Their faces beamed as they stood there staring at the drawing, shoulders brushing, each man relishing the nearness of the other, although neither chose to say so out loud.

Wyeth breathed in the pervasive scents of paste and finger paint. He stared at the handmade chains draped across the ceiling, painstakingly crafted with loops of multicolored construction paper, pasted together and carefully swagged from one overhead light fixture to the other. He admired the row of brass coat hooks where the students would hang either their coats or their backpacks—or both—during class and which also brought memories flooding back from Wyeth's own childhood back in Indiana.

After Wyeth took it all in, he let his eyes drift to Deeze's face. Deeze too was gazing about as if he had never seen this place before.

Perhaps it was the surprising silence. With not a student in sight and the night peering in through windows that usually sifted sunlight onto young heads, the empty desks seemed sadly barren. Still, pride of ownership lit Deeze's eyes and almost took Wyeth's breath away.

"You really love working here, don't you?" he asked quietly.

Only then did Deeze's gaze slide back to the man beside him. "I do. If you love your own job, Wy, half as much as I love mine, then you must be a happy man too."

Wyeth's glance skidded away. He pretended to study the drawings on the wall again. "I'm happy. I love the library. It's not exciting like this must be, but it's what I wanted, what I studied to do. I have no regrets, and that's about the best most any of us can say about our careers, right?"

They turned toward the sound of a shuffling footstep behind them. An old gray head poked through the doorway. Below the head, a priest's white collar shone bright around a scrawny neck. Worried eyes above quickly turned from trepidation to delight.

"Oh, it's you, Mr. Long! I saw the light and wasn't sure who was sneaking around."

Deeze laughed. "Not sneaking, Father. Just showing off my classroom to a friend." He plucked at Wyeth's sleeve and tugged him closer to the door. "Father Mike, I'd like you to meet Wyeth Becker. He works at the library downtown."

Wyeth stuck out his hand, and the old priest pumped it a few times, grinning broadly. "Glad to meet you, son. Any friend of Mr. Long's is a friend of the school. And that new library is a wonderful addition to the city. I envy you working there."

"Thank you, sir," Wyeth said. "We're very proud of it."

Father Mike gave each man a last perusal, then shot Deeze a wink. "Now that I know you aren't burglars or terrorists or Methodists, I'll leave you to it. Don't forget to lock up when you go, Mr. Long."

"Aye, aye, Father," Deeze said, shooting him a merry little salute. "And you have a pleasant evening."

When the priest was gone, Wyeth commented, "Nice man."

"He's more than a nice man. He's been my champion from the beginning. The Catholic hierarchy was leery about hiring a non-Catholic to teach their five-year-old students. Father Mike rather forcefully reminded them the greatest teacher who ever lived wasn't Catholic either."

"Really? And who was that?" Wyeth asked.

Deeze's eyes sparkled. "Jesus, of course."

Both men laughed, then Deeze lifted his hand and rested it against Wyeth's cheek. His thumb scraped across the blond stubble that had sprouted there during the course of their long day together.

"You must be getting hungry," Deeze said. "I know I am. Let's go have dinner."

Wyeth tilted his head slightly into Deeze's hand to better feel it pressed against his skin, then gave his head a more businesslike nod. Deeze was right. He *was* hungry.

"Yes," he said, chewing on a grin, wondering what Deeze had planned. "If it's to be anything like the rest of this crazy day, I'm sure you'll surprise me."

"If I don't, it won't be for lack of trying," Deeze said, flipping off the ceiling lights and ushering Wyeth through the classroom door before locking it tight behind them. Then he breathed in a gulp of night air and leaned in to steal a quick kiss, after first glancing around to make sure Father Mike was good and gone.

The unexpected kiss jarred Wyeth's glasses, so he pushed them back up his nose.

Reclaiming Wyeth's hand and pulling him toward the street, Deeze added, "Now then. Dinner. I hope you know how to cook."

Wyeth stopped in his tracks. "Say *what?*"

NOT THREE blocks farther up the street, Deeze steered them into a steakhouse tucked in among neighborhood shops and a string of bustling fast-food joints. Wyeth had never noticed the restaurant before in his long walks around the city with Chaucer trailing along at his heels. Once inside, Wyeth was surprised to find a lovely, quiet restaurant with a large flaming grill placed in the middle of the room. Unsure what the grill was doing there, it all became clear when they ordered their dinners, only to find moments later that raw cuts of meat were delivered to their table.

Deeze grinned at Wyeth's look of surprise. "Like I said, Wy. Hope you know how to cook."

Laughing, they moved to the grill and threw their steaks onto the flames. While they carefully prepared the main course, still laughing and trying not to set themselves on fire, along with several other strangers who were doing the same thing, their baked potatoes and side dishes were delivered to their table by a waitress who cast them a wink now and then as if they were old friends.

Despite their best efforts to ruin it, dinner was delicious. And just as Wyeth suspected it might, it turned out to be an astonishing experience as well.

They savored their meals in silence since it had been a long day and both men were starving. As the feeding frenzy began winding down, Wyeth sat back, emitting a dainty burp, then peered shyly across the table at Deeze, who was just finishing up his meal. While Wyeth was barely halfway through his steak, Deeze was already gnawing diligently at his bone like a rabbit munching on a carrot. There had been something Wyeth had wanted to say for hours. He figured this was as good a time as any to get it off his chest.

"You're always smiling, Deeze. I've never met *anyone* so filled with happiness. I hate to be the one to tell you, but it's not normal. I can barely crank up happiness six minutes out of any given day. How do you do it? How can you be so insufferably mirth-riddled all the time? How is it that everything you do becomes a merry adventure?"

Deeze blinked in surprise, then threw his head back and barked out a laugh, startling an older couple at another table. Even the waitress, halfway across the restaurant, looked up, bemused. Deeze saw the reaction of all these strangers to his hoot of laughter, but it clearly didn't bother him. He turned his back on the room and leaned across the table, lowering his voice. "Life *is* an adventure, Wy. And I enjoy adventures. Don't you?"

"I—I've never really had any." *Not until today*, he failed to add. "And don't call me...."

Deeze shot him an innocent moue, all wide eyes and deep dimples. There was a smear of steak sauce on his chin. "Hmm?"

Resigned, Wyeth shook his head. "Never mind. Call me whatever you want."

"All right, then," Deeze said. "I'd like to call you my friend."

Wyeth chose that moment to concentrate on sawing off another chunk of his own steak. "Fine. Friend it is."

"Really?" Deeze reached across his plate and laid his hand over Wyeth's, capturing his knife in midslice. "And what if I should decide 'friend' doesn't quite cover it? What if I take it into my mirth-riddled pea-brain to want more than friendship?"

Wyeth was embarrassed and startled, but he was pleased too. He didn't want to be, but he was. "Then I'd say you were jumping the gun. Unless you've forgotten, we've only just met."

"Not true," Deeze said. "I've spent more time with you, just today alone, than I've spent with anyone else in a month. I've watched you go from pale-faced librarian to bronzed sex god."

Wyeth felt his ears begin to burn. He was glad the restaurant was dark so Deeze couldn't see him blush. "Oh Jesus, Deeze, do shut up."

But of course Deeze didn't. "I've seen you digging your toes into the sand on a Southern California beach and looking scrumptious doing it. I've seen you pick a winning horse out of a field of twelve, while I chose the only horse of the day who ended up riding an ambulance off the track." He molded his face into a vaudevillian glower. "And *I'm* the one who knows how to *gamble!*"

Wyeth wiggled his fingers in Deeze's grip while he sat patiently waiting for the guy to wind down. It looked like it might take a while, but Wyeth didn't mind. He was actually beginning to smile at Deeze's tirade.

"I've also shared my life with you, Wy. You met one of my students, you charmed the good Father who got me my job, you've seen where I spend my days, you've learned during the course of our time together to smile when I compliment you and stop acting like you've been offended, and last but not least, your kisses are more delicious than any kisses I've ever sampled. And I mean *ever*."

Wyeth sat speechless, and if the truth were known, a little breathless too. Finally, he sputtered the only two words he seemed able to capture on the spur of the moment. "You're crazy."

Deeze applied pressure to Wyeth's hand. The insipid grin fell from his face, and he leaned farther across the table to capture Wyeth's gaze with his.

"Look at me," Deeze muttered under his breath.

So Wyeth looked. He had never seen such hypnotic eyes. He was a bird under the thrall of a snake, only this snake wasn't a threat. Well, yes he was. And maybe the very worst kind. But still he couldn't look away. Wyeth sat stupefied under Deeze's gaze; even his equilibrium felt thrown off balance, like he was about to tumble over the side of a cliff to crash bloodied and lifeless on the rocks below.

Weakly, Wyeth slid his hand from beneath Deeze's. Deeze let it go, but his warm brown eyes never once left Wyeth's face.

"You're the most beautiful man I've ever seen, Wyeth Becker."

"Y-you're nuts."

"I'm smitten."

Wyeth tried to ignore the pounding of his heart. "Nobody says smitten anymore. It's archaic."

"I resurrected it."

"You're certifiable."

"You keep saying that. How is your steak?"

"Huh? What?"

"Your steak. How is it? Don't you love this restaurant?"

Wyeth looked around the dimly lit room. "Uh, sure. It's great. I've never been in a place where you cook your own meal."

"Stay with me tonight. Stay with me tonight, Wy, and let me spend the day with you tomorrow. I don't want to let you go quite yet."

"I don't underst—"

"Yes, you do. I want to fall asleep tonight with you in my arms. I want to breathe in the scent of you while I nod off. I want to feel you smile against my chest. I want to lay my hands at your back, pull you close, and feel your heart hammering against my own. I want you naked in my bed, Wy. I want it more than anything in the world."

Wyeth laid his knife and fork at the side of his plate. He sat back and wiped his napkin across his mouth, simply because he didn't know what else to do. It was a struggle to get the words out, but he managed it in the end. He was ashamed to speak the words, but he was more afraid of *not* speaking them. The happiness he had felt during the course of their long day together sloughed away in a matter of moments. He felt suddenly empty inside. Empty and resigned.

"And then what, Deeze? I've caught this show before, you know. After our weekend's over, you won't call. I'll see you on the street and you'll look away, pretending I'm not there. There won't be any more crayoned notes on your window. I won't spot you jogging. You'll disappear. And there I'll be, wondering what I did wrong."

Deeze frowned. He tried to take Wyeth's hand again, but Wyeth slipped them under the table out of reach. Deeze's voice flowed softly among the muted sounds of other diners, weaving around the distant clatter of cutlery, the piped-in music, the hiss of flames on the grill, the bustle of busboys clearing tables and filling water glasses and schmoozing the clients.

"Please," Deeze whispered, "tell me you don't believe that."

Wyeth gave a cool shrug, already furious with himself for saying what he had. He worked his mouth into a sardonic smile, trying to make light of his words, while what he was really doing was attempting to spackle over the holes in his facade he'd just allowed Deeze to peer through.

"I don't know what I believe, Deeze. You're a little overpowering for someone like me. I can't keep up with your energy."

"You've been hurt," Deeze said. "I'm sorry. But I've been hurt too. You don't have a monopoly on dating assholes."

At that, Wyeth did laugh. And it was an honest one. "Are you sure?" he asked around a grin. "I thought I did."

Deeze reached all the way across the table, practically climbing out of his seat to do it, and patted Wyeth's cheek. "Good. You're smiling again." He plopped himself back in his seat and gazed down at their plates. "Let's eat up, Wy, before our dinners get cold."

So they resumed their meals. And later, when their plates were empty and Wyeth began to look around for the check, Deeze asked softly one more time, "Stay with me tonight. Please, Wy."

Wyeth sighed. Staring across the table, he spoke almost without thinking, even while his heart clenched itself into a knot inside his chest.

"All right, Deeze. If that's what you want."

CHAPTER SEVEN

DEEZE'S APARTMENT was larger than Wyeth's, but he was clearly just as reliant on IKEA for his decorating ideas. Napoleon, Deeze's Maine coon cat, was the biggest, fluffiest, snottiest cat Wyeth had ever met. It shot him a single condescending glance, then yawned, turned its six-inch whiskers and golden brown back on him, and haughtily flounced off, disappearing under the couch.

"Yep," Deeze said with mock pride. "That's who I share my life with."

"Lucky you," Wyeth drawled, unimpressed.

The cat was forgotten a moment later when Deeze pulled Wyeth into his arms, and with one pleading look, laid his mouth over Wyeth's lips before he had a chance to say anything. Ten seconds into the kiss, Wyeth had forgotten what he was about to say anyway.

His body went limp—well, *most* of it—as he relaxed in Deeze's embrace. His fingertips, as if living a life of their own and acting entirely undirected by him, gripped the tail of Deeze's shirt and tugged it from his pants. A moment later, Wyeth dipped his hands beneath the shirt and laid his palms to the heat of Deeze's broad back. Both men shuddered at the touch.

Deeze lazily broke the kiss and muttered through moist lips, "Maybe you're not so shy after all."

Wyeth stepped back, shocked by his reaction to Deeze's kiss. The sensation of Deeze's warm, strong back still burned on his palms, and he longed to feel the heat of it again. But he was ashamed of his reaction too. Ashamed and frightened. Only Deeze's grip on his shoulders prevented him from backing away.

"Please don't be afraid of me," Deeze pleaded, holding him in place. "We can take it as slow as you like. I just want to be with you."

Wyeth stared at Deeze's open, handsome face. Because he couldn't seem to restrain himself, he lifted his hand and slid a thumb across Deeze's bottom lip, stirring up a smile. His pulse pounded in his temples. His erect cock strained for release down below. His entire body vibrated with need. Too turned on to worry about shame anymore, he stepped forward and pressed his body to Deeze's. When he felt Deeze's cock, as hard as iron, against his own, Wyeth's knees almost buckled. Once again, he slid his hands beneath Deeze's shirt and sought the heated skin he'd discovered before.

Deeze tasted his mouth yet again, and as their lips met, Deeze began to tug at Wyeth's clothing. In moments Wyeth's shirt was unbuttoned and pushed back off his shoulders, exposing his torso for the first time. Deeze broke the kiss to step back and stare at him. Wyeth stood trembling under Deeze's gaze. When Deeze began to smile, Wyeth swallowed hard and reached out to pop the buttons on Deeze's shirt, but his hand was shaking so badly, Deeze finally finished the job himself. With the last button undone, he whipped his shirt off and flung it aside.

Wyeth gaped at the dark pelt of hair shadowing Deeze's chest from one bronze nipple to the other, then to the line of hair that trailed down his lean stomach to disappear behind his belt buckle, promising all sorts of wonders below.

Still trembling, Wyeth started to unbuckle Deeze's belt, then stopped as if surprised by his own boldness. He lifted his eyes to Deeze's face and saw a smile there that was so beautiful it almost stopped his heart.

"Come to bed," Deeze whispered.

Wyeth nodded, trembling and mute.

WYETH STOOD naked and aroused at the foot of the bed as Deeze dropped to his knees before him. In the first rush of heat when Deeze's warm hands cupped the back of his thighs and Deeze's questing lips surrounded his aching cock, Wyeth let himself go. He no longer feared the man kneeling before him. He wanted only to be with him—to be with him more than he had wanted to be with anyone for a very long time, to share himself in every way he could. And to lose himself in Deeze's beauty, even if it was just for one night.

Slowly, so slowly, Deeze savored Wyeth's cock, taking it deep, releasing it to plant kisses along the pulsing shaft before taking it in again. Loving the way Wyeth's legs trembled when his tongue slid across the seeping slit. Relishing the way Wyeth craned his head back and groaned when Deeze cupped his balls, caressing them gently as he took in every inch of Wyeth's erection.

Lost in the heat of Deeze's worshiping mouth, Wyeth knew he couldn't hold back his release much longer. In fact, he couldn't hold back another second. It had been less than two minutes since Deeze first tasted him, and Wyeth was already too far gone to pull himself away.

"Oh no," he gasped. "Deeze, I'm sorry!" No sooner were the words stammered than Wyeth's body tensed. He wrapped his hands tightly to either side of Deeze's face, holding him in place. He bit down on his cheek to keep from screaming out in shame as his hips thrust forward and his seed exploded prematurely.

Deeze clutched Wyeth to him, cupping the back of his thighs, bracing his bucking body, never once pulling his mouth away. He suckled and relished the jetting streams of come, his own cock aching with need at the same time. He wasn't bothered one little bit that the eruption had come before either man was ready. In fact, Deeze loved it even more this way. He pressed his forehead to Wyeth's heaving stomach while he savored Wyeth's juices. Even when Wyeth's fingers clutched Deeze's hair, damn near pulling it out by the roots, Deeze almost laughed at the wonder of it all. When this librarian let himself go, he really let himself go. While Wyeth's body quaked and rocked and lurched against him, Deeze made himself a greedy receptacle for every drop of passion Wyeth spilled.

With the last pulsing jet of semen, which was weaker than the others, but still heart-stoppingly intense, Wyeth could no longer maintain his silence. He cried out, and when he did, Deeze, still on his knees before him, pulled him ever closer, still drinking from Wyeth, still relishing every sip.

When Wyeth stood empty and shuddering, he gazed down at Deeze's face staring up. There was a beatific smile on Deeze's moist lips, and a shimmering rope of semen splayed across one cheek from mouth to ear that had somehow escaped Deeze in the explosion. While Wyeth watched, his knees still threatening to buckle beneath him, Deeze dipped his fingers into the precious smear and dragged it toward his lips, where he licked it away with a groan of lust.

"You," Wyeth managed to mutter, his throat dry, his pulse still hammering inside his head. "I want you."

Still trembling on rubbery legs, Wyeth pulled Deeze to his feet and, twisting him around, pushed him down on the bed. Deeze landed hard, bounced, and spit up a laugh. Wyeth didn't mind at all. He grinned too, while with trembling fingers that were still not completely under his control, he managed to unbuckle Deeze's belt and peel Deeze's jeans and undershorts down over his long, furry legs. With a little help from Deeze, the jeans were flung aside and Deeze lay there before Wyeth wearing nothing now but a pair of white socks and his gay pride bracelet.

Deeze's eyes were bright with need. He squirmed farther up the bed and tucked a pillow and one arm under his head, the better to watch. His fingers brushed his own iron cock because at that moment he couldn't bear not to touch it, but Wyeth eased Deeze's hand away and circled Deeze's erection with his own cool fingers.

"Oh my God," Wyeth muttered in awe, feeling the heft and girth of Deeze's erect cock for the very first time. With his thumb, he eased the foreskin back and exposed Deeze's cockhead, glistening with its own spilled nectar. "You're beautiful," Wyeth whispered, easing himself onto the bed between Deeze's legs. Hunkered there, as happy as he had ever been in his life, he tilted Deeze's cock upward and tucked that shiny moist head between his lips.

While Deeze shook and gasped beneath him, Wyeth never took his eyes from Deeze's face. To Deeze, the warmth and softness of Wyeth's mouth was a thundering revelation. This wasn't his first blowjob by any means, but this man—this man. The care he took. The way his gentle eyes never left Deeze's face. The way his tongue lingered and his lips teased. And the way Wyeth's free hand roamed everywhere at once— over Deeze's leg, across his flat, heaving stomach, through the brush of hair in his armpit, his fingers lingering there as if Wyeth had never felt anything so erotically beautiful in his life. Before the hand came to rest there, in Deeze's armpit, Deeze lay quivering and practically senseless under Wyeth's caresses.

A heartbeat before Deeze's release, Wyeth slid his hand down Deeze's rib cage and delicately slipped his fingers under Deeze's heavy balls, supporting them, cupping them in the heat of his palm.

It was then that Deeze exploded beneath him. Deeze gasped and arched his back high. After one delicious moment of anticipation, during which not a sound could be heard anywhere, Deeze cried out and sprayed Wyeth's mouth with jets of delicious warm cream. Deeze flung his legs wide, then brought them together again around Wyeth's waist, clamping him in place as he emptied himself into that heavenly, hot mouth. Now it was Deeze's turn to clutch Wyeth's hair and shudder his way through release.

When his convulsions slowed and he collapsed with a tiny whimper onto the bed, Wyeth slid his lips from Deeze's softening cock and crawled up the length of the man to tuck his face against Deeze's neck. While he settled in, Deeze's arms folded around him, cocooning him in place.

They spoke no words. They only lay there, the room still lit as bright as day in the glare of the ceiling lamp over their heads. A stirring on the mattress down below told them when Napoleon climbed onto the bed to join them. Wyeth smiled against Deeze's heated skin when the cat snuggled up to his foot.

Wyeth was surprised by the smile stretching his own lips. He wondered when it had come, how long it had been there. He breathed in the scent of Deeze's skin, tasted again the musk of come on his tongue, and all shyness suddenly gone, he traced his tongue gently across the five o'clock shadow on Deeze's cheek. It was the same spot where, moments before, his own juices had been splattered. Making a sound that was close to a purr, Deeze pulled him more snugly into his arms.

Deeze reached over and grabbed a remote off the nightstand. A second later the overhead light went out, and they were lying in the muted glow of streetlights sifting through the curtains on the bedroom window.

Each man settled in against the other, their bodies still stricken with wonder by all they had just discovered, all they had just experienced. The heat of their joined bodies was a glorious burning. They lay satiated, exhausted, content. Nevertheless, Wyeth's thoughts raced among the stillnesses inside his head. What would happen now? Where would they go from here? But even those unwieldy thoughts were pushed aside when Deeze pressed a kiss to Wyeth's forehead.

Muttering low, Deeze said, "Thank you."

Barely perceptibly, Wyeth nodded. Closing his eyes, he pushed all thoughts away. He lost himself in the softness and strength of the man holding him. For the moment, he would let Deeze's satin flesh and the memory of what they had done together be enough.

If it all disappeared tomorrow, he would at least have this. This moment. To look back on. To remember.

He closed his eyes as their two hearts gradually ceased racing, one in unison with the other. Content in Deeze's arms, Wyeth dozed.

Holding him close, Deeze buried his lips in the fragrant red hair and smiled a gentle smile when Wyeth's breath slowed and a tiny snore erupted. He lay still, letting Wyeth sleep, as the night settled quietly around them and the man in his arms seeped deeper into his heart, right where he had been since the first time Deeze spotted him on that park bench in Seaport Village. Back on the day when that handsome freckled face hovered over him while the guy's stupid book gurgled to the bottom of the lagoon and Deeze lay half-conscious on the cobblestones, knocked senseless by his stupid dog. Even now, as happy as he was at this moment, Deeze smiled, remembering that day.

And now here they were. Together.

Soon Deeze let the memories go as his body dragged him into sleep. When he awoke an hour later, his hunger for the man in his arms awoke with him. But he lay still, not wanting to disturb Wyeth's sleep.

Then his heart quickened at the feel of an eyelash fluttering across his skin.

IT WAS barely midnight when Wyeth opened his eyes. Somehow in his sleep, he had slid down in the bed. His head now rested low on Deeze's stomach, and Deeze's sleep-softened cock lay gently against his lips. As he breathed in the clean scent of it, relishing its silky heat, he felt it stir and lengthen against his cheek.

Strong hands gently gripped him at the waist and pulled him up in the bed. Wyeth felt so small in Deeze's arms. So weightless. In the darkness, Deeze's mouth found his, then Deeze lazily broke the kiss and pressed his lips to Wyeth's ear. "I knew you'd taste heavenly."

Wyeth cuddled. He was already so turned on his voice was weak with it. Still, he found himself apologizing. "I'm sorry. I came too fast."

"So did I," Deeze whispered, the edge of his hand dipping into the crevice of Wyeth's ass. A fingertip settled lightly on Wyeth's puckered opening and gently massaged him there. "But this time I won't."

A tremor stuttered through Wyeth's body, jarring him from one end to the other. He pressed his already erect cock against Deeze's leg, loving the feel of Deeze's broad hand cupping his ass, his gentle fingertip teasing his most tender spot.

"God yes," he gasped. He breathed the words against Deeze's neck. Once the words were uttered, his lips slid a kiss across Deeze's throat. As Deeze swallowed, his finger pressing more insistently to Wyeth's opening, Wyeth nipped lightly at Deeze's jaw. He released his tongue to taste the stubble on Deeze's chin. Again, both men shuddered. Deeze eased his finger away.

"No," Wyeth quietly pleaded. "Don't be afraid. Touch me there. Do—do you have lotion? Condoms?"

Deeze slid a kiss over Wyeth's ear. "Yes," he muttered. "But only if that's what you want." He reached down and slipped his fingers around Wyeth's cock. He laughed when it lurched in his hand. "Or is this telling me everything I need to know?"

Wyeth clutched Deeze tighter, driving his cock deeper into Deeze's fist. "What an asshole," he groaned, squeezing his eyes shut, lost in his own pleasure.

Deeze muttered his way back to a kiss, his mouth eager but his eyes alight with mischief. "That's what I was thinking," he crooned. "What an asshole indeed. Lovely actually." Their lips met. Then he quickly pulled away and rose up on the bed, easing Wyeth over onto his stomach and straddling him with his long legs.

Wyeth lay sprawled out, facedown, lazy and expectant, excited by the sense of Deeze hovering over him, thrilled by the hunger he could feel in Deeze's caresses. His legs hemmed in by Deeze's warm thighs, he tried to make himself more comfortable. He raised his arms to embrace the pillow beneath his head and peered back over his shoulder as Deeze's large hands slid across his back, massaging his taut muscles. Wyeth's cock rubbed deliciously against the warm sheets beneath him. His legs opened slightly, and Deeze murmured something. Not a word. Just a sound. A gentle exhalation. Another purr.

Deeze scooted himself down in the bed and opened Wyeth's legs wider to settle himself down between them. At the very first touch of his lips on Wyeth's butt, Wyeth tensed, but at the same moment, Wyeth's legs opened even more, this time of their own accord. He reached back and dug his fingers through Deeze's hair, holding him in place, guiding him.

With a wondrous smile, Deeze kissed his way inward. At the moment his mouth settled its moist heat over Wyeth's opening and his tongue tasted him there for the very first time, Wyeth's fingers tightened in his hair. Wyeth lifted his ass to meet that gently probing tongue, and when he did, Deeze clutched Wyeth's hips, lifting him high and claiming him for his own.

Deeze explored the secret places of Wyeth's body with gentle kisses and moist proddings, and Wyeth quaked and shook beneath him.

While Deeze reached over to the nightstand and fished around, pulling things from the drawer, Wyeth continued to vibrate beneath him, his face buried in the pillow, his hand still reaching behind him, waiting to reclutch Deeze's hair, waiting to steer him once again to where he most needed Deeze to go.

With his hand asserting gentle pressure at the small of Wyeth's back, Deeze rose up on his knees between Wyeth's legs. In the darkness, Wyeth heard the sound of tearing foil, followed by a moment of tense expectancy during which he knew Deeze was rolling the condom down over his cock. And while he did that, Deeze's hand slid down, and once again his hot fingertip came to rest on Wyeth's opening, as if reserving his spot, marking his territory. Again Wyeth trembled, biting his lip to keep from crying out.

When a lubed thumb brushed his hole, lingering, massaging, Wyeth squirmed around on the bed, ecstatic. More lotion was applied, and Wyeth could feel Deeze's hairy legs brushing against the tender skin of his inner thighs as he eased Wyeth's legs wider. Without warning, a fingertip gently slid through the muscled ring protecting Wyeth's opening. A moment later, a second finger joined it, sliding deep.

Wyeth groaned and lifted his ass higher, his mouth full of pillow, his free hand reaching behind him, trying to make contact with Deeze's skin. Anywhere. A leg, a shoulder, a forearm.

When Deeze lowered himself over him and slid an arm beneath Wyeth's stomach, anchoring him in a tight embrace, Deeze's cock pressed gently against Wyeth's opening. Then it nudged against him a little less gently, seeking entry.

Wyeth forced himself to relax. He reached around and found Deeze's hip, clutched him there, tugged him closer, silently begging.

Deeze, sensing that unspoken plea, pushed forward and his long, heavy cock slid deep inside the man beneath him.

Wyeth sucked in a great gout of air as he twisted his head around to find Deeze's mouth with his own. They kissed. They held the kiss while Deeze's cock sank deeper. Gently. Carefully. But hungrily too. Mouths together, they shared an exquisite moan.

Wyeth gripped Deeze's hip more firmly. Latching on, trying to anchor the man against him, *inside* him. He shifted his ass around to allow Deeze to settle deep. To fit his cock inside him like a hand inside a glove.

Deeze could barely find his voice. "Am I hurting you?" he asked inside their still-lingering kiss.

"God no," Wyeth gasped. "D-do it," he stammered. "Just do it."

Deeze chuckled and slid his cock deeper. "Nike it is, then," he giggled around a gasp, and before Wyeth could fully prepare himself, Deeze began a slow luscious slide, burying himself as far as he could go, then slowly pulling away. Just before they parted completely, he eased his straining cock back inside. Every loving stab of Deeze's long cock set a fire inside Wyeth that left him almost senseless with need.

Deeze was the perfect size. He filled Wyeth's opening, stretching him tightly enough to make the redhead cry out with every piercing, every withdrawal. But there was no pain in his cries. He loved every second, every inch, every thrust.

And Deeze loved it even more.

They were both nearly breathless now. Deeze's thrusts increased in tempo. Their kisses deepened. Their tongues probed. Deeze slipped his hand under Wyeth, gliding his heated fingertips across Wyeth's smooth stomach until he could wrap them around Wyeth's cock, feeling it stiffen and swell in his grip. The second he did, Wyeth bucked and filled Deeze's hand with come.

In the throes of his own orgasm, Wyeth stammered, "Oh Jesus, Deeze. Fuck me."

Deeze rose up onto his knees, clutched Wy's hip with his come-soaked hand, the fingers of his other hand clutching Wyeth's hair like a rider gripping a horse's mane. As Wyeth laughed and sobbed beneath him, so lost in desire he didn't know *what* the hell he was doing, Deeze drove his long cock deep, over and over again, into that delectable well of silken heat.

With Wyeth's face crammed into the pillow, his mouth open, gasping for air, Deeze pounded him relentlessly from behind. Wyeth's breath was snatched away when Deeze's cock suddenly swelled to an even greater girth, and at that moment, at that *very* moment, it was Deeze's turn to cry out.

He slid his cock to its deepest point and held it there, his whole body trembling. With both hands still holding Wyeth in place, he gave a final uncontrollable lunge and erupted into orgasm. His gushing come filled the condom. His legs shook; every muscle contracted. He fell forward and buried his face in Wyeth's hair as his come continued to spill out.

Through it all, Deeze clutched Wyeth to him as if afraid he would slip away. As if terrified he might escape.

But Wyeth wasn't going anywhere. He tightened his grip on Deeze's hip and held him close while Deeze emptied himself inside him. Wyeth swallowed, gasped, and twisted his head around for another kiss. Their lips met just as they collapsed full force onto the bed. Wyeth still lay prisoner in Deeze's arms. Deeze's cock still pierced him from behind, still anchored deep, still probing, still firm and filled with blood. In their kisses, Deeze's sweet breath flowed hot across Wyeth's mouth.

Still joined, their bodies slowly relaxed. They settled onto the bed, muscles unclenching, still connected, still clutching, not wanting to part even now. Long moments passed, moments while their nerve endings hummed, their overtaxed muscles quivered and strained and eventually began to unknot. Deeze's cock softened, grew smaller, and eventually slipped free of Wyeth's gripping heat. The moment they slid apart, Wyeth twisted around in Deeze's arms and buried his face in the sweat-dampened hair on Deeze's chest. Deeze dragged him into an embrace and both men lay there, breathless, clinging to each other while their bodies grew calm, their hearts quieted.

"Teacher," Wyeth whispered, cuddling closer, finding his voice at last.

"Librarian," Deeze answered, wrapping his arms more snugly around Wyeth's back.

Holding on tight, they let their incredible day together—and the even more incredible night—waft away to memory, sadly letting it go, each mourning its loss in his own private way.

Later, Deeze slipped from Wyeth's embrace long enough to clean himself up, then returned from the bathroom with a damp washcloth for Wyeth. When both men were pristine, they burrowed back into each other's arms.

In Wyeth's final seconds before sleep at last took him, he relished Deeze's warm chest against his cheek, his breath stirring Wyeth's hair, the gentle organic thud of Deeze's heart mere inches from his ear, as if its rhythm was being played for only him to hear, a worshiping audience of one.

Wrapped snugly inside Deeze's arms, Wyeth squeezed his eyes shut, trying not to let the sadness take him as he wondered when it all would end.

For it always did. It always, always did.

Chapter Eight

Yet oddly enough, it didn't end at all.

What began as a reluctant dinner date and a one-night stand, turned into an extended liaison between two men who really had nothing in common, who were as different as night and day, but who still could not seem to get enough of each other.

As the days passed, it never ceased to amaze Wyeth that Deeze continually sought him out. Why he should do so, Wyeth was afraid to contemplate. So he accepted the circumstances like he would accept any streak of unnatural good fortune. Enjoy the luck while it lasted, and try not to get too comfortable along the way.

Still, there could be no denying that Deeze filled Wyeth's every waking thought. The olive-skinned dreamboat was entrenched inside his head from that very first night. Something about opening his eyes on that first morning in Deeze's embrace had changed Wyeth. When Deeze's warm mouth slipped over his at the moment their eyes squinted into the light of that new day, with that first wonderful night behind them, Wyeth had known something fundamental in his life had changed. Tectonic plates had shifted. He was afraid to analyze it too closely, but he knew he would be a different person from that day forth.

That unquantifiable change scared him to death, but the idea of being dropped from Deeze's orbit scared him even more. To think he would never have sex with the man again was enough to terrify him. But there was more to it than that. It wasn't just the sex.

It was Deeze himself. The happiness he exuded. The pure, undiluted joy that spilled out of him. Joy, Wyeth admitted, that had long been absent from his life. If it had ever really been there at all.

The day after their first night together, which was Sunday, they lounged between their two apartments, caring for the pets who still had yet to meet. Best let the humans get to know each other first, they seemed to silently agree. Wyeth spent the day fending off Deeze's exuberance, because he really didn't know how to handle it. He wasn't used to being around such unbridled optimism. The fact that Deeze also continually reached out to touch, to pet, to croon gentle words plucked a nerve in Wyeth that hadn't been tweaked in a long time.

On Sunday evening, Wyeth excused himself, returning home under the pretense he had work to do, but in reality he needed to get away from Deeze long enough to assess the situation and try to figure out what the hell was going on. He simply could not understand why Deeze was so attentive to him. Yet even Wyeth admitted his confusion said more about his own faults than it did about Deeze's.

So after a romantic weekend like none he had ever experienced before—one that left him literally weak at the knees—Wyeth spent that first day back at work humming around the library, forgetting what he was doing, acting scatterbrained, smiling absentmindedly at anyone who looked his way, losing books left and right and having to go off searching for wherever it was he left them, sometimes finding them, sometimes not. It got so bad his fellow librarians began snickering behind his back, but Wyeth didn't care. He didn't care because he didn't know. He was too lost in his own thoughts—in thoughts of Deeze—to pick up on what everyone else was doing.

Deeze was not unaffected either. He spent his working hours giggling with his students, acting just as childish as they did, and sometimes worse. He fulfilled his teaching duties but did it with a laugh bubbling up out of nowhere every time he turned around. More than once Father Mike had to pop into Deeze's classroom and ask the whole lot of them to hold down the racket. Deeze was suddenly so outrageously happy—and truthfully Deeze had *always* been happy, but not like *this*—that even the other priests and teachers began to notice, smiling to each other, wondering what had gotten into the young kindergarten teacher.

While the two men's lives had inexplicably changed, their work weeks had not. They still completed the tasks appointed to them. They did the jobs they were paid to do and then bustled home to care for the pets who relied on them. But afterward, either one or both would step to the window of his apartment and stare out across the street at the window of the other. Often, Wyeth would find a note for him there, propped on Deeze's windowsill or taped to the glass. Always in crayon, always on colored construction paper, always in blocky childish letters. The notes ranged from *Meet me at the cafe on the corner* to *Walk with me to the bay* to *Thank you for last night*. One merely said *Yum*. In truth, the messages didn't matter, for regardless of what was printed on those ridiculous notes, they always made Wyeth smile.

Once, Deeze stared out his window and found Chaucer with his feet up on the windowsill, gazing back at him with a sappy grin on his face. Wyeth was nowhere around. Deeze laughed for twenty minutes over that.

A routine developed. On the three nights a week when Deeze attended his college classes, Wyeth reverted to the life he had known before Deeze came along. He read. He listened to music. He spent time walking Chaucer around the city. The only difference was that now those pastimes were no longer enough. Every moment he spent on his own was like a knife piercing his gut. It didn't take a minor in psychology (which Wyeth held) to know it was Deeze's absence that made him feel that way.

On his nights *away* from college, Deeze pleaded and cajoled until Wyeth relented and joined him for coffee, or dinner, or a movie, or just a quiet walk around town. After those meetings, they tumbled into bed together. For that, at least, Wyeth needed no cajoling. There, Wyeth felt no shyness whatsoever. Not anymore.

The old Wyeth would have been terrified by that realization. But not this Wyeth. This Wyeth still suspected his happiness was hanging by a thread, that one day Deeze would tire of him and turn away without a backward glance, that fate would snatch his happiness away like fate always did. But he tried not to think about it. That fear was too heart wrenching to contemplate.

Still, the tiny frightened voice in the back of Wyeth's head was always there, gnawing away at him, making him wonder when the bubble would burst. Making him wonder when Deeze would wake up and realize he could do better than this shy, introverted librarian with the freckles and red hair who wasn't very adept at letting himself go— although he was learning; he was definitely learning.

Wyeth spent his days hungering for the feel of Deeze's body next to his, aching for the sound of Deeze's whisper, the brush of Deeze's hand. And there were other things he hungered for too. More intimate things. The softness of Deeze's kiss, the taste and heat of Deeze's come gushing across his lips, the gentle way Deeze caressed him as his long cock slid deep, filling Wyeth in a way no one had ever filled him before. But even more than that, there were those quiet moments when they lay wrapped together, desperately hanging on, bodies wet with sweat, nerve endings tingling, while their hearts thudded down to a more sustainable tempo.

It was in those moments, the immediate moments after sex, when the true connections were born. Whispered endearments, cuddled caresses, lazy thoughts gently expressed. When words were less guarded than they were at other times. When gestures came from the heart, unplanned, uncensored. The slide of fingertips on a cheek. The bump of hard knees and the tickle of cool toes. Silences that were as calming as the shimmer of moonlight on still water. Silences that burrowed deep into Wyeth's heart to a place where he knew they would remain, forever cherished, endlessly remembered, eternally his very own—never to be shared even with Deeze, the man who had planted them there.

Deeze spent his days wondering what it was about the young librarian that had captured him so completely. Why the line of Wyeth's strong jaw stirred him so. Why the brush of blond hair on the back of Wyeth's pale hands was such a turn-on. Why his kiss tasted so sweet. What it was about the man that left him so hungry for more that it was an ache every time they stepped away from each other.

Deeze spent three or four nights a week with Wyeth, in one apartment or the other, trying to find out, trying to understand. Those nights together were the times that meant the most to both men, although neither was willing to admit it yet, even to themselves. In Deeze's mind, it was all an astonishing revelation. In Wyeth's mind, Deeze was a blessing doomed to eventually end, one way or another.

This wasn't to say Deeze wasn't also annoying. Wyeth learned this basic truth less than three weeks into their—whatever the hell it was.

It started with a simple conversation one evening over tacos at a street-side cafe not thirty feet from Wyeth's apartment building....

"YOU DID it," Wyeth said. "I didn't think you would."

Deeze looked up. "And what might that be?"

Their knees were touching under the table and for that reason alone, Wyeth had an erection that sent an ache shuddering through him all the way from the soles of his feet to the top of his head. He tried to ignore the ache. It's not like he wasn't used to it. After all, it popped up every time Deeze was in sniffing distance. Still, it was distracting in the middle of dinner.

"You bought old Mrs. Mulroney, my annoying three-thousand-year-old neighbor, a subscription to the *San Diego Union-Tribune*. Tenants on floors 2, 3, and 4, are planning a party to celebrate. They've even considered submitting your name to the Catholic archdiocese for sainthood. Of course, they've never seen you with a dick down your throat. At least I hope they haven't."

Deeze leaned across the table. A flake of cheese peppered his chin. "God, I love it when you talk dirty."

Wyeth blushed. "Yes, well, be that as it may, sainthood is out, but we are all grateful for your largesse nevertheless. Now that our papers won't be stolen off our doorsteps anymore, I can go back to my *New York Times* crossword puzzles, and everybody else can catch up on world events and find out what Dagwood's been up to."

"Good to know." Deeze reached over and brushed a fingertip down Wyeth's cheek, dismissing out of hand the kindness he'd shown in buying an old lady a newspaper subscription she either couldn't afford or was too cheap to spring for. "Let's talk about more serious matters, Wy. For instance, your spray tan is pretty much gone. Did you know?"

Wyeth blushed even deeper, darkening his freckles. He nudged his glasses higher on his nose, a nervous habit he always fell into when he was at a loss for words and needed a moment to think. This time it didn't work very well.

"Don't worry about it" was all he said. He stared up into the tree hanging above their heads as if admiring the tiny white Christmas lights wrapped around every limb for atmosphere, although it was only August.

Deeze stopped gnawing at his taco long enough to study Wyeth's face. "I can read you like a book, you know, which is kind of funny since you're a librarian."

"And your point is?"

"My point, young Wyeth, is you aren't sneaky enough to be duplicitous. Admit it. You've already made an appointment for another tan."

Wyeth dabbed at his mouth with a napkin, took a moment to straighten his shirt collar, stared up at the sky to see if maybe a comet was due to tear across the heavens, and finally admitted, through slitty eyes after nudging his glasses up his nose *again*, "So what if I did?"

Deeze splayed his hands in front of his face as if fending off an oncoming bus that was careening straight for him. "Don't get so defensive. No reason. Just making conversation!" But he had a victorious gleam in his eye that finally made Wyeth grin right back. Deeze leaned in and whispered, "I have to admit though, as much as I love chewing on your artificial tan line, I enjoy the taste of the real you far better. Save your money. Cancel the appointment. I prefer you in the original packaging."

Two spots of color rose on Wyeth's cheeks. He knew they were probably there but decided to act like they weren't. "If that's what you want," he said quietly, secretly relieved. He had never felt like himself with that tan. Then his face perked up and he forgot the tan completely. "By the way, Deeze, your cousin at the Tan Banana said I should dump you while I still have my sanity."

"What a bitch."

Wyeth laughed. "I like her."

A gleam lit Deeze's eyes. "What's to like? The woman spends her days painting people. It's not exactly a cerebral occupation. Besides, you can only dump me if you admit we are actually in a relationship to begin with." One sly eyebrow climbed upward. "Is that what you're saying?"

This had been a subject they had touched on more than once. And one Wyeth always avoided.

Wyeth blinked. The ingredients of his taco spilled out over his hand and landed on his plate. "I wasn't implying we had a relationship at all. I was just kidding. We've only known each other a couple of weeks. I still barely like you."

"Oh, I must be mistaking you for the *other* guy I've been sleeping with."

Wyeth's eyes opened wide. "The other guy?"

The teasing light in Deeze's eyes softened. He gave Wyeth that special look that always made Wyeth's heart stutter. "It was a joke, dumbass. But back to us. It's been a great two weeks, almost three, actually. Don't you think it's been great?"

Wyeth couldn't have convincingly denied it, even if he wanted to. "Well. Yeah, Deeze, but—"

Deeze reached over and brushed his fingertips through the hair on Wyeth's forearm. "Let's stop talking now before you have a stroke."

"I'm not having a—"

Still twiddling the hair on Wyeth's arm with one hand, he stretched his other arm across the table and tapped Wyeth's lips with an index finger. "Shush. By the way, I learned that from you. Shush. I use it with the kids in my class now. It never works, of course. You can shush yourself into a coma and a five-year-old won't give a shit. But I use it anyway, just because it reminds me of you."

Wyeth eased his arm out from under Deeze's hand, but he tried to do it calmly. He didn't want to appear as terrified as he suddenly felt. "Deeze, I know we've just met. I know we're just friends." He heard himself talking and cringed. But still he couldn't shut up. "I know there's nothing between us. I wasn't trying to imply we have a relationship. I really wasn't."

Wyeth stared down at his plate, concentrating on his food. He didn't notice when Deeze's eyes darkened. He didn't notice when Deeze's smile suddenly lost its spark. That smile was simply window dressing now. It didn't come from the heart. It was a facade, a spray-on tan, not an ounce of realness to it. Deeze knew it even if Wyeth couldn't be bothered to look up and notice.

"Then I guess it's true. There really isn't a relationship here," Deeze whispered, folding his hands in his lap. He gazed around at the other diners. Deeze decided he would give Wy a few days to muddle over what he had just said. In the meanwhile, it was time to stop horsing around. He had something he wanted to say, and by God he was going to say it. Now. The smile on his face became a little more real.

"Come jogging with me, Wy. Let's knock off a few miles together."

Wyeth lifted his head and stared. From the look on his face, he had still been lost in the relationship conundrum, and the request to go jogging was like a surprise kick in the nuts. "You mean *run*? *Tonight*? Are you fucking crazy? I don't run. I don't *want* to run. I *hate* running."

Deeze flashed a few snowy teeth, hoping it would help. "Only because you haven't tried it."

"We just ate," Wyeth said sounding a little desperate.

"By the time we get home, change into our running gear, and gather up the dog, our dinners will have settled. Stop stalling. Let's go." He turned to the waiter, who was standing in a corner by a potted plant scratching his ass. "Check, please, Itchy."

Wyeth all but blubbered. "But, but, but—it's *night*."

Deeze shrugged. "I thought you'd be more comfortable in the dark."

"Why would you think that?"

"Well, when I turn all the lights off when we're in bed together you certainly lose all inhibitions." He grinned. "That's the only reason I do it, you know. If I had my way, I'd have every light in the apartment blazing so I won't miss that perfect O you make with your mouth every time you're about to come."

Wyeth gazed desperately around as if to see if any other diners were listening. "Shush, Deeze! Jesus!"

Deeze threw his head back and laughed. He took a minute to calm himself. Once he did, he leaned forward and placed his hand on Wyeth's forearm again.

"Just looking at you makes me happy," he said softly. "I want you to know that."

Wyeth wasn't buying it. "Your cousin said you've always been happy. She said if you seem happy now, it has nothing to do with me."

"Wow, she really is a bitch. But she's wrong. It has everything to do with you. I might have been happy before, but I was never this fucking delirious. Ask anybody. Just the thought of you naked in my arms and I want to rush out and buy flowers. Or lease a car. Or build a house. It's extraordinary, really."

"You're nuts."

Not bothering to deny it, Deeze got back on track. "So. About running. I assume you do exercise occasionally. You didn't get that magnificent ass by sitting around eating corn chips all day."

And just when the blush was draining from Wyeth's ears too. "Leave my ass out of this."

"Never!" Deeze hissed, as if appalled by the very idea of leaving Wyeth's ass out of *anything*. His eyes emitted that sexy heat that Wyeth sometimes dreamed about while he was moping around the library acting like he was working. It was the same heat the memory of which made Wyeth quickly seek out his desk and plop desperately down behind it so no one could see he was growing a hard-on. Librarians with boners are a puzzlement to most library goers.

Now, sitting under the stupid illuminated tree waiting for the scratchy-ass waiter to bring them their check, Wyeth tried to ignore that sexy gleam in Deeze's warm brown eyes while he seriously considered the question. He did exercise, of course. He wasn't a complete slug. He even owned a set of Richard Simmons tapes he kept hidden in a cupboard and danced along to now and then when the mood struck, although he always kept the volume low so none of the neighbors would hear the old queen screaming for him to "Wiggle it, honey! Make it move!"

On the other hand, Wyeth had never won an argument with Deeze yet, and he was pretty sure he wouldn't win this one either. Wyeth was a college graduate, after all. He wasn't a complete dunce. He knew when he was in over his head.

He heaved a great, long, put-upon sigh. "You'll have to go slow or I won't be able to keep up."

Deeze's dimples popped into view, cratering out like sinkholes. "No problem."

"And bring your Band-Aids in case I get a blister."

"Happy to." Deeze grinned. "On one condition."

"What condition is that?"

"Kiss me," Deeze said. "Here. Now. Kiss me. In front of all these people."

Wyeth gazed around. There must have been fifty diners in the place. No one was looking in their direction. And he really did want to kiss Deeze. He'd been watching that scrumptious mouth for over an hour.

"Fine," Wyeth said, surprising even himself. "I'll kiss you. Right here. Right now."

Without hesitating, Deeze scooted his chair out from under him with a horrendous squeak and leaned as far over the table as he could. Clutching Wyeth's necktie (they were still dressed from work) he dragged him close and covered Wyeth's mouth with his.

At the first touch of lips, Deeze smiled. So did Wyeth. Five seconds into the kiss, neither man was smiling anymore. When Deeze's hand came up to stroke Wyeth's cheek, tongues came into play. The restaurant around them went silent. No conversation, no clatter of cutlery, nothing. Waiters became statues, forks loaded with food hovered forgotten in midair, jaws stopped chewing. It was like a cold snap had suddenly engulfed the establishment, freezing everybody solid.

Wyeth waited a good fifteen seconds before breaking the kiss. When he did, he simply sat back down and fished around for his wallet, not caring what the people around him thought, or at least he pretended he didn't.

"Wow," Deeze mumbled, licking his lips.

Wyeth got thanked with a gentle bump of Deeze's knee against his beneath the table. With the floor show over, the restaurant noise ratcheted back up to its normal level, and people went back to minding their own business.

"We'll run tomorrow," Deeze quietly said, his eyes eager, the pink tip of his tongue still darting across his lips as if retasting the kiss. "I have other plans for tonight."

"Thank God," Wyeth muttered, as sober as Deeze, his heart already thundering inside his chest in anticipation. Not in anticipation of running tomorrow, but of what awaited him tonight.

Hand in hand, they left the cafe. Every diner in the place watched them go.

CHAPTER NINE

"PICK YOUR feet up!"

"Blow me!"

It was a week later. Wyeth had managed to evade the jogging issue for seven days, but now his reprieve had expired. Grumbling under his breath while his heart *kaboom*ed and flopped around alarmingly inside his chest cavity, he reluctantly trailed Deeze up Sixth Avenue in a pair of red sweatpants and a yellow tee. He wore the sweatpants in eighty-degree heat because he had taken Deeze's advice and not returned to the salon for his spray tan booster. Deeze might love Wyeth's pale hairy legs, but Wyeth still didn't.

As far as running went, the only redeeming factor in the whole enterprise was the fact that he got to stare at Deeze in his cute little running shorts, thudding along in front of him. He knew he ran a pale second (no pun intended) as far as sexiness went, but how could he not? he thought wryly, staring once again at Deeze's ass. *Just look at the guy. The man's a god.*

With downtown behind them and Wyeth worn out already, they slipped through some trees and jogged into Balboa Park with all the other insane people who rose at the crack of dawn to batter their joints to mush in the pointless quest of outrunning their own mortality. Or more likely, hurrying it along.

Wyeth had to admit it was sort of lovely being in the park this early in the morning, with the sun barely up and the birds chittering in the bushes. Jewels of dewdrops spotted the grass, and remnants of the last mowing stuck to his shoe tops. The long sloping lawn smelled like a field of hay, which for a city boy was kind of nice. Still, he would have enjoyed it more if he hadn't been waiting to fall flat on his face the moment his legs gave out or his tendons started snapping like rubber bands or his heart suddenly exploded like a roadside bomb. His eyes burned with sweat, his shirt was stuck to his chest, he had bitten his tongue after jumping off a curb, he couldn't be more than fifteen steps away from heat prostration, and he was annoyed that without his spray-on tan, he looked like a sweaty little albino next to Deeze, who apparently never perspired (or faded) at all.

Chaucer wasn't looking too thrilled either. Wyeth had released him from his leash so they wouldn't trip each other up, but the dog was lagging behind already, and they had barely gone five blocks. Deeze, of course, was prancing around having the time of his life, flinging his arms about, sucking in great gulps of morning air, goading Wyeth to run faster, and singing one fucking ABBA song after another as if begging Wyeth to hurl a sneaker at him and smack him upside the head.

Expecting a lung to collapse at any moment, Wyeth called out in jittery little oxygen-deprived gasps, "Could you be slightly less happy? It's pissing me off and depressing the dog!"

Deeze sang all the louder for about a minute just to be annoying. Then he shut up and grudgingly slowed his pace to let Wyeth catch up. They settled in side by side at a more reasonable speed, clomping along the sidewalk, their footfalls sounding like gunshots on the morning air.

"Now you're bookin'," Deeze said, barely out of breath at all.

Wyeth gave an exasperated grunt. "I'm a librarian. I'm always bookin'."

Deeze was undeterred. "Be honest. Isn't this fun? See what you've been missing?"

Wyeth snarled. "You mean the coronary? I think I feel one coming on even as we speak. It should be a doozy. I hope you know CPR."

"But don't your legs feel stronger?"

"No. They feel like Jell-O, and my ass is cramping up."

"Think of it as tightening the glutes."

"If I recall, we tightened my glutes last night. You even used your grease gun." He had the good grace to blush at his off-color joke, although it was up for grabs whether he was really blushing or just wending his way toward a massive heart attack.

Deeze edged a little closer and gave him a good-natured elbow to the ribs as they jostled along. A broad grin spread across his face, and he reached out to swipe the back of his fingers along Wyeth's sweaty arm. His voice dropped to a crooning register usually reserved for more intimate moments—moments with fewer clothes and far less pain and where the gasping was caused by more personal endeavors. Like sex. "Speaking of that, you were incredible last night."

Wyeth found himself smiling, even while another rivulet of sweat stung his eyes and his jockey shorts crawled up his ass. Then he frowned when Deeze ruined the moment by urging him again to pick up the pace a bit, prompting Wyeth to grouse about the night before, "I've had better, you know."

Deeze sputtered a laugh. "Liar!" And as if Deeze was trying to prove he could be even more annoying than he already was, he proceeded to run a few more circles around both Wyeth and Chaucer while Wyeth veered across a grassy patch of parkland looking for a place to die.

"Don't you ever sweat?"

Deeze shot him a wink. "I was sweating last night."

Wyeth had to bite back a snort. Jeez, even in the midst of agony Deeze could make him laugh. "We both were," he said. Then he lost his rhythm (if he ever had any), tripped over his own feet, and almost landed facedown in the dewy grass. Deeze caught him just in time, and together they stumbled to a stop, arm in arm.

As soon as all forward momentum ceased, Chaucer plopped down on the ground like someone had clubbed him over the head. Deeze stroked Wyeth's arms, standing close enough that Wyeth could feel Deeze's warm breath wafting over his face.

Again Deeze softly said, "You really were incredible last night."

Wyeth blinked back a drop or two of sweat. He bent over with his hands on his knees, trying to catch his breath. He finally rose up and leaned in to give Deeze a kiss on the cheek.

"Thanks," he said, slipping a hand under the tail of Deeze's shirt and stroking his hairy belly. He licked his lips while his eyelids drooped dreamily. "Let's go home and fuck, baby. I want you so bad. I can't wait another minute."

"Oh man," Deeze gasped. He edged closer and started to nuzzle Wyeth's ear. Then he pulled back and squinted his eyes. "Wait a minute! I'm not falling for that. You don't want to go home and fuck. You just don't want to run anymore."

Caught off guard, Wyeth muttered something about some people being too smart for their own good, and the next thing he knew, Deeze was tugging him down a hillside into a grove of trees where the shadows lay deep and the dawn hadn't reached quite yet. This must be where the serial killers hang out, he thought. Somewhere in among the tree trunks, murderers crouched, slews of them probably, waiting for a couple of idiot joggers to come stomping along so they could beat them to death and eat their power bars.

Although at that particular moment, it wasn't his own impending demise that bothered him most. All Wyeth could *really* think about was this: *if we're running downhill now, later we'll have to run uphill to make up for it*. He wanted to cry. Suddenly death at the hands of a serial killer didn't sound so bad.

Thank God Chaucer chose that moment to reel against a pachysandra bush and, with a pitiful whimper, halfheartedly lift his leg to relieve himself. Deeze and Wyeth stopped to wait. While Chaucer stood there on three trembling legs, splattering the bush, he glared at Deeze.

"Your dog doesn't look too happy."

"Who can blame him?" Wyeth bent and patted Chaucer's head. "Pee slower, boy. I need a break." Wyeth then collapsed against a tree, wiped his face with his shirttail, and tried to catch his breath.

Deeze laughed and leaned into his own tree to execute a few hamstring stretches. He then dropped to the ground and did a couple of push-ups to get the kinks out—like Deeze really had kinks. After the push-ups, he did a series of jumping jacks that would have killed a lesser man, and it didn't even leave him out of breath. Still bouncing around like a basketball, Deeze watched Wyeth stroke his aching calf muscles and groan.

"Sore?" Deeze asked kindly. "I can massage you when we get home."

"Really?" Already Wyeth's imagination was dragging him to the place where a massage would likely lead. It was a steamy place where body fluids were likely to be swapped, and Deeze's grease gun would come into play yet again. Frankly, Wyeth couldn't wait to get there. It was certainly better than running. "All right. Can I massage you too?"

Deeze stopped stretching and walked into Wyeth's arms. "Baby, you can do anything to me you want." With those words hovering in the morning air around them, mixing with the hum of insects and the rustle of leaves overhead and the quiet patter of serial killers lurking in the bushes, Deeze cupped the back of Wyeth's head and tucked his face into the side of his neck. His hands slipped under Wyeth's shirt, and he stroked Wyeth's lean frame as Wyeth stood cradled in Deeze's arms.

"Are you having fun?" he asked softly.

Wyeth snickered. "You must be joking."

Deeze slapped his ass and embraced him tighter. "I'm not talking about running, silly. I'm talking about—*in general*. Are you having fun *in general*? I mean, you know, with *me*?"

Wyeth swallowed. Suddenly he didn't feel like joking anymore. He squeezed his eyes shut, enjoying the sensation of Deeze's broad hands on his back. Their legs touched; their hips bumped together. Already Wyeth felt his cock—and Deeze's too—hardening in response to the closeness. The freshly shaved cheek against Wyeth's face, the scent of the man holding him, the taste of Deeze's sweat on Wyeth's tongue when he ran his lips over Deeze's jaw—all of it made Wyeth tremble. But not from exertion this time. This tremble came from a deeper place. A hungrier place.

Wyeth hesitated, then said softly, "Y-yes. I'm having fun."

He waited, wondering if Deeze would answer, but he didn't. So raising his hand to the back of Deeze's neck to dip his fingers into his hairline, Wyeth rose up on tiptoe and lifted his head to whisper in Deeze's ear, "Everything you do makes me happy, Deeze. I've never been with anyone like you."

Deeze dropped his head and brushed his lips over the tender skin under Wyeth's ear. He gently nipped at Wyeth's earlobe with his teeth, sending another shudder through them both.

Deeze's voice was husky and fractured, as if he had just woken from a long sleep. Or as if he had been planning what he was about to say for a very long time, and now that it was time to speak the words he was overcome with stage fright. "Wy. We have to talk. We—we have to decide what we want to do. I don't think we can go on much longer the way we are. I need to know what we are going to do about it."

Wyeth pressed his hands to Deeze's chest and pushed himself away, just far enough to stare into Deeze's eyes. "Do about what? I don't know what you mean," he said, his voice uncertain, his eyes suddenly wary.

Deeze studied Wyeth's face and smiled a sad little smile. "I think you do."

"Explain it to me," Wyeth drawled, his throat suddenly dry, his cock withering. Already his heart was growing small inside his chest. Burrowing deeper to protect itself from pain. Forming a protective shell. Preparing for the worst. Preparing for what he had known all along would come sooner or later. "I don't understand what you're getting at, Deeze. I really don't. Spit it out. What are you trying to say?"

Deeze sighed. His eyes flitted through the branches above their heads as if searching for an answer there. "I'm just trying to say that we have something between us. I can feel it, and I think you can too. But it's not enough. We're reaching a crossroads. Things can't go on the way they are. Decisions have to be made." He gave his head a tiny shake as if unhappy with the words he'd chosen. He tried again, a little more desperately this time. "I-I just don't want us to end up hurting each other, Wy. That's all it is." Then he said the same words over again, sadly, as if the very act of uttering those words admitted the defeat he felt inside. "I just don't want us to end up hurting each other."

Wyeth dropped his head to Deeze's chest, trying to comfort Deeze even as his own anguish swelled inside him. "Shush," he said, fighting back a wave of pain but determined to hold on to his dignity until he could get away. Away from this place. Away from Deeze. "If you want to break it off, Deeze, I understand. You don't have to worry. I won't make a fuss."

Deeze stiffened in his arms. "Wait. What?"

Wyeth used all his willpower not to let the ache in his heart tear at his voice. He had to be strong or he'd never get through this. "I said I understand. You don't have to worry. I'll bow out gracefully." He spat up a mirthless chuckle that was as patently false as the look of weary boredom on his face. "I knew it would happen sooner or later. No point in putting off the inevitable, right? If it's stillborn, it's stillborn. Best to let it go."

Suddenly Wyeth could no longer hold back the tears. His vision blurred. His breath caught in his throat. He briefly tightened his grip on Deeze's arms as if clawing for balance, then he tried to turn away, racked with shame and hurt.

Deeze held on to him, refusing to let him go. He snatched him back around and dipped a finger under Wyeth's chin, dragging his face up to his. He waited until their eyes were locked before he spoke. "What the hell are you saying?"

Only then did Wyeth's tears spill out, skittering down his cheeks. Horrified, he tried to turn away, but again Deeze wouldn't let him go.

"What's wrong?" Deeze pleaded. "What did I say?"

Wyeth wrenched himself from Deeze's arms. He realized suddenly how cool it was under the trees. How fragrant the woods were, how quiet it was with the city noises sifted to silence amid the hush of the trees. He also realized how empty he suddenly felt. It was a familiar emptiness. One he had lived with before. One he had *always* lived with. It was an emptiness he hadn't felt since Deeze crashed into his life.

When he found the words he wanted to say, they simply tore out of him. He couldn't have stopped them if he'd tried. "I knew you'd break my heart the first night we slept together, Deeze. I knew it, but I took the risk because I wanted to be with you. At least for a while. I understood the rules the minute I threw myself into your bed."

"Threw yourself…. *What* rules? What the hell are you talking about?"

Wyeth angrily brushed the tears from his cheeks. He threw his shoulders back and tried to be brave about the whole thing. Jesus, if he couldn't hold on to his pride, what the hell did he have left? "Deeze, nobody knows better than me that you're out of my league. Hell, I never did understand what you saw in me. I just thought maybe I could hang on to you for a while and enjoy the ride. You're the most beautiful man I've ever been with. For that reason and a million others, I knew it couldn't last. If you want to end it now, then I understand. Really. You don't have to tear yourself up over it. Let me just get my dog and try to find my way out of these stupid fucking trees."

His voice gave out and the tears welled in his eyes again. He took a sharp little intake of breath, and just stood there, drained.

Deeze gripped Wyeth's shoulders and shook him so hard Wyeth's teeth rattled. The fury of it startled Wyeth, and his tear-filled eyes popped open in surprise. Deeze loosened his grip on Wyeth's shoulders, but still he didn't let him go. "Is that what you think I'm doing? Breaking up with you?"

Even as the tears rolled down his cheeks, Wyeth's face finally tightened in anger. "Aren't you?" It was an accusation, not a question.

Deeze cringed as if a stone had been hurled his way. "No! Jesus, Wy! I think about you all the time. You're never out of my head. Don't you know that? I don't want to lose what we have. I don't want us to end up hurting each other. Don't make that mocking face, Wy. Don't ever think you can't hurt me. Hell, you're hurting me *now*."

"Deeze…. I don't underst—"

"I'm not trying to break up with you, Wy. In fact, I'm trying to do the opposite. I don't want us to see anybody else. I don't want us to date other people. Not until we decide how we really feel about each other." Suddenly, it was as if all the air had gone out of Deeze. He gripped Wyeth's waist and dropped to his knees in front of him. Dragging him close he buried his face in Wyeth's stomach and gazed up into his face. "I want you for myself, Wy. I want us to make some sort of commitment to each other. I'm not trying to own you. I'm not trying to marry you. I just don't want to share you with anybody, not until I figure out what is happening *in here*."

Squeezing his eyes shut, he struck a fist against his chest, against his heart. "I know it's selfish, Wy. I know! But it's what I need right now.

I need to *know*," he added lamely. Then he looked up into Wyeth's eyes again, his own eyes shimmering with passion, with confusion, with a dozen different emotions. "Please tell me you want that too."

Wyeth stared down into Deeze's upturned face. As he stared, a tear slid from his eye and splashed across Deeze's lips. Deeze licked the tear away, smiling weakly.

"Yummy," Deeze whispered in a broken voice. Then his face grew serious. "Talk to me, Wy. Please. Tell me what you're thinking."

But Wyeth couldn't speak. He was so stunned, so relieved, and so deeply, deeply touched, there was no voice left in him. He slipped his fingers through Deeze's curly hair, and, swallowing hard, he closed his eyes, squeezing back another onrush of tears. A moment later his strength gave out and he dropped to his knees on the trail in front of Deeze and squirmed his way into Deeze's arms.

With dawning expressions of relief, they kissed, and just as Deeze had done a moment before with him, Wyeth tasted Deeze's salty tears. By that alone, Wyeth knew he wasn't dreaming.

At the same moment, his voice returned. His words were right there waiting for him. He had to break the kiss to speak them. "Yes, Deeze, I want the same thing as you. You know I do. I want it with all my heart."

A minute passed while they listened to the birds chittering in the branches overhead. Still on their knees, still embracing, Deeze pressed his lips to Wyeth's ear.

"Time to move on," he crooned. "We've only just begun."

Wyeth burrowed more deliciously into Deeze's arms. "I love the Carpenters. So romantic."

Deeze gave an uneasy laugh. "I mean we've only just begun the run. We still have miles to go."

Wyeth tensed. "Are you fucking nuts? After everything you just put me through? After everything we just talked about?"

Deeze looked uncertain, like he didn't quite know what to say to that. "Well, we still have to stay healthy, don't we?"

Wyeth couldn't help himself. He coughed up a chuckle. "My God, your cousin was right. You really are nuts."

Deeze's eyes brightened. His dimples popped into place. He slid a fingertip over Wyeth's smile, clearly entranced. "I'm nuts about *you*. Does that count?"

"If you're so nuts about me, why are you scaring me to death and running me into the ground?" Wyeth groused, hauling himself to his feet.

Deeze remained on his knees a little longer, smiling broadly. He gathered Wyeth's legs into his arms and once again pressed his face to Wyeth's stomach. He lifted Wyeth's shirttail, dragged the red sweatpants down a smidgeon, and planted a kiss just above the spot where the fiery bush of ginger pubic hair began.

"Keep that up and we'll be arrested for public indecency," Wyeth sputtered, staring down and chewing on his lower lip, feeling the blood already surging into his nether regions.

Deeze grinned up at Wyeth. "A small price to pay for such perfection." His eyes grew serious yet again. "Are we committed now? Are we dating only each other from this day forth?"

That was all it took for Wyeth to choke up again. He swallowed and caressed the sides of Deeze's face. "Are you really all mine now, Deeze? I mean as far as us seeing other people? Are we really an exclusive item, you and me?"

"Mm-hmm." Deeze's gentle smile twisted up, and he planted another kiss on Wyeth's abdomen. "You're mine and I'm yours."

"Wow," Wyeth sighed through a shuddery breath.

Deeze tugged Wyeth's sweatpants down a little farther and placed a gentle kiss into the very midst of that heavenly bush of ginger pubes. Then his nose twitched like it had been tickled, and he laughed. Wyeth's waistband snapped into place as Deeze released it and bounced to his feet. Smiling broadly, he planted a second kiss on Wyeth's nose.

He snuggled close to Wyeth's ear again, his voice sexy and deep. "It's true, though," he said in a sexy whisper.

"What's true?" Wyeth gasped, shivering under the gentle pressure of Deeze's lips at the side of his neck.

"We really have only just begun," Deeze whispered.

In the process of melting, Wyeth could barely utter the words. "You mean us?"

Deeze barked out a merry laugh. "No, dipshit. I mean our run. Let's go!"

Wyeth stared in appalled amazement as Deeze took off down the trail. Trying to pull himself together after everything that had just happened, he patted his leg for Chaucer to follow. Chaucer didn't look too happy about it, but he reluctantly obeyed.

Gazing down the path, Wyeth spotted Deeze a hundred yards ahead already. He looked so handsome and sexy, Wyeth could hardly stand it. He sucked in a breath of bracing morning air and set off in hot pursuit, his poor little rubbery legs pumping up and down like badly damaged pistons.

Fifty feet farther on, he yelled out, "I've changed my mind. I want to date a lazy guy instead. A fucking couch potato. A slug!" Chaucer barked in agreement while Deeze, down the trail, merely laughed.

"Asshole," Wyeth muttered to himself, swatting away a bug.

"DID YOU have fun?"

Wyeth settled his back against Deeze's naked chest, slid his hands over Deeze's bronze, soapy legs, which hemmed him in on either side, and let the warm bathwater soak away his aches. He hadn't taken an actual tub bath for ages, and he had *never* taken one with a man who looked like Deeze, so this was quite an experience. It would have been even more fun if he wasn't so damned exhausted and his legs didn't feel like overcooked noodles.

He closed his eyes and enjoyed the moment as best he could while Deeze dug his chin into his shoulder and lazily reached around to lather up Wyeth's chest with a bar of soap. Deeze's slick hands roamed everywhere, and already the head of Wyeth's cock was peeking out of the soapy water and begging for a little attention. A moment later, Deeze slipped a soap-slicked fist around it, and every muscle in Wyeth's body went rigid at the sensation.

"My baby likes that," Deeze crooned in his ear.

Wyeth also liked the iron cock pressed against his back beneath the water. He unpeeled his ass from the bottom of the tub and slid his dick deeper into Deeze's fist. Trying not to gasp but failing miserably. "And to think I used to prefer showers."

Deeze slid a thumb over the tip of Wyeth's dick, which made Wyeth buck against him in a testosterone-charged shudder. With a smile, Deeze returned his hands to Wyeth's chest. Slowly, Wyeth relaxed as Deeze cradled him in his arms. He laid his head back, and Deeze pressed his cheek against Wyeth's damp hair. With one hand splayed over Wyeth's chest, and the other on Wyeth's stomach, ignoring Wyeth's dick for the moment, Deeze held him close. Once again, Wyeth let the warm bathwater soak through him, relaxing tense muscles.

They were in Deeze's apartment. Napoleon sat on the commode watching them. He seemed pretty bored, but Wyeth ignored him, too wrapped up in Deeze to care about the cat.

Wyeth dropped his head back and turned just enough to tuck his head under Deeze's chin. Sliding down in the tub, he rested his cheek at the base of Deeze's throat.

"Deeze?"

"Hmm?" Deeze sighed, seeming lost in the moment.

Wyeth brushed his lips against Deeze's wet throat. "Did you mean what you said in the park? About us not dating anyone else while we're seeing each other?"

Deeze's arms slid more snugly around Wyeth's chest. He pressed his mouth to Wyeth's forehead. Wyeth wasn't sure, but he thought he felt a smile in the kiss. "You know I meant it. Why? Are you having second thoughts?"

Wyeth considered that. "N-no. I just don't really understand what made you say it."

"Do you *want* to see other people?" Deeze asked. The smile against Wyeth's skin seemed to have disappeared, even while the arms around his chest grew tighter. Deeze brought a soapy hand up to lift Wyeth's chin and twisted him around so they could peer into each other's eyes. "You're not about to break my heart, are you, Wy?"

Deeze's smile was back, but it was a wary one. Wyeth couldn't bear to see it, so he kissed it to make it go away. Twisting around in the tub even more, sloshing a little water out onto the bathroom floor, which startled the cat, he positioned his head more firmly against Deeze's chest. Slipping his arms around Deeze's waist at the same time, he said, "Just hearing you ask that question astonishes me, Deeze. To think that someone like me could break the heart of someone like you. It's incomprehensible to me."

Deeze cupped a soapy hand against Wyeth's cheek. Pulling back, he studied Wyeth's vibrant blue eyes. "And why do you think that is, baby? Why do you think it's so hard for you to believe you have the power to break my heart?"

Wyeth dropped his gaze. He couldn't hold it any longer. It was too much like looking into a mirror, seeing his own insecurities staring back. And the words. Deeze's words. They tore at him in a way no one's words had ever torn at him before. And he wasn't even sure why. That was the confusing part. "I-I don't know."

Deeze offered a gentle smile. "Yes, you do. Somewhere deep down inside you do. But I don't want you to think that way anymore. It isn't necessary. What might have once been true, at least in your eyes, isn't true anymore. Not with me. All right? Will you trust me? When I say I want to see only you, will you at least give me the joy of believing me when I ask it?"

"The j-joy...." Wyeth stammered.

"Yes," Deeze said. "The joy. That's what you bring to me. Don't you know that?"

Wyeth closed his eyes. To shut out the room. To shut out the man holding him. To shut it all out. He knew he had to say the words. They were truth. He had to admit them, not only to Deeze, but to himself as well.

"I thought it was you who brought the joy, Deeze. I've changed since I've been with you. Maybe you don't see it, but I do. Sometimes I look in a storefront window when I walk by, and the shock of what I see stops me in my tracks. It's a different person staring back, Deeze. A different person than who I used to be. The one I see now is happy. He's smiling. I never walked down the street smiling before. Never. I-I just want you to know that."

"Wy—"

Wyeth pressed a finger to Deeze's lips. "Shush," he said. "I want to say one more thing."

Deeze smiled and kissed the fingertip, the open gaze in his warm eyes telling Wyeth to go ahead, to get it off his chest, to say what he wanted to say.

So Wyeth did. "I just need to tell you that no matter what happens between us now, I will always be grateful for the time we've had together. Nothing is permanent in life. I know that. But spending these weeks with you has been something I'll never forget. You've changed me. You've made me a different person. And it's a person I like a whole lot better than the person I used to be. I just want you to know that."

Deeze cupped a hand to the nape of Wyeth's neck, and once again they settled back against the cool porcelain tub, the warm water swelling up to Wyeth's shoulders, the bubbles brushing his chin.

THE TWO men sat in the bathtub in silence for long minutes while Wyeth lay in Deeze's arms, wondering if he'd said too much, and Deeze held Wyeth close, wondering if it was time for him to say even more.

But in the end, they let the cooling bath water make the decision for them. With their silence quickly turning to lust, they climbed from the tub and dried each other off. From there they moved to the bed and let their bodies take over the conversation.

What began as a soothing massage to ease the tautness in Wyeth's calves, ended with those same strong hands exploring farther afield. Wyeth lay pliant to Deeze's pleasure. Wherever Deeze wanted him to be, whatever Deeze wanted him to do, that was what Wyeth wanted too. They were two souls with a single need.

When Deeze entered him, with Wyeth on his back, his pale legs clamped tight to Deeze's sides, he sought Deeze's mouth in a kiss. They stared into each other's eyes while Deeze's cock delved to his deepest parts, deliciously searing through him.

At the moment of climax, when they cried out in unison, Deeze's mouth once again sought Wyeth's, and while their bodies bucked with orgasm inside their long breathless kiss, Deeze muttered, "Thank you, baby, thank you," over and over again.

Later, they burrowed into each other's arms while the sun streamed through the bedroom window and the cat snoozed on the sill.

While Deeze slept the afternoon away, childlike in Wyeth's arms, Wyeth lay wide-awake listening to the gentle thunder of Deeze's heart thudding softly against his ear.

When the tears came, Wyeth let them fall.

Tears of happiness were a new experience for him. He wanted to enjoy them while he could.

CHAPTER TEN

THE WEEKS that followed brought about a whirlwind of new emotions for Wyeth, and for Deeze too, maybe, although neither spoke of it. It was too new. Too all-encompassing. They settled into their exclusive dating arrangement without a single hitch. While Wyeth might still sit back occasionally and marvel at his good fortune, he no longer fought against accepting the fact that Deeze wanted to be with him. Deeze made that fact crystal clear at every turn.

Wyeth was so amazed by the way his life had changed since he and Deeze began to see each other that he thought it only fair to try to enjoy the same pastimes Deeze enjoyed. Since Deeze's greatest passion (aside from teaching) was running, Wyeth pulled out all the stops and immersed himself in the sport as well. He stopped griping every time Deeze asked him to go for a jog. He even let Deeze teach him the proper warm-up stretches so he could run without doing any damage to himself.

He bought new running shoes, and yes, he wore shorts now when they jogged. After a lifetime of hating his pale skin, he had finally begun to accept the fact that maybe, just maybe, he wasn't so ugly after all. If someone like Deeze could find him sexy, what the heck did Wyeth have to complain about?

On the nights when Deeze had classes at the college, Wyeth began running in secret. He and Chaucer, who still hated exercise with every fiber in his being but could be bribed into participating with a Milk-Bone and a belly rub, clomped along miles of city streets, weaving through the high-rises of downtown, seeking out new places to explore from the bay to the park and beyond. Wyeth sweated buckets even while his leg muscles hardened and his stamina grew. And while his strength and form improved, he also began to appreciate the simple joy of forward motion, the wind in his hair, the sun on his back, the pistoning of his strengthening legs, the healthy thunder of his pumping heart.

One Wednesday evening, Wyeth happened to glance in a supermarket window at his own reflection racing past. He stopped in his tracks and stood there on the street corner staring at himself. At his lean frame. At his heaving chest. At his surly dog sitting grumpily at his feet.

At the smile on his own rosy-cheeked, sweating face.

It was at that moment that Wyeth realized for the first time that he was actually beginning to *like* running. That night he told Deeze, who was ecstatic.

The next day Deeze upped the ante and signed them up for a marathon.

Wyeth stared at the entry form Deeze had just handed him. "You have to be joking. A *marathon*? You want me to jog *twenty-six miles*? At *once*?"

Deeze grinned. "It's 26.2 miles actually. And not jog. Run. I'll help you train for it. It'll be fun."

"It'll be a disaster."

"Ye of little faith. I'll buy you a new outfit. Maybe we'll wear matching clothes."

Wyeth rolled his eyes. "Nothing gay about that."

Deeze snuggled close. "I'm proud of you. I *want* people to know we're together."

Wyeth stopped griping on the spot. Wyeth melted when Deeze got romantic. Every single time. "Do you really?"

"You know I do. And to prove it, I won't even try to outdistance you during the race. I'll stick right by your pokyass side."

One of Wyeth's eyebrows climbed up into his hairline. "That's assuming you really *could* outdistance me during the race. Maybe I'm no longer as poky as I used to be. Ever think of that?"

Deeze laughed. "Ooh. Cocky."

Wyeth's bravado suddenly petered out. "How many people will be racing?"

Deeze shrugged. "I don't know. Hundreds, maybe."

"Good. No one will notice me. I'll be lost in the mob. Are there hills? Where is this race anyway?"

"Downtown to Point Loma, around past SeaWorld and back through Balboa Park. No hills, or almost none. Don't worry. You can do it. It'll be a great run."

At the word "run," Chaucer crawled off the couch and slouched into the bedroom, where he ducked under the bed with his tail between his legs.

"What's wrong with him?" Deeze asked.

"You said *run*. He hates that word. It has replaced the word *bath* as his all-time favorite word to hate. Tell me he won't be going with us."

"He won't be going with us. Nothing can suck the fun out of running like your dog."

Wyeth gave a wry smirk. "He really does, doesn't he?"

"Speaking of Chaucer, I think it's time he met Napoleon. I'm tired of you having to crawl out of my nice warm bed to come back here and take him for a walk, or feed him, or try to soothe his damaged ego because you left him alone all night."

Wyeth frowned. "They'll kill each other."

Deeze wormed a hand down the front of Wyeth's jeans, his mind clearly no longer focused on pets. "You don't know that. Maybe they'll love each other," he said, licking his lips. "Ooh, what have I found here?"

Wyeth's eyes closed of their own volition while Deeze's fingertips did magical things inside his trousers. "What were we talking about?" he asked as sweat popped out on his upper lip. "I seem to have forgotten."

Twelve seconds later his pants were flying through the air and ended up hanging on a pole lamp in the corner of the room. Simultaneously, his undershorts went sailing off in the opposite direction and came to rest in a bowl of apples on the dining room table.

"How did you get my clothes off so fast," Wyeth asked, his legs already wobbly in anticipation.

"Trade secret," Deeze grinned, and dropped to his knees to demonstrate a few other trade secrets. All of which were greatly appreciated and more than happily returned in kind.

"DOES NAPOLEON like dogs?"

"Only if they've been slathered with tuna first."

"Really?"

"That was a joke. Actually, he's never said."

Wyeth coughed up a nervous grunt. "I guess we'll find out soon enough."

It was early morning. Deeze had just spent the night in Wyeth's apartment. Because of that, he was a little uneasy about Wyeth's proposal to introduce the pets today. Napoleon had a tendency to hold a grudge, and leaving him on his own from dusk to dawn wasn't the best way to get on his good side.

Deeze stared down at Chaucer who was sitting trustingly between him and Wyeth in front of Deeze's front door. As long as they weren't running or giving him a bath, not much of anything bothered Chaucer. He didn't appear to suspect he was about to be thrust into a cage match with a large Maine coon cat of indeterminate temper and an ax to grind after being abandoned all night and left alone with an empty food bowl and a dirty litter box—*again*. Actually, Wyeth didn't appear to suspect the gravity of the situation either.

"I want you to play nice," Wyeth said, bending down and dragging Chaucer's chin around so they were facing eye to eye while he wagged a disciplinary finger in the mutt's face. "We're a family now. Try not to kill the poor little defenseless pussycat you're about to meet."

Chaucer didn't make any promises, but he did give Wyeth a swipe across the nose with his tongue to let his master know he understood the request and would give it the proper consideration. Deeze, on the other hand, got even more worried and started energetically gnawing at his lower lip.

"Umm, Wy. You may be misreading the facts a bit. Napoleon is neither little nor defenseless. In fact, for an animal with gonads, he can be a real bitch."

Wyeth slapped a dismissive hand through the air. "Don't be silly. He's just a kitty. How unfriendly can he be?"

At that moment a brindle paw stabbed outward into the hall from the bottom of Deeze's door. The paw had extremely long claws, and the claws were fully extended. Through the door they could hear a grumbling roar, which clearly came from the throat of a pissed-off feline. Napoleon was mad already, and they weren't even through the door.

"Uh-oh," Deeze said.

"Oh, relax," Wyeth said, but this time he didn't seem quite as sure of himself. "He's just excited, don't you think?"

Deeze sucked on his front teeth. "Napoleon? Oh, he's excited all right."

Chaucer took matters into his own hands and stepped boldly forward. He sniffed at the paw, which was now blindly slapping the floor and frantically groping this way and that, looking for something to disembowel. Not having a lick of sense, and never *having* had a lick of sense, Chaucer wagged his tail and gave the marauding paw a playful nip with his teeth.

Something extremely heavy and extremely pissed off crashed against the other side of the door, rattling it on its hinges. Chaucer soared straight up into the air with a terrified howl, and when he came back down he had two bleeding slash marks crisscrossing his nose. He stared up at Wyeth's horrified face with pouting eyes, as if deeply hurt that his master had not warned him of the danger. He then turned away and curled up into a ball by the hallway wall, as far from the still rattling door as he could get without ripping the leash from Wyeth's hand. There he lay like a deep-fried shrimp, nose to nuts. Whimpering in self-pity, he administered to his poor nose, still casting occasional accusatory glances in Wyeth's direction.

Napoleon continued to fling himself at the door with such force that Deeze reached out to pat the hinges, hoping to lessen the racket before his neighbors started poking their heads out into the hall to see what the hell was going on. He tapped his chin with a thoughtful forefinger. "Hmm. Maybe we should introduce them another day."

"Yes," Wyeth agreed, clearly appalled by that banging, clattering door and the growls and spitting to be heard on the other side of it. "Maybe we'll try again after your cat has been tranquilized and put in a straightjacket."

"He *is* a little high-strung."

"You think?" He gazed down at his trembling dog, clucked his tongue in sympathy, then all but growled at Deeze. "Chaucer's bleeding, thank you very much. I hope you're still packing Band-Aids."

THE NEXT day they tried introducing the animals again. This time they planned ahead. Chaucer wore a loose muzzle, more to protect his nose from being savaged again by Napoleon than to preclude any damage he might inflict with his teeth on the damn cat. This put Chaucer in a bad mood right off the bat, because he loathed wearing a muzzle.

For his part, Deeze had spent the night before clipping Napoleon's claws to better blunt their ability to rip Chaucer's face off. This activity on Deeze's part was a two-edged sword. While it did make Napoleon's claws marginally less lethal, it also pissed the cat off no end. Napoleon hated having his nails trimmed as much as Chaucer hated jogging. And when Napoleon was mad, it took him days to get over it.

By the time the appointed hour for the meeting came around, the two animals were already furious. By the same token, the two humans seemed blithely unaware of that fact and so for lack of a better plan decided to go ahead with the meeting anyway. Because, really, they both agreed, how bad could it be?

Needless to say, they were about to find out.

Wyeth stood outside Deeze's door with Chaucer straining at the leash. He was straining at the leash trying to get *away* from the door, not *through* it. Every sinew in Chaucer's body wanted nothing more than to get back in the elevator and go the fuck home.

On the opposite side of the door, a growling Napoleon lay trapped in Deeze's arms. He was so mad he was puffed up to three times his normal size. It was like holding a squirming goat. Napoleon had already drawn blood on Deeze's forearms in three places, but Deeze, the perpetual optimist, took a stoic breath to steel his nerves, flipped the lock on his front door, and sang out to Wyeth standing in the hall, "Come on in! Let's get this over with!"

Wyeth strode through the door dragging a terrified Chaucer along behind.

At the first sight of the strange dog on his home turf, Napoleon wrenched himself from Deeze's arms and launched himself through the air like a Sidewinder missile, a spitting, snarling ball of fury with dangerous, pointy ends protruding in every direction.

"Close the door!" screamed Deeze. "Don't let them out!"

Wyeth kicked the door shut behind him just as Chaucer's eyes got as big as baseballs and his hackles shot up like porcupine quills. In full terror mode, he took off running, ripping the leash from Wyeth's hand and emitting a howl that made both men cringe.

Napoleon shot after the dog like a cheetah chasing down an antelope on the plains of the Serengeti. In less than three strides he was close enough to sink a claw into Chaucer's tail, which gave poor Chaucer a shot of adrenaline rather like a supercharger pouring extra fuel into a GTO. In a split second, Chaucer was airborne.

Trailing his leash, which snagged on everything he passed, Chaucer tore through the apartment like a tornado, leaving a path of destruction in his wake. Table lamps flew. Knickknacks crumbled. A humongous box of school supplies leapt skyward, and hundreds of assorted crayons shot into the air, adding an explosion of color to the festivities.

As the animals flew around the room in circles, both screaming and wailing to high heaven, Wyeth and Deeze stood in the eye of the storm, speechless, wondering just what sort of biblical hell they had unleashed.

Chaucer howled like a banshee while Napoleon tore straight up the living room curtains, leaving rents and nubbins behind in the fabric before his weight tore the curtains from the windows completely. Chaucer bounced across the sofa, scattering cushions, and became mired in a stack of throw pillows. Napoleon saw his chance and leapt with all twenty claws extended right onto Chaucer's back, sticking to the poor hapless beast like a furious swath of homicidal Velcro. Chaucer howled and shot into the bedroom, upending the coffee table along the way, sending a bowl of malted milk balls rolling across the floor. By hurling himself under the bed, he scraped Napoleon off his back, and the moment the two were separated, Deeze slammed the bedroom door closed, locking them both inside.

Wyeth stood staring at the devastation, jaws agape. At that moment the last curtain still hanging slid from the rod and landed in a tattered puddle of red on the living room floor.

Calmly, Deeze licked a dribble of blood from his arm and said, "Well, that went pretty well. How about some tea?"

WYETH GLANCED at his watch as he paced the marble floor of the library's domed reading area. The murmur of whispered voices and the papery flutter of carefully flipped pages filled the massive space beneath the vaulted ceiling like the startled hush of bird's wings flurrying into flight. The air around Wyeth was alive with the scent of old books, new books, dusty books, and just a tinge of body odor from the scattered homeless people who came into the air-conditioned library, not only to read and pass the time, but to escape the summer heat outside, as they came to escape the cold and rain in winter. Most of the homeless who frequented the library were, despite their circumstances, lovers of the written word. Or maybe they just came to forget their own troubles for a while, to separate themselves from the stark realities of their own disappointing lives by losing themselves in the stories of others.

Wyeth knew many of the homeless by name. He even sought them out to say hello, to ask how they were doing, to see what they were reading. They were invariably polite and humble and treated the books with respect. Wyeth only wished some of the "regular" library patrons would be so civilized.

He lifted a hand and smiled at one of his favorites, Crazy Bill. Crazy Bill, as always, wore a greasy overcoat and a battered deerstalker hat on his head like a down-on-his-luck Sherlock Holmes. Sitting next to him, perusing the same book as Bill, sat Itty Bitty Bob, Bill's best friend. Itty Bitty Bob reached four foot six standing and two foot two sitting. He was a dwarf. The book they were perusing was an illustrated copy of *Treasure Island*. Apparently they were in the mood for pirates.

"Hi, Bill. Hi, Bob," Wyeth said, leaning in and whispering so as not to disturb the other readers.

Bill and Bob gave him two sweet smiles that were very much alike, then turned back to their book as if they were getting to the good part and couldn't be bothered right then, thank you very much. Wyeth gave each a congenial pat on the shoulder and left them to it.

Heads throughout the reading room lifted at the clatter of tiny footsteps and the chorus of high-pitched, childish giggles coming from the stairway leading down from the floor above. Off in the distance, Wyeth heard a series of sibilant *shush*es coming from other librarians, but they didn't seem to reduce the noise much.

"Can it!" boomed a familiar voice, and Wyeth grinned. Immediately the *shush*es increased dramatically while the giggling ceased altogether.

Peeking around the corner of the stairwell, Wyeth spotted Deeze at the same moment Deeze spotted him. They gave each other a cheery wave, and Deeze turned to beckon forward the crocodile of five-year-olds following along behind him in an undulating line of tiny excited humanity.

The kids were all in little brown school outfits consisting of khaki shorts and little tiny chestnut-colored polo shirts. Some even wore little brown baseball caps on their heads that read St. Luke's across the front.

The kids were craning their necks, gazing with awe at the domed ceiling and over at the long shelves of books stretching out seemingly for miles in every direction. A few were more interested in all the homeless people sitting around watching *them*. Wyeth couldn't blame the kids for that. Some of the homeless were rather eccentric in their dress. To a five-year-old, they must have looked like fairy-tale creatures. Ogres maybe. Or trolls one might spot lurking under a bridge.

Deeze, still leading his unruly troop, strode across the reading room floor and walked right up to Wyeth to give him a hug. Wyeth quickly broke the hug, thinking maybe they had better shake hands instead, then turned along with Deeze to the twenty-four little terrorist Catholics who were straining to break ranks and take off in twenty-four different directions to see what they could tear apart.

Deeze managed to snag their attention by clearing his throat rather pompously, and as soon as most of them were looking in his general direction, he pointed to a doorway off to the left. The sign above the door said Children's Corner.

"Everyone quietly go thataway," Deeze commanded. With a grin, he added, "The key word in that sentence is *quietly*. And yes, Mary Lou"—he pointed at a giggly girl with freckles and no front teeth who seemed to be capable of making an inordinate amount of noise even when she stood there unmoving with her mouth clapped shut and her hands tucked safely into her armpits—"that includes you."

The kids broke ranks and stampeded toward the door Deeze had pointed to. All but one.

Wyeth gazed down to see a familiar face staring up at him. It was little Jake. The boy from the beach. Jake tugged at the crease on Wyeth's trousers, so Wyeth knelt to face the boy to see what he wanted.

"Hi, Jake," Wyeth said. He stared down at the kid's bony knee. All sign of his former injury was long gone. "I see you don't need a Band-Aid anymore."

"No, I healed. People do, you know."

Wyeth laughed, not at Jake, but at himself. Someday he'd learn not to talk down to kids. "So did you want something?"

Jake nodded, eyes wide. "My mom said you must be Mr. Long's boyfriend. Her and Daddy were talking about it after we saw you that day on the beach."

Wyeth stared up at Deeze, then back at the boy. "Is that really what she said?"

Jake nodded, his eyes wide and innocent. "Uh-huh."

It was Deeze's turn to kneel down and intervene. "You must have misunderstood her, Jake. Mr. Becker and I are just friends."

"It's okay," Jake said. "Mommy's brother has a boyfriend too. It's not like she's a homeyphone."

Deeze visibly struggled not to laugh since the kid was looking so serious. "I think you mean homophobe."

"Yeah, that." Jake grinned. "She said she thought you guys were cute together. My mom's kind of sappy sometimes when she talks about lovey-dovey stuff. Even Daddy says so. But don't worry. He's not a homeyphone either."

"Well, that's nice, but we're just friends," Wyeth said again.

Deeze leaned in and whispered into the boy's ear. "Don't listen to him, Jake. Your mom's right. Wyeth *is* my boyfriend, and I like him about as much as you like Jujubes."

Jake's little face lit up. "I *love* Jujubes!"

"I know you do."

They heard a woman's voice as she strove to get the kids' attention. She was sitting in a straight-backed chair in the middle of the Children's Corner, asking all the little boys and girls to gather around so she could read them a story. She had a slightly harried look in her eye, Wyeth noticed. Not that he could blame her for that.

"Run along now, Jake. It's story time," Deeze said, pointing to the lady in the chair. "Go join your classmates. Try not to do anything that will entail a SWAT team rappelling down through the ceiling or me having to explain to your mommy why you've been sent to Sing Sing for thirty years."

"You talk funny," Jake said, and two seconds later he was flying across the reading room, little tiny Keds smacking the floor beneath him as he narrowly missed an elderly man in a sport coat with leather patches on the elbows, who chuckled and called, "Whoa there, son!" as the boy sailed past.

Deeze and Wyeth rose to their feet and gazed at each other.

"You are, you know. My boyfriend, I mean," Deeze said around a smile.

Wyeth blushed and meekly nodded.

Deeze plucked at his shirtsleeve. "Come listen to the story with us," he pleaded. "I don't want to leave you just yet. The library can do without you for a half hour or so. Think of it as public relations."

Wyeth had a concerned look on his face. "Aren't you worried about what Jake's mother said?"

Deeze shrugged. "No, but you have to admit she's perceptive. I suppose it helps that she has a gay brother." He glanced toward the reading room. "Come on. The story's beginning. I hate missing the start of a story. Or the opening scene in a movie. Or foreplay. Ooh, listen. It's Dr. Seuss too. He's my favorite. Wyeth? You coming?"

Wyeth stared dreamily into Deeze's eyes. "I love…." But his words trailed away before he could finish.

Deeze's gaze softened. A tiny smile played at his mouth. "You love *what*, Wy? What is it you're trying to say?"

Wyeth reddened, but for once in his life he didn't care. He was determined to say what he wanted to say no matter what sort of shitstorm it unleashed. Still, at the last minute he couldn't do it. Hating himself for being a coward, he sought out words that weren't really what he meant to say at all, but were as close as he dared to get. "I-I love it when you say my name," he feebly muttered.

Deeze's smile broadened. "And I love *you.*"

Wyeth's heart stopped. He was almost sure it did. "You've never said that before, Deeze."

Deeze winked. "No, but I'm saying it now."

Wyeth stammered out a reply. "I-I love you too, Deeze. That's really what I started to say before I chickened out."

Deeze smiled gently. "I know."

"We can rewind the last couple of minutes and pretend like you didn't answer me at all if you want. I didn't mean to make you say something you didn't want to say."

Deeze cocked his head. "Are you nuts? I meant what I said, Wy. It wasn't a mistake. I've been waiting for the perfect opportunity to say it for weeks. Thanks to you being a sniveling wuss who was too chicken to say it himself, this turned out to be the day."

Wyeth didn't care that Deeze had just called him a sniveling wuss. His eyes misted over anyway. "Well then, if it wasn't a mistake and you really meant to say what you said, would you mind saying it again? I wasn't ready for it the first time. I want to memorize every moment of you uttering the words."

"My God, you really are nuts." But Deeze was smiling again, which was no big deal since his previous frowny face had surely all been for show anyway. "Okay. Here goes. You ready? You listening?" He rested his hands on Wyeth's shoulders, massaging him gently with his fingertips, edging just close enough that they wouldn't be arrested for smooching in public. "I love you, Wyeth Becker. I think I've loved you since the very first time your dog stepped out in front of me and knocked me on my ass."

"You should have been watching where you were going."

"Shut up. Now, tell me you love me back."

Wyeth sniffed. He was getting teary-eyed again. "I do love you back. I'll never forget how beautiful you were lying there unconscious at my feet, concussed to within an inch of your life in your little mauve shorts. You were so nice and quiet."

"I wasn't unconscious. I was faking."

"I knew that."

"And I can be quiet when I want to be."

Wyeth rolled his eyes. "No, you can't."

Deeze paused for a second. "You're right. I can't."

"Deeze?"

"Yes?"

"Am I mistaken, or have we just ratcheted our relationship up *another* notch by saying we love each other?"

"You're not mistaken. I'd kiss you, but I don't want to get you fired. I can barely support *myself* on a teacher's salary. So come on, Wy. I have to get back to my kids before they dismantle your wonderful library brick by brick and I find myself on a street corner peddling all my surplus crayons and construction paper to make a living while you get fired anyway and we end up just two more homeless guys sitting in the library sucking up the free air-conditioning and pretending we don't stink to high heaven."

"Wow. Dr. Seuss has nothing on you."

Still holding hands, Deeze tugged Wyeth toward the sound of the lady in the children's room who was now giving her best impersonation of Yertle the Turtle, which was so over the top that Deeze's kids were roaring with laughter. Wyeth barely heard a thing the woman said above the pounding of his own heart. Still stunned by current events, his was the only somber face in the crowd. If there was a laugh in him anywhere, he would have been hard-pressed to find it.

He stared over at Deeze, at his bright-eyed grin, his joyous, handsome face. Their eyes met briefly as they settled cross-legged on the floor next to Jake, who had patted the floor at either side of himself in the hope they would join him.

Deeze's fingers brushed Wyeth's as they both ruffled the boy's hair before all eyes turned back to the lady with the big colorful book in her lap and the Yertle the Turtle voice. Deeze and Wyeth laughed with the kids, pretending to be as rapt at the story as all the five-year-olds sitting on the floor around them. In truth, Wyeth had eyes only for Deeze, who seemed to feel the same if his eyes locked on Wyeth's were anything to go by.

Later, Wyeth couldn't recall a single word the woman said. Not one. In fact, he had no idea what the story had been about at all. Not a clue. She could have been reading *War and Peace* or the operating instructions for her new Maytag washing machine for all he knew.

On the other hand, Deeze had said he loved him.

That was a much better tale to contemplate anyway.

CHAPTER ELEVEN

IT WAS Tuesday evening. Deeze was at class, and Wyeth had just finished a five-mile run around the harbor, with a reluctant Chaucer bitching and moaning at his heels every step of the way. The moment they stepped through the apartment door, Chaucer made a beeline for the bedroom, where he crawled under the bed, all the while growling obscenities to himself and the world at large.

Wyeth peeled out of his sweaty running clothes and was about to fish Chaucer out with a broom handle to apologize, when his cell phone rang. Naked, he padded across the living room to dig his phone out of the puddle of damp running clothes piled on the floor where he'd dropped them.

The caller was Deeze.

"Have you tried to find me?"

"No," Wyeth answered. "Aren't you at class?"

"I didn't make it. I'm with Agnes."

"You mean the old lady next door?"

"None other."

"I always knew you'd leave me, but I thought it would be for someone younger. And richer. And possessing a dick."

"Funny. Get down here and wait with me."

"Wait with you? What are you waiting for? Where are you?"

"Mercy Hospital. The emergency room."

Wyeth tensed. "What happened?"

"I'll tell you when you get here."

"Okay. Give me fifteen minutes."

Wyeth was there in twelve. He found Deeze sitting at the back of the waiting room next to a Coke machine, sipping a Diet Sprite and looking worried.

"Baby," Deeze said when he spotted Wyeth approaching.

Wyeth dropped into a chair beside him. "So what happened?"

"I found her on the street in her housecoat, walking around in a daze, talking funny, and acting all out of it. I immediately shoveled her into the car and brought her here. She cussed me the whole way."

Wyeth tried not to smile. Agnes could be cranky. "So what's wrong with her?" he asked. "Did her insanity finally take a turn for the worse? Was she speaking in tongues? Chasing squirrels through the park?" Wyeth suspected he was being a bit sarcastic, so he toned it down. "Sorry. Have you talked to a doctor?"

Deeze cast his eyes around the room, which was filled with miserable people sitting there like they were. Waiting. Waiting. "It's the chemo. The doc said her body is too old to accept it any longer. They may have to lower the dose."

"Chemo? You mean she has cancer?"

Deeze's eyes skittered back to Wyeth's face. "Yeah. She's had it for several years."

"She never said."

Deeze shrugged. "That's Agnes. She never talks about the important stuff. Just bitches about the ketchup dispensers at Denny's and how they never squirt properly. Or the price of eggs. Or how they always air commercials on TV for disposable douches while she's trying to eat dinner."

Wyeth stuck his tongue in his cheek. "Yeah, I don't like that either."

Deeze grinned, then he just as quickly frowned. "This isn't good news, Wy. Without the chemo, the cancer will gain a foothold again, and that'll be it."

"You've known this all along," Wyeth said.

Deeze nodded. "About the cancer, yeah. Once in a while she'll tell me something important. Just sort of slips it in among all the crazy stuff. You have to be paying attention to catch it. I really do like her, you know. I feel it's my duty to be a friend to her. Poor thing doesn't have very many. None, actually, as far as I know."

Wyeth reached out and clutched Deeze's hand. "Then I'm sorry." He didn't add that he was also sorry for all the times he had dissed Agnes in front of Deeze, or maybe Deeze forgave him for that already. Even he had to know how infuriating the old lady could be.

"Are they going to admit her?" Wyeth asked.

"No. I'm waiting to take her home."

"Then I'll wait with you."

Deeze's eyes burrowed into Wyeth's. He looked tired, Wyeth thought. But Deeze smiled anyway. "I was hoping you would." He brought his hand up and ran his fingers through Wyeth's wet hair. "You were running."

"Yeah, don't get too close. I haven't showered yet."

"I noticed," Deeze said, wrinkling his nose. Wyeth slapped his arm.

Together they settled back, trading sips from Deeze's Diet Sprite and waiting for Agnes to be brought out to them.

"I'm sorry she's sick," Wyeth said, pulling himself from his thoughts. "If I'd known, I might have been a little nicer to her."

Deeze grunted a laugh. "What are you talking about? She loves you. Told me if I didn't claim you for myself, she was going after you."

"You have to be shittin—"

Before Wyeth could finish, the sound of carpet slippers slapped their way toward them, and Wyeth looked up. Agnes was on the arm of a handsome young orderly. She was wearing a housecoat with tea roses all over it, and her hair was poked up under a snood. Wyeth wasn't sure, but it looked like she was naked under the housecoat.

Spotting Deeze and Wyeth back against the wall, she cried out, "There's my boys! Ain't they cute together? They love each other, you know. I'm the one that got them together."

The orderly said that was nice and, with a secretive smirk, passed the old lady into Deeze's care after giving each man an appreciative glance.

Well, he's gay, Wyeth thought.

Agnes patted her snood, waiting for someone to tell her how nice she looked.

It was so blatantly obvious, Wyeth dragged the words out of his throat as a concession to all the times he'd been snippy with her. "You look nice," he said with all the enthusiasm of a man being led to the gallows.

Of course, she was instantly offended. "Nice? I've just been prodded from one end to the other! They even lost my nightgown and knickers! I'm lucky I still have my teeth!"

DEEZE BIT back a grin at Agnes's retort, pleased that she was clear-headed enough now to complain. He'd been deeply concerned when he found her on the street, though he wasn't going to let her see that. "Sorry about your knickers," he said. "How do you feel?"

"I'm weak as a kitten," she announced, putting on a brave face. "But as soon as they adjust my meds, I'll be right as rain. Good as new. Fresh as a daisy."

Deeze made a funny face for her benefit. "So you OD'd on the drug that makes you speak in clichés, and now you won't be doing it anymore. Is that what you're telling us?"

"Ass," Agnes growled. Turning her back on Deeze, she took Wyeth's arm and started dragging him toward the exit.

Smiling, Deeze trailed along behind, carrying the old lady's folded-up walker and admiring Wyeth's ass while they headed for the door.

A tap on the shoulder stopped Deeze in the hallway outside the emergency room. It was the young doctor who had treated Agnes. The doctor spoke in hushed tones while Agnes and Wyeth strolled off through the front doors toward the parking area, both apparently still thinking Deeze was right behind them.

When the doctor finished explaining things to Deeze, they shook hands, and the doctor headed back from where he came. Deeze hustled out the door to find that while he had sat inside the hospital waiting room, day had turned to night, blue skies to stars.

He spotted Wyeth waving to him from the parking lot and took off at a jog to catch up, enjoying the flexing of muscles after sitting on a plastic chair for the past three hours.

"Well, where the heck have *you* been?" Agnes grumped when he huffed up to them. Then she gave him a slightly gentler gaze. "Did the doctor talk to you like I asked him to?"

Deeze patted her shoulder. "He talked to me. Now then, let's get you home," he said quietly.

"IT WAS sweet of you to help Agnes, Deeze."

Deeze shrugged. "She's a friend," he said, as if it was the most obvious thing in the world. "She'd do the same for me."

"Are you sure?"

Deeze coughed up a tiny laugh. "Well, not entirely."

Deeze and Wyeth lay in bed. A sheen of after-sex sweat glistened on their bodies, drying in the breeze coming through the bedroom window. It was hours after they had carted Agnes home. The moon was high in the sky outside, and they were snug and comfortable. Wyeth dreaded going back to work the next day. The cool air wafting over them heralded the beginning of autumn, and he was thrilled to death about that. It had been a hot summer.

Hot in more ways than one.

Wyeth lay cradled in Deeze's arms, his back to Deeze's chest, Deeze's sated cock nestled unthreateningly against his ass where only minutes before it had been anything *but* unthreatening.

Deeze brushed a kiss across the nape of Wyeth's neck. "The doctor told me she won't last long with the current dose of chemo, but she refused to let him cut it. It's a toss-up now as to which will kill her first. The cancer or the meds."

"I'm sorry. I hope she knows how lucky she is to have you caring about her. Without you, she'd be going through this alone, and that would be truly sad. You're a good person, Deeze, and I'm just as lucky to have you as she is."

Deeze snuggled closer, pressing himself to Wyeth's back. His voice was a contented rumble, his breath hot on Wyeth's shoulder. His strong arms circled Wyeth, clinging tight, holding him so close he could hardly breathe.

"I love you so much," Deeze muttered, sending a rush of desire coursing through Wyeth's system like a shot of adrenaline.

The words fell from Wyeth's lips. He couldn't have stopped them if he wanted. "I love you too, Deeze. I love you more than anything."

A momentary silence settled over them. When Deeze stiffened behind him, Wyeth wiggled around to face him, burying his face in the luscious forest of hair on Deeze's chest. It was his favorite place to be. "What is it?" Wyeth asked. "What are you thinking about?"

Deeze's fingers played through Wyeth's locks. He scooted down in the bed so their faces were aligned. Their leg hair bristled together, their flaccid cocks nestling side by side. Deeze's warm eyes fixed on Wyeth's, and a tiny smile twisted his mouth.

"As far as I'm concerned, our trial period is over, Wy. I know what I want. I'm hoping I know what you want too. I think it's time we start thinking about moving in together. I mean, if you'll have me."

Wyeth swallowed hard, melting under the longing expression on Deeze's handsome face. He traced a thumb across Deeze's lush lips, lips still swollen and red from kissing the stubble on Wyeth's face since he hadn't shaved since that morning. Wyeth knew his lips probably looked the same, since Deeze's stubble was even thicker than his own and Deeze hadn't shaved since morning either.

A trace of Wyeth's old insecurities struggled to break free, but he forced them into the shadows where they belonged. He had changed a lot since being with Deeze. He was a stronger person now, and he knew it. He was also a person who understood love. He trusted it now. No one had ever taught him that before. Or maybe he had simply never let himself give into it so completely before. Until Deeze came along, love was a concept that had no place in real life. Not Wyeth's life, at any rate. Now love was the driving force of everything he did. Everything. It lived inside him through every second of every day. It steered his every move, consumed his every thought.

And it made him truly happy.

"Yes," Wyeth answered immediately, not even considering his reply. He leaned in to taste those swollen lips, to wrap Deeze more securely in his arms. "Yes, I'll have you. You're all I've ever wanted, Deeze. Living with you would be…."

"What, baby? What would it be?" There was tenderness in the question. Wyeth wasn't fooled by the mischievous glint in Deeze's eyes. Deeze fooled around about a lot of things, but he wasn't fooling around now. He was dead serious.

At that moment, Wyeth loved the man so much he thought his heart would truly burst, shattering into a zillion pieces, like Alderaan after the Death Star zapped it out of the universe. A tremor coursed through his body. He fought the urge to throw himself out of bed and dance a jig around the bedroom. Or laugh like a maniac. Or maybe just lie there and blubber like a baby from sheer adoration. If it hadn't meant he would have to peel himself from Deeze's embrace, he might have done one or all of those things. As it was, he wouldn't have moved from where he was for anything in the world.

"A dream," he whispered, his lips on Deeze's chest. "Living with you, Deeze. Knowing you're really mine. It would be a wonderful, perfect dream."

Wyeth lifted his head and watched as Deeze absorbed the words, his dark eyes studying Wyeth in his arms, seeking the truth in what Wyeth had said. By the smile that touched his lips, Wyeth knew when Deeze found it. Deeze's large, gentle hand came up to cup the back of Wyeth's head while he planted a soft kiss on the tip of Wyeth's nose. "It's a dream for me too, baby. I love you so much I have to fight screaming it to the world a dozen times a day."

"Me too."

"I love you so much, I want to hire a plane to skywrite it across the heavens."

"Me too."

"I love you so much I think we should make love again as soon as I can replenish my testosterone after the last fuck we shared, which was—what, twelve minutes ago?"

Wyeth grinned. "Hmm. That last one wasn't quite as romantic as the others, but I think I like it anyway."

Deeze grinned back. "Goody."

They snuggled cozily in each other's arms while the night deepened around them. The sounds of the city drifted through the bedroom window, along with the cooling breeze. The hue of a blinking traffic light flashed a spot of red on the dresser mirror, sending it ricocheting across the room. An ambulance screamed a few blocks away, announcing to the city that not everyone was having a good night. Some homeboy's lowrider blasted rap music as it rumbled past the apartment building. The sound of laughter growing louder as people spilled from the bar down the street indicated it was two in the morning and the drunks were headed home.

Wyeth pressed his lips to Deeze's chin, inhaling the scent of the man he loved so much, not minding the stubble one little bit.

"I'll take good care of you," Deeze whispered. "I promise. I'll never hurt you, Wy. Never."

Wyeth couldn't speak since there was a lump in his throat the size of a softball. He could only nod.

They lay contentedly in the darkness while the city gradually quieted around them and the night rolled its way to dawn. Eventually, Deeze slept.

Wyeth lay awake until the sun peeked through his bedroom curtains. Quietly, he slipped naked from Deeze's arms and tiptoed to the window to gaze out on the coming day. He was standing there when Deeze opened his eyes.

"You're so beautiful," Deeze muttered, patting the mattress at his side. "Come back to bed for a few minutes before we have to go to work. Please, baby, I want you next to me."

Wyeth didn't need to be asked twice. He threw himself back into bed and wormed his way into Deeze's arms. They lay like that until the jangle of Chaucer's leash and the scratching of Chaucer's toenails on the front door told them someone needed to go out.

And so began a day neither man would ever forget.

A day one of them would barely survive.

CHAPTER TWELVE

WHILE WYETH jumped into the shower and did everything he needed to do before heading off to the library, Deeze raced back to his apartment to feed the cat and dress for work. After a hurried clean-up, he donned his school clothes, gathered up a supply of children's jigsaw puzzles he had ordered from Amazon more than a month earlier that finally came in, and carted it all out to his car. Deeze was used to spending his own money for school supplies for his classroom. Sometimes, that was the quickest way to get them. He wasn't the only teacher on the planet supplying his students from his own pocket, so he didn't think anything about it. It was simply part of the job. Besides, he knew the kids would love the puzzles he'd bought. And that was incentive enough for Deeze to spend a few bucks of his hard-earned money.

He drove off under an overcast sky, the puzzles and other school supplies stacked in the back seat of his Honda Civic. As he drove, he hummed a little song. He drove by rote along the same streets he traveled every morning, his mind taken up not with the traffic around him but the night behind. The night he had spent in Wyeth's arms. Thinking back, he remembered everything he and Wyeth had talked about. And the new commitments they had made.

The commitment of actually living together. Of being truly lovers!

Deeze imagined he could still smell Wy's musk on his skin, but he had showered, so that was probably imagination. Or maybe Wyeth's sweet scent had burrowed its way into his genetic memory, and it was there inside his head all the time whether Wy was present or not. Deeze smiled at that thought. It pleased him to think a part of Wy had embedded itself somewhere deep inside his chromosomes, not unlike the way the man had settled inside his heart. Deeze knew he had never been this much in love in his life. He risked closing his eyes for a moment to cast a quick thank-you skyward to whichever fate had coaxed Wy's dog into his path by the lagoon all those months ago.

Opening his eyes again so he wouldn't drive through a light pole, he punched the radio, and out popped Adele, singing her lovely head off, filling the car with her perfect voice. Deeze sang along, fucking up her rendition of "Set Fire to the Rain" considerably in the process, but Adele didn't seem to mind.

Strangely, during the chorus, the first drops of rain Deeze had seen in months splattered his windshield. He smiled, immediately thinking how cool it would be to walk with Wyeth along the bay, talking quietly, cuddled beneath Wyeth's umbrella, watching the whitecaps slap the shore while Chaucer scampered in the downpour, barking at the sea gulls.

Still smiling, he parked in his space by the cathedral, gathered up his school supplies from the back seat, and ducked through the rain to his classroom door. There, he took an inordinately long time to fish out his key, and by the time he opened the classroom door, he was laughing at himself for being soaked to the skin.

"I really should buy an umbrella of my own," he chuckled to himself, dripping his way through the door.

WYETH HAD a pretty standard morning. In essence, all he did was kill time, vamp to the music of the library's rhythm, and wait to be reunited with Deeze at the end of the day. He unpacked several boxes of new additions to the history section on the second floor and shelved them in their proper alphabetical spots. He removed tags and time cards from a dolly filled with older books. The books would be retired and sold at the monthly book sale, which not only raised additional funds for the library but helped clear out discarded stock as well. In this fashion, Wyeth dragged his way to lunchtime. Amazed to see raindrops on the shoulders of patrons bustling through the front doors, he dug the umbrella from his locker in the employees' lounge and popped it open to see if it still worked before he left for his customary noontime stroll.

The girl who had a crush on him appeared out of nowhere and wagged a finger in his face. "It's bad luck to open an umbrella inside," she chided in a flirty voice.

Wyeth shot her a wink and said, "I won't tell the gods if you won't."

The wink left her mesmerized for the rest of the afternoon.

Forgetting the girl immediately, Wyeth took his customary walk around the bay with Chaucer and a book, sitting once again by the lagoon where he had first met Deeze. The memories of that meeting ran so rampant through his head that he sat on the same bench, with his book forgotten in his hand, while Chaucer slumbered peacefully beneath him, safely out of the rain, undoubtedly grateful he wasn't being dragged around the city at a gallop. Hunkered under his umbrella, Wyeth watched the koi skimming below the raindrop-spotted surface of the tiny lagoon. He thought of Deeze the night before, holding him in his arms and whispering in his ear. Saying it was time they started looking for a place to live together. To be proper lovers. To commit themselves completely to each other.

While the rain peppered down, pattering on the umbrella above his head, Wyeth watched a sailboat skim across the bay toward the Coronado Bridge, its sails puffed up fat, listing in the breeze. As he stared, a rush of emotion coursed through him. His vision blurred with tears. He remembered the sincerity in Deeze's voice when he spoke the words Wyeth would never forget. He remembered how Deeze's arms had tightened across his back, holding him close, claiming ownership, declaring his love by nothing more than pressing his heart to Wyeth's chest and muttering gentle words in his ear.

But most of all, Wyeth remembered how he had once doubted Deeze. How he had once waited, day after day after day, for Deeze to come to his senses and realize he could do better than court this skinny, pale librarian with the inferiority complex and a fear of being hurt. Wyeth remembered the time he had spent waiting to be dumped. The weeks he had wasted waiting for his heart to be broken, as it had been broken so many times before.

He stared down at Chaucer—who was gazing up, squinting into the rain—and tried to cover the poor animal a little better with the umbrella. Chaucer thumped his tail in appreciation, peering up into Wyeth's face with limitless love, not even really minding that he was getting wet.

"We're a family now," Wyeth said, causing Chaucer to perk up his ears. "He loves us, and we're all going to live together from now on. Please don't kill his cat."

Chaucer looked so confused, Wyeth laughed.

"Come on, boy," he said, still smiling. "Lunch hour's over. Let's get you home and dried off."

TWO HOURS into his afternoon shift, Wyeth ducked behind a shelf of art books, ignoring the one or two random guys who were always there, perusing the volumes for pictures of naked women—painted, drawn, photographed, or sculpted, it made not a whit of difference to them. But who was he to judge? Wyeth thought back to his own adolescence, tirelessly digging through old copies of National Geographic for the occasional photograph of a naked Amazon tribesman or a Masai warrior clad in nothing but a leopard skin and a spear.

Oh, the heady days of his youth!

He chuckled inwardly, and gazed up to see Agnes Mulroney bearing down on him across the broad expanse of the library's reading area like a torpedo heading straight for its unsuspecting target.

Wyeth started to smile and wave, then he truly looked at the woman. She was slumped over her walker, desperately determined, pushing it wearily before her in fits and starts. The chemo was taking a toll. Just since he'd seen her yesterday, she looked older and more beaten down by age and illness. Peering closer, he realized it wasn't only her illness that was twisting her face into a semblance of pain. It was something more. It took him a moment to place what that something was.

It was fear. The woman was scared to death.

As she drew nearer, he heard the squeak and rattle of the walker over the patter of her house-slippered feet. She was in her primrosed housecoat again, but the snood was gone. She had obviously been to the beauty shop she went to every Monday morning. Her hair was finger waved across her head in crisp, sharp ridges, not unlike a corrugated tin roof. Sprayed to within an inch of its life, it didn't seem to have absorbed so much as a drop of rainwater. But then Wyeth glanced at the windows high above his head and saw the rain had stopped. Agnes halted twenty feet short of where Wyeth still stared at her from behind the shelf of art books. She stood there, eyes wide and frightened, her grizzled old hand clutching at the collar of her robe. Only when she swayed on her feet did Wyeth spring into action.

"Agnes!" he exclaimed, rushing toward her. When he was a few feet nearer, he grabbed a chair from one of the reading tables and dragged it to her, the chair legs making a horrendous screeching sound as they screamed across the tile. Everyone within fifty feet lifted their heads to see what was going on.

She ignored the chair, clamping her fingers around Wyeth's wrist, causing him to wince. He saw now that there were tears in her eyes.

"What is it?" he asked. "What's wrong? Do you need to go to the hospital?"

"A TV set!" she bellowed. "You must have one. Where is it?"

Confused, Wyeth pointed to a doorway leading to the employees' lounge. "Over there," he said. "Why?"

She released his hand and headed for the door he'd indicated, her squeaking, rattling walker once again annihilating the serene silence of the library's vast reading room. Again, heads jerked up, more than one face frowning at the racket. When an old homeless guy started to gripe about the noise Agnes was making, Wyeth shot him such a look of fury that the poor man clapped his mouth shut like a mailbox. Cowed, he stuck his head back in his book as if he had suddenly decided maybe the sound of Agnes's walker wasn't as annoying as he thought it was.

Wyeth trailed along behind Agnes, even more confused than he was before. "Agnes, stop! What is it? Tell me what's wrong!"

She ignored him but kept leading him toward the door he'd indicated.

By the time they were inside the employees' lounge, Wyeth was surprised to see several library employees sitting rapt, huddled around the TV in the corner.

Agnes saw them and pointed. "There!" she said, her eyes fierce. Turning back to Wyeth, her old face softened. She reached up and laid a withered hand to his cheek. "Try not to worry," she said softly. "They haven't given any details yet. We'll just have to wait."

"Wait? Wait for what?" Wyeth asked, tearing his eyes from Agnes's harried face to the television that was the focus of everyone's attention. Only then did he spot the Breaking News logo plastered across the top of the screen and the two words printed at the bottom in bold red font: Active Shooter.

Between the two banners, the news crew carried a live feed of a church and the scattered complex of buildings surrounding it. The coverage came from a news helicopter hovering high above the scene. A long line of police cars and a row of ambulances were lined up in front of the church. Crowds had already gathered, held back by dozens of police officers, arms raised, clearly urging calm.

Wyeth stared at the compound. The layout. The three prefab buildings erected to the left of the old church.

His breath caught. He recognized the place immediately. It was Deeze's school!

Only then did Wyeth hear the voice of the announcer. "The shooter has been taken into custody, the police tell us. The danger is over. It looks like there are casualties, though. We won't be sure of the number until the police release more details."

A second announcer, a woman this time, wormed her way into the broadcast. She sounded sad, her voice stricken. "The shooting took place around the preschool at the back of St. Luke's church. Here's a helicopter shot of the premises. Oh dear." She spoke to the reporter in the helicopter. "Are we seeing what I think we're seeing, Dave?"

"I'm afraid so, Kimberly," Dave said from high above the city streets, his voice blunted by the whapping of helicopter rotors and the rush of wind. "And there may be more casualties inside the building. We just don't know."

Wyeth stepped closer, peering intently at the screen. He saw it then. While the cameraman in the helicopter panned a wide shot over the grounds, the camera suddenly zoomed in, affording a shaky shot of a prone body lying in the rain-soaked grass of the school lawn. A few feet away lay another, face up, arms flung wide. Too far away to recognize their facial features, the bodies appeared to be those of adults, not children. Both lay perfectly still. They were clearly dead.

"Oh God, no," Wyeth muttered, his heart hammering.

Agnes dropped into a chair. Squeezing her eyes shut, she began to weep.

"Poor Deeze," she sobbed. "Poor Deeze." Dropping her hands into her lap, she gazed up into Wyeth's stricken face. A hint of her old determination surfaced in the lines of her face, but still it clearly hurt her to wrench the words from her throat. "Those bodies…. They weren't…." She sucked in a breath of air, clearly trying to calm herself. "I'm sure he's all right," she finally uttered, her old fingers pawing at Wyeth's shirt now, trying to get his attention. "He *has* to be, honey. He *has* to be."

A look of disbelieving fury burned through Wyeth. A tear slid along his cheek, and he angrily wiped it away. Clenching his fist, he jerked away from Agnes's touch as if he couldn't bear to be touched by *anyone*.

He balled his hand into a fist and struck himself in the chest. Once, twice, three times.

When the pain of the blows finally reached him, he yelled, "No!" at the top of his voice, startling everyone in the lounge.

Agnes, sobbing silently, reached out and stroked his arm.

CHAPTER THIRTEEN

FOR DEEZE, the day had been going just fine.

He sat at his desk, reading the day's newspaper and quietly turning the pages so the rattle of newsprint wouldn't wake anyone. His students, back from the cafeteria, were spending the rest of their lunch hour as they always did—heads down, napping. Some at their own little desks, others curled up side by side on the interlocking rubber tiles of the play area in the corner of the classroom.

Two boys in the back, one of which was little Jakey Armbrewster—naturally—were snorting back and forth in quiet laughter until Deeze chucked a wad of paper at them to get them to shut up. A few minutes later, both boys were sound asleep.

Deeze grinned. Sometimes the little scamps weren't as rebellious as they thought they were.

Relaxing and killing time, he stared through the classroom windows. The rain had stopped, but the day was still gloomy under a pewter sky. The foliage in the courtyard was glistening, washed clean by the unexpected downpour. Shimmering puddles, reflecting the glowering sky above, still stood on the sidewalk that wove its way around the church to the school grounds on the other side of the compound, where grades one through eight were taught.

Still staring mindlessly, fighting back sleep himself, Deeze suddenly spotted movement inside the copse of pepper trees that graced the grounds. A flash of color. A spark of light, reflecting off metal.

Curious, he rose from his desk and stepped silently toward the window, weaving his way in and out among his dozing students.

Pressing his forehead to the window pane and looking out, Deeze spotted the gun barrel almost immediately. It protruded from around a tree trunk, but from the opposite side of the tree where he couldn't see the person holding it. Before the reality of what he was seeing truly registered in his mind, the tip of the gun barrel exploded with sharp little pops, which didn't sound like much of anything, really, other than tiny claps of indeterminate noise, rather like the tip of a blind man's cane rapping at the edge of a curb. The windows at either side of Deeze exploded inward with a horrendous crash, sending sprays of glass shards shooting through the air, sprinkling the heads of the kids closest to him.

Every child in the classroom jumped. Some giggled, confused and half-asleep, while others grew big, frightened eyes, their mouths forming Os of burgeoning horror. All of them looked to Deeze for guidance. Innocent, helpless, terrified.

Deeze dove for the nearest kids and scraped them from their seats, dragging them to the floor.

"Everybody down!" he bellowed. "Get down on the floor!"

A girl, one of the ones he had raked from her desk, wailed in pain when a sliver of glass from the shattered window pierced her knee. Deeze desperately shushed her, pulling her into his arms.

Over her head, Deeze cried again, "Get down, everybody!" and most of the students obeyed. The ones still at their desks dropped to the floor and covered their heads with their hands. The ones napping on the floor in the play area crawled off in one direction or another, disoriented and scared to death. Many were crying now. Tiny mewlings of terror filled the room.

Deeze released the girl, and with broken bits of glass digging at his palms, he crawled as quickly as he could to the far end of the room, where the windows ended at the door. Once there, he reached up and switched off the light so it would be harder for the shooter to see into the classroom. That done, he risked reaching up one more time and flicking the lock on the door, securing them inside.

There was no other escape route from the room. Anyone trying to get out—or in—was restricted to the one door and the bank of windows on the left side of the classroom. By the same token, the left side of the classroom was also the shooter's only avenue of attack.

Deeze scrambled about on hands and knees, grabbing kids left and right and dragging them toward the corner of the room farthest from the windows, the corner where his massive oak desk stood. There, he strained to slide the heavy desk, angling it so it afforded as much protection to his students as possible. He wasn't sure if it would stop bullets, but maybe it would shield the children enough to keep them safe until the police arrived. Surely the cops were on the way. *Someone* must have reported the shooting.

Horrible thoughts tore through Deeze's mind. Horrific memories. Unforgettable names and dates. Body counts. Endless lists of injured students. Columbine, 1999, Sandy Hook, 2012, Roseberg, 2015.

This can't be happening. It can't.

Two more windows exploded inward. One of the children screamed. The shooter apparently shifted targets, aiming at the other classrooms now. Deeze heard windows shattering farther away in the complex.

Deeze threw himself over the pile of kids, mumbling apologies for hurting them, but hissing for them to be quiet at the same time. One child latched on to the collar of his shirt with his tiny hand, and gazing down, Deeze realized it was Jake. His eyes were as big as silver dollars.

"Hush now," Deeze whispered. "It'll be all right."

Jake nodded, trying to look brave.

At that moment several things happened at once.

They heard another *pop* of gunfire and a scream outside. A man's scream. Then another of his own classroom windows exploded inward, and a child roared in fright. Deeze watched a bullet hole blossom in the wall in front of him, not six inches from a child's head. At the same moment a splatter of blood struck Jake's face, startling both man and boy. Deeze had no idea where the blood came from. Jake whimpered as Deeze dragged him against his chest, still trying to protect the boy, along with all his other students. Only then did he feel a sharp pain and look down to see a furrow of bloodied skin where a bullet had grazed his wrist.

Was it his own blood that had splattered the boy?

He pushed the pain away, concentrating on the kids. Keeping them safe was all that mattered.

Just as he was about to plead to God for a little help, a blaze of white hot agony sliced across his leg. The moment the pain tore into him, an 8 x 10 glossy of Wyeth's beautiful face flashed before his eyes, as clear as day.

No, Deeze bellowed inside his head at the unfairness of it all. *Not now. Not fucking now.*

Instantly consumed with fury, he raised his head and squinted above the desk at the shattered windows in front of him. Pleading with the kids to stay down, to stay quiet, Deeze crawled and crabwalked below the lip of the windows toward the classroom door. Too mad to be slowed by the pain in his thigh and wrist, he reached up and quietly unlocked the door. Pulling it open just enough to peer through the crack, he scanned the courtyard outside.

At that moment, the sky opened up and it started raining again. Deeze squinted into the downpour. Then he saw it. Out among the trees, the gun was raised again. More gunshots smacked the side of the building. Glass shards tinkled as another window smashed in the distance. Another child cried out, but it wasn't one of his students. It was one of the younger students farther away. In the nursery, maybe. My God, the man was shooting at *babies*!

Screaming with rage, with nothing inside his head but his own murderous fury, Deeze hurled himself through the classroom door and into the rain. Head down, he ran straight for the shooter. Along the way he spotted Father Mike, lying motionless on the grass, his eyes wide open, staring sightlessly at the brooding sky, unblinking as the rain peppered his face. Not ten feet away lay another man, this one facedown so that Deeze couldn't see who it was. Without pausing, he stumbled over them both, skidding in the wet grass. He quickly regained his footing and made a beeline for the gunman.

Deeze's eyes opened wide in horror as the barrel of the gun pivoted directly toward him. Too furious to stop or cower, he dove straight for it, wrenching the gun from the shooter's hands before another shot could be fired. Deeze and the shooter tumbled to the ground in a heap. Madder than he had ever been in his life—so mad he was weeping tears of fury—Deeze pummeled the shooter's face with his bloodied fists.

He only stopped when the gunman whimpered beneath him. It was a childlike whimper, a sound he'd least expected to hear. Forcing himself to jerk away, he stumbled back, putting some space between him and the shooter. When he did, he saw a boy of maybe thirteen curled up at his feet, crying into the ground.

Confused but still furious, Deeze grabbed the gun lying in the grass and hurled it as far as he could into the bushes.

In the distance, he heard the wail of sirens. A chorus of them split the air.

In the classroom behind him, his students still cried softly. He could hear them over the rain. As he stood there getting soaked, still trying to quell his own fury, a final pane of glass dislodged from its mooring and shattered on the sidewalk, making him jump. Deeze remembered the blood he had seen on little Jakey's face. He reeled in horror, fear stuttering through him like another spray of bullets. Racing back in the direction from which he'd come, he flung himself through the classroom door to where his terrified students still lay huddled in the corner behind his massive desk, right where he had left them. A bout of dizziness made him falter as relief flooded through him. He stumbled to a halt when his legs wouldn't move anymore.

Gazing down at himself, he saw a rivulet of blood seeping from the gunshot wound to his wrist. His pant leg was sodden with blood. He was wracked with pain from one end of his body to the other. Through sheer willpower, he took two more steps toward his kids before his strength gave out completely.

Like a spectator with a front row seat, Deeze watched the ground rush up toward him. His vision closed in upon itself like a camera shutter winking closed.

At least the shooting has stopped. And it's raining again. That's nice.

By the time he hit the ground, his mind had closed down completely.

WYETH AND Agnes Mulroney and a cluster of other library patrons and staff stood glued to the TV in the corner of the employees' lounge while the news crews on the screen painstakingly extrapolated all the facts—and some of the fiction—from the story unfolding before them. Wyeth knew there were casualties, but he didn't know how many or who those casualties were. He sat on an old Naugahyde couch next to Agnes, twisting his tie into a sweaty, wrinkled mess, listening to one mindless newscaster after another jabber on and on but never say one single thing that gave him hope that Deeze might be all right. He had tried calling Deeze's cell phone a dozen times, but his messages were sent to voicemail. Deeze turned his phone off when he worked.

At least the shooting had ended. He could see by the camera shots from the news helicopter that the area around the school was cordoned off with yellow crime scene tape now. A veritable wall of squad cars still filled the streets surrounding the church, but most of the ambulances had left. He knew it would be pointless to go there. He would just be in the way. All he could do was sit here and watch these stupid news announcers, wringing his hands and wondering what the hell was going on.

It dawned on him that perhaps he should go back to his apartment. He could escort Agnes home as well. She was clearly distraught. Wyeth studied her with new concern as she sat there beside him staring mindlessly at the TV, all the while shredding a tissue into confetti and letting it drift down around her feet like snowflakes. This was perhaps the first time he had ever seen the woman worried about anyone other than herself. And it wasn't only Deeze she was worried for—it was Wyeth too. He could see it in the way she reached out, petting him, continually cooing a sort of comforting tuneless melody as she sat there at his side, telling him over and over again that everything would be all right, warning him not to give up hope, not to give in to fear.

Finally, her kindness tore a hole in Wyeth's terror.

"Let me take you home," he said softly. "You look worn out. As soon as I get you safely back to your apartment, I'll go to the school. I have to find out what's going on. Where Deeze is." His voice almost faltered. "What's happened to him."

To his surprise, she didn't argue. He took her hand, positioned her squeaky old walker in front of her, and once she was securely on her feet, steered her through the library toward the street.

Agnes moved so slowly that the walk toward their apartment building seemed endless. Oddly, Wyeth found comfort in the old woman's presence. There were words on the tip of his tongue that he needed to speak. Words he needed to utter into existence, if for no other reason than to hear them on the air. At least with Agnes there, he had someone to say them to.

"I don't know what I'll do without him if—" But that was as far as he got. He couldn't bear to finish the sentence, or even to finish the thought. He bit down on his lip and fell silent.

The rainstorm had lessened. It was merely sprinkling now. Apparently the storm was almost over. Wyeth didn't care one way or the other and neither, it appeared, did Agnes. In fact, they hardly noticed the rain at all.

"You won't lose him," Agnes said sharply. "God won't let that happen."

There was such conviction in her old eyes, Wyeth was strangely reassured. "No," he said. "He won't." Then a more horrible thought struck him, searing through his head like a bolt of lightning. "My God, his kids! His students. I hope they're all right. It would kill Deeze if anything happened to them."

He was startled to see a tear slide down Agnes's wrinkled cheek. "Maybe it's time I stop fighting this damnable cancer and just let myself go." She gazed along the sodden street as if she had never seen it before, as if she had no idea where she was. "The world has grown cruel since I was a girl. It's not the way it used to be. I'm not sure I want to live in it anymore. All these shootings. All this hatred."

Even in the midst of his own heartache, Wyeth unearthed concern for the woman beside him.

"If Deeze were here, he'd tease that thinking out of you. He'd tell you to fight and be strong just like you've always done."

Agnes smiled even as her gaze hardened and her back straightened. A smidgeon of the old fire returned to her eyes. "Yes," she said through pale, thin lips, impatiently wiping the tears away with a handkerchief she'd plucked from her sleeve. "He'd tear me a new one, he would."

Wyeth grinned through his own sadness. "You're right. He would."

Agnes turned to him. Once again, past her tortured smile, Wyeth could see the weariness in her eyes. The illness. She was clearly worn out by her constant battle with the cancer devouring her from the inside. And now this new worry over Deeze. She suddenly appeared too frail to fight so many battles at once. There were too many enemies, too many terrors, closing in from all sides. Tears once again welled up in her eyes. She stumbled and almost fell.

"Agnes, take my arm," Wyeth whispered. "Lean on me. Let's get you home."

She did as he asked, ceding control of the walker, which he folded up and tucked under his arm. Wrapping his free arm about her waist, he was startled to feel how thin she was. She weighed almost nothing. She was also clearly at the end of her strength. Muttering encouraging words, he ushered her along the street, letting her cling to him, hoping to get her home before she collapsed.

Just shy of the front door to their apartment building, another body snugged up close and took Agnes by the other arm. It was Laurie, Deeze's cousin. The one who ran the tanning shop.

"I was at the library looking for you. They told me you'd gone home," Laurie said to Wyeth while together they steered Agnes through the door and led her to the elevator at the back of the lobby.

Perhaps too weary for once in her life to butt her way into someone else's conversation, Agnes stood silently against the elevator wall, clutching her heart, as the car rose quickly through the bowels of the building. Still, her eyes never left off shifting between Wyeth and Laurie at either side of her. A stray thought flashed through Wyeth's mind that despite how sick and worried she was, Agnes was probably curious about Laurie. He would make a point to tell her more about Deeze's cousin later.

"What have you heard?" Wyeth asked, desperately peering into Laurie's eyes, looking for the truth. "Tell me, Laurie. Please. Is Deeze okay? Those bodies on the lawn...."

Laurie's spikey hairstyle had been laid flat by the rain. It made her look diminished somehow. Not as dauntless as she usually appeared. But there was the same tenacious snap of fortitude in her eyes that had been there the one and only other time Wyeth had met her—on the day of his first and last spray tan at the Tan Banana.

"He's hurt, but no one would tell me how badly. They've taken him to the emergency room, along with several other people. I was coming to get you and take you there with me when I saw you guys on the street." Laurie reached around the old woman and patted Wyeth's arm. "Don't worry. Deeze will be all right. He's strong. He'll survive this."

The elevator dinged, and the doors opened. Agnes heaved herself off the wall and plucked her walker from under Wyeth's arm. "You two go," she said. "Go to the hospital. Deeze will want you there." She stepped closer to Wyeth and laid her old head against his chest, then just as quickly stepped away. "Now go. Get out of here. The man you love needs you. Don't make him wonder why you haven't come."

"No," Wyeth said, touched by the gentle sincerity in the woman's eyes and the simple truth of her words. "I won't."

Without speaking again, she took a firm grip on her rattling walker and took off at a snail's pace down the hall.

Wyeth and Laurie watched her go.

"She's dying, isn't she?" Laurie asked quietly.

"Yes," Wyeth answered, and taking Laurie's hand, he pulled her back into the elevator. With a jolt and the ding of the doors closing in front of them, they headed down.

THEY WOULDN'T let them see Deeze. Not yet.

Deeze lay out of sight on a gurney in a treatment room in Mercy's ER. It was the same place he had brought Agnes only the day before. While Laurie and Wyeth waited, they sat saddened and stunned, holding hands, staring at the television hanging high on the waiting room wall. Local news gave a steady stream of updates about the shooting at St. Luke's. It didn't take long before they were reasonably well informed about everything that had happened.

All the newscasters seemed to agree on one thing. It could have been a lot worse than it actually was. Two men, a priest and a teacher, had lost their lives. Still, the body count could have been much higher. And most importantly of all, not one child was harmed.

Of course, a lot about the incident was still unknown. The biggest question being the shooter's motive and identity. For with all the information flying around about the event, so far the police had released nothing about the person who started it all.

Still, both Wyeth and Laurie had to smile when one of the announcers called Mr. Long, the kindergarten teacher who singlehandedly stopped the shooting by disarming the gunman, a hero. Wyeth did even more than smile. He swelled with pride.

He turned to Laurie and quietly asked, "Where's his family? Deeze never talks about them, but they should be here, don't you think?"

Wyeth watched Laurie fiddle with a button on her overalls, clearly uncomfortable with the question. Dropping the button, she slouched back in the chair and stared once more at the TV in front of them. It was airing a Tylenol commercial now, like a headache pill would help them get through this horrible fucking day.

"Deeze's folks died in a car crash a few years ago. Deeze was grown when it happened. He had no siblings, just a couple of distant cousins like me. He's made it on his own ever since."

"He never told me."

"He doesn't like to talk about it. Deeze can be private with the things he feels strongly about. It runs in our family. I'm not a blabbermouth either."

Wyeth considered snickering at that but thought better of it. "But what about aunts and uncles? Where are *your* parents, Laurie? Do they live out of town? Why aren't they here?"

"My parents are probably sitting in church somewhere, blaming Deeze's lifestyle for what happened to him. Just like they blame my lifestyle for everything bad that happens to me."

"Oh," Deeze said, understanding completely. After all, there was a pretty potent strain of homophobia in his own family back in Indiana. Like Deeze, he too had turned his back and walked away from the hatred.

"Poor Deeze," he mumbled to himself.

Laurie stared down at her hands. "It's hard being different. Don't let anybody tell you otherwise."

Wyeth couldn't have argued with that statement even if he wanted to. He had lived it long enough to know she was right.

A moment later, a nurse beckoned them toward the back.

At the treatment room door, a doctor intervened and informed them the police had finished questioning Deeze for now. While Deeze's injuries were superficial, the doctor still requested only one person see him at a time. Laurie immediately pushed Wyeth toward the swinging doors, telling him to go, to hurry, she'd wait for him in the waiting room.

Wary, Wyeth peeked around the treatment room door. Deeze lay on a gurney. He was still dressed in his blood-spattered trousers, but his shirt and shoes and socks were gone. His hair was wild and his face gaunt. He looked like he had aged two decades since Wyeth saw him that morning.

"Father Mike is dead," Deeze said, spotting Wyeth at the door. They were the first words out of his mouth.

Wyeth stepped to the edge of the gurney. Deeze's pant leg was slit to the thigh where the doctors had bandaged the wound from a shard of window glass that had pierced Deeze's leg, cutting deep but missing any major arteries. His wrist, where a bullet had grazed his skin, was neatly wrapped in gauze as well. His hands and knees were stained with yellow disinfectant applied to the countless cuts and abrasions he'd inflicted upon himself by crawling back and forth over the broken window glass on the classroom floor. Strangely, every injury he received was little more than a flesh wound. Deeze had been lucky. Even he knew it.

Wyeth had heard about Father Mike's death on the news while he and Laurie were waiting. He remembered the day Deeze introduced the priest to him.

"I'm sorry," he said now, resting a consoling hand on one of the few uninjured spots he could find, Deeze's bare shoulder.

Even with his raw and battered hands, Deeze rolled toward Wyeth and clutched his arm, his eyes pleading. "The kids," he said. "Are they all right? The police said they are, but I don't know whether to believe them or not, and no one will talk to me. Tell me, Wy. Were the kids all okay? Did they—survive?"

Wyeth leaned down and laid a gentle hand to Deeze's cheek. "Your students are all safe, Deeze. They are saying on the news that you saved them by hustling them into a corner and using your desk and your body to shield them from the bullets."

"Jakey," Deeze said, his eyes filling with tears. His hands were shaking as he gripped Wyeth's wrist. "There was blood on him, Wy. It splattered across his face. I saw it."

Wyeth smiled and stooped to brush a kiss over Deeze's forehead. "Then it must not have been his blood, Deeze. Jakey's fine. They're all fine. I saw it on the news. None of the kids was hurt. A few scratches from the glass is all. Nothing serious." He gazed at the numerous injuries on Deeze's body. "Maybe the blood was yours."

Deeze seemed to accept Wyeth's words as truth. The terror on his face lessened. He relaxed on the gurney, but his bandaged hand never left Wyeth's wrist. His fingers still held on tight. His eyes took on a faraway cast, as if he were suddenly somewhere else, as if he were reliving the hours behind him.

"It was a boy," he said. "The one I took the gun from. A student. I've seen him before. An eighth grader, I think. Some poor Mexican kid. I-I punched him. I beat the shit out of him, Wy. Is-is he still alive? Did they arrest him?"

Deeze looked as if his heart were breaking. The tears in his eyes spilled onto his cheeks. He clutched tighter at Wyeth's arm, making a blush of red appear on the gauze surrounding his wrist where the bullet had furrowed the skin. The way he was grabbing at Wyeth must have reopened the wound.

Wyeth took Deeze's hand in both of his and forced it down onto Deeze's chest, muttering soft words, urging Deeze to calm down, wishing someone would give Deeze a sedative, administer something to help him relax.

"They're all fine, Deeze. The boy with the gun too. You didn't hurt him. Lie still, okay? We're going to take you home soon, Laurie and me. But if you get yourself all worked up, they won't let you go. It's over, baby. Okay? You saved a lot of lives today, Deeze. They're calling you a hero on the TV."

"I wasn't a hero. I was terrified."

"Maybe that's what made you a hero. You did what you had to do, terrified or not. Now rest. Sleep if you can. All right? I'll be right outside.

Me and Laurie. We'll take you home as soon as they let us. So shush for now. Try not to think about anything. Lie still."

A tiny pout twisted Deeze's mouth. "You're still shushing me. Even after everything I've been through." Then he offered a tremulous smile.

Wyeth smiled in return and planted another kiss on Deeze's forehead. He started to pull away.

"No," Deeze said. "Wait with me here. Don't leave."

"All right," Wyeth said. "I'll stay until they throw me out."

"Good," Deeze said.

STILL CLINGING to Wyeth's hand, Deeze had begun to close his eyes in exhaustion when he heard a sound behind him. His eyes popped wide open again when he saw Laurie standing in the treatment room doorway, peeking in.

She looked embarrassed, like maybe she'd had just one job to do and had somehow managed to muddle that. "Sorry, cuz, but I'm going to let this kid in," she said. "Otherwise he threatened to kick me in the leg."

Squeezing past her, little Jake came running into the room. His tiny face was twisted in nervous fury. He gazed around, then spotted Deeze on the gurney. Taking off like a shot, he dove onto the gurney right under Wyeth's nose and burrowed into Deeze's arms.

"Ouch," Deeze grunted, then he laughed and hugged the boy back. A nurse hurried over to pull the boy off, but Deeze waved her away. "Let him be," he said softly. "The kid's had a rough day."

The nurse stepped back, although she was clearly unhappy about it.

"Are you okay, Mr. Long?" Jake asked, not seeming to care one little bit about all the people staring at him.

Deeze grinned at the boy in his arms. "I'm fine, Jakey. Just fine. Are you okay too?"

Jake nodded. "Uh-huh. But I was scared."

Deeze sighed. Sadly. "Me too."

Deeze eased the boy to arm's length to make sure he was really unharmed. What he saw satisfied him, and he relaxed.

At the sound of more footsteps behind them, Deeze turned to find Jake's parents, the people he'd seen on the beach that day so long ago when he and Wyeth were first beginning to know each other. Jake's mom and dad both looked shell-shocked. The mother stepped forward with the obvious intention of plucking Jake out of Deeze's arms, clearly afraid the boy would hurt him, but Deeze waved her away as he had the nurse.

"It's okay," he said quietly. "He's not hurting me."

The boy's father still clutched a magazine from the waiting room. He wrung it, forgotten in his hands. He must have been wringing it a long time. The cover was wrinkled and spongy with sweat.

He cleared his throat, clearly uncomfortable but determined to say what he'd come here to say. "We…. We wanted to thank you, Mr. Long. Jakey told us what you did."

At that, Jake's mother stepped forward shyly, staring down at her son wrapped so lovingly in the arms of the man who had saved his life.

"Thank you for our son, Mr. Long. We'll never forget what you did today." A lump formed in Deeze's throat. Before he could speak, Jake lifted his head from his chest and peered at him with two of the bluest eyes Deeze had ever seen in his life. While he watched the boy, Jake turned to study Wyeth, who was standing at the edge of the gurney with tears of pride and joy and misery and a thousand other emotions streaming down his cheeks.

"You got Band-Aids for him?" Jake asked, his face serious.

Wyeth nodded. "As many as he'll ever need," he answered softly.

Reassured, the boy burrowed back into Deeze's arms and closed his eyes.

Jake's father blew his nose into a hanky with the sound of a goose honking his way south for the winter, causing Jake to dig his face into Deeze's armpit and giggle.

Even Deeze grinned at the sound of the boy's innocent laughter.

"And life goes on," he whispered, more to himself than anyone else. Reaching out, he once again grasped Wyeth's hand.

WYETH STARED around him while a spark of the old terror lit his eyes. A crushing weight of dread settled over him. Or was it euphoria? He wasn't sure.

This cubicle they were all in—the whole emergency room, in fact— was awash in misery, in the permeating reek of medicine and desperation. Cries could be heard in different areas of the ER. Whimpers of pain. The soothing murmur of doctors' voices. But there was death here too. He couldn't see it, but he knew it was here somewhere, lurking around the next corner, perhaps. Waiting to cull the herd. Waiting to swoop in when it saw an opening.

But not today. Not with my Deeze, Wyeth thought, his eyes narrowing with hope, with determined certainty.

A rush of gratitude so intense it was almost painful clenched Wyeth's insides as he stared down at the man and the boy on the gurney.

He had come so close—*so close*—to losing Deeze! And this boy too. They both could have lost their lives so easily today. And so many others as well. A tremor shuddered through him. He swayed on his feet. The next thing he knew, Laurie was there, wrapping him in her strong, capable arms.

He dropped his head to her shoulder and tried to get a grip on his emotions.

In the end, it was the feel of Deeze's hand, still resting snugly in his, that brought Wyeth back, that anchored him.

He turned at the sound of weeping and saw Jake's mother sobbing into her husband's chest.

Glancing down, Wyeth met Jakey's eyes staring up at him. The boy wore the only smile in the room. It was a gentle smile. Gentle and trusting.

Wyeth thought it appropriate that only the child would winnow the group's emotions down to its most basic element. Gratitude. Gratitude that his friend and teacher had done a wonderful thing today. He had saved Jake's life. Jake's and countless others'.

Still smiling, the boy dropped his head back to Deeze's shoulder.

Over the top of Jake's head, Deeze shot Wyeth a wink. Then the weariness kicked in and his eyelids fluttered. Gradually, his body stilled. He dozed.

On tiptoe, all but Wyeth left the room. Even little Jake allowed himself to be lifted away from Deeze's embrace, nestling comfortably in the crook of his father's arm.

While Deeze's breathing quieted, Wyeth sat in a straight-backed chair at Deeze's side, never so much in love as he was at that moment. Even the surrounding bustle of a big city emergency room couldn't draw his attention from Deeze's peacefully sleeping face.

But a tap on his shoulder finally did.

He looked up to see Laurie standing over him. She tilted her head toward the treatment room door. Not wanting to disturb Deeze, she whispered, "You should come and see this."

Reluctantly, Wyeth eased his hand from Deeze's grip and, without waking him, followed Laurie toward the door.

She urged him forward. "Look."

Wyeth pushed the swinging door aside and peered out into the waiting room. As before, the seats close at hand were taken with people waiting, people sick, people crying quietly, looking worried, looking exhausted. But in the back of the large room, back toward the hallway leading into the emergency room, stood a wall of people that hadn't been there before. Many of them were children, each and every one standing patiently with their small hands either folded in front of them or clutching a parent's hand. Others, like Jake, were safely in their fathers' or mothers' arms, their weary heads resting on a familiar shoulder. Many of the heads lifted when Wyeth peeked through the door.

"His students," Laurie whispered in his ear. "They're waiting to see if Deeze is okay."

The door squeaked behind them, and Deeze peeked through. Clutching the doorframe for support, he stepped quietly into the room, squeezing himself between Wyeth and Laurie, who both reached out to steady him.

The second he appeared, a hush fell through the crowd of waiting students and parents. Here and there a smile appeared. Then it began. Softly at first, then not so softly. Applause. Applause for the man who had saved their children's lives.

Deeze lowered his head, blushing. Reaching out, he groped for Wyeth's hand. Raising his other hand in silent thank-you to the parents and children before him, he shyly turned away.

CHAPTER FOURTEEN

THE NIGHTMARES began on the second night after the shooting.

Deeze tore himself awake, flailing in the darkness at some invisible threat. His hand struck flesh other than his own, and Wyeth gasped in surprise, wrenched from sleep by the blow.

His mind logy from the sleeping pill he had taken earlier, Deeze stammered an apology, then threw himself furiously out of bed.

Staring down at the mess of covers, slashed with a streak of red from the stoplight down on the street corner reflecting off the dresser mirror, he thought for one horrifying moment it was blood he was seeing. Then he recognized Wyeth's pale body rising from the sheets, reaching out for him in the shadows.

Still confused and only half-awake, Deeze pulled back out of reach. "Don't touch me," he hissed, staring at Wyeth's hand as if he had never seen anything more terrifying in his life.

But Wyeth would not be stopped. He climbed from the bed and wrapped his arms around Deeze's naked back, pulling him close, making shushing noises as if soothing a child.

"It was a nightmare, Deeze. You're all right. Calm down now. Shush, baby. Shush."

Slowly Deeze's muscles unknotted. He began to relax in Wyeth's arms. They stood in the flush from the stoplight. In the blink of an eye, they were brushed with green instead as the light changed to Go. They heard the rumble of traffic as cars began to move, obeying the traffic light, sheep heading off in one direction or another.

Deeze buried his face in Wyeth's neck. He was still trembling from the nightmare as he stared about the room, getting his bearings.

"I thought I was back at the school," he murmured, his mouth on Wyeth's sleep-warm skin. "The shooting. It was starting up all over again. I just sat there at my desk, frozen in fear, while the children were falling around me. There was blood everywhere. Blood and tiny, still bodies. No one cried. No one moved. I just sat there, Wy! I sat there and did *nothing*!"

He shuddered. Letting out a feeble sob, he tucked his head under Wyeth's chin as if hiding from the world.

A hot tear spilled onto Wyeth's throat. He clutched Deeze more tightly to him, gently shushing him, calming his fears. "That's not how it happened, baby. You saved them. You saved them all. It's over now. You don't need to think about it anymore."

"But Father Mike. And the other teacher. They were dead in the grass. I saw them."

Wyeth stroked Deeze's back as they stood there in each other's arms, their naked bodies pressed together. Deeze still trembled, but he was less tense now. Less manic. Wyeth could sense Deeze's nightmare receding. He continued to hold on tight. Soothing Deeze. Muttering gentle words in his ear. Humming softly. Slowly, Deeze relaxed in his arms. Deeze's fingers began a gentle stroking along the wales of Wyeth's spine as if his senses were coming awake, rememorizing familiar haunts, beginning to reconnect to the man who loved him, returning the comfort being offered him, paying it back as best he could.

The stoplight outside changed twice more before Deeze murmured into the darkness. "I'm better now. Thank you, Wy. I-I don't know what happened."

Wyeth stroked Deeze's curly hair. It was damp with sweat. "It was just a nightmare. After all you went through, I'm not surprised. Come on now, let's go back to bed. All right? You think you can sleep?"

"Will you hold me?"

The question was so innocent and so unexpected, Wyeth's pulse quickened to hear it. "My favorite pastime," he whispered, pressing his lips to Deeze's temple, clutching his hand, tugging him gently toward the bed.

THEY COLLAPSED side by side onto the rumpled mound of blankets and sheets, not even attempting to straighten out the mess. Deeze rolled into Wyeth's waiting arms and pressed his face to Wyeth's chest. Wyeth cupped the back of his neck, holding him there, his lips in Deeze's hair.

Barely audible, Wyeth's gentle words filled the silent shadows around the two men. While Wyeth spoke, Deeze listened intently, inhaling Wyeth's familiar scent. Loving the feel of the strong, capable hands stroking his back. Feeling the love Wyeth offered him, knowing it was real, knowing it was from the heart. Absorbing Wyeth's strength.

"That day doesn't have to scare you anymore, Deeze. You survived it. It's over. And thanks to you, your students survived it too. It was a sad thing to have happened, but the world sees sad things all the time. What's important is how we comport ourselves while they're taking place. You did everything you could have done. You saved a lot of young lives, Deeze. There is nothing for you to be afraid of anymore. And certainly nothing to feel guilty about. There'll probably be more nightmares. Why wouldn't there be? Just remember who you are and what you did. And remember me too, please. I'm the man who loves you. Don't ever forget that. All right?"

Deeze pressed a kiss to the sharp nubbin of Wyeth's Adam's apple. Rather than speak, he merely edged closer. Scooting farther down in the bed, he laid his cheek to Wyeth's lean stomach, enjoying the feel of the hair there tickling his skin, the gentle rise and fall of Wyeth's breath. The heat of the man beneath him. The soft thudding of Wyeth's heart blending with the silent pulsing of his own.

He stared through the bedroom window at the stars outside. They were back in the sky now that the storm was over and the clouds had retreated. Life was as it should be again. Or most of it.

Deeze lifted his head and peered over the side of the bed. There on the windowsill next to the bed lay Napoleon. With his tail lashing back and forth in agitation, the cat was staring down at Chaucer curled up on the floor beneath him, innocently snoring away like a steam engine. Clearly plotting mayhem, Napoleon had a mean glint in his eye and a low growl stuttering in his throat. Deeze wasn't sure, but he thought he could see the animal flexing his claws like switchblades. Oblivious to his peril, Chaucer snored on, his toenails scraping the hardwood floor, chasing dream bunnies in his sleep.

Napoleon hissed from his perch.

"Jesus, cat, give it a rest," Deeze muttered.

Turning back to a happier place, he laid his head on Wyeth's stomach again. Perhaps it was his warm breath blowing across the tender skin of Wyeth's belly that began it. He wasn't sure. But Deeze smiled to himself as he watched Wyeth's cock in the moonlight, slowly filling with blood and lengthening before his eyes. His own cock hardened in response as he pressed it to Wyeth's shin.

When Wyeth's blossoming erection gave a final tiny jerk and came to rest against Deeze's lips, Deeze opened his mouth and took it in. And as easily as that, the nightmare was forgotten, Deeze's fears laid to rest. At least for now.

"Baby," Wyeth muttered, his body already trembling. "It's been so long."

Later, when Wyeth arched his back and Deeze drank from him, Deeze squeezed his eyes tight, relishing the heat and taste and *life* of the man beneath him.

Yet even at that moment—that incredible moment—Deeze could feel the guilt waiting to claim him. It lurked there, just beneath the passion, on the other side of love.

Survivor's guilt they called it. Deeze had never known it before, had never really understood it. But now that he did, he wondered if he would ever be free of it.

DEEZE AND Wyeth sat by the lagoon in Seaport Village. Their favorite spot. In the distance, they heard the calliope music from the carousel where the two had twirled their way into romance on that first date so many months ago. A Navy destroyer thrummed majestically along in front of them, heading out across the bay to the open ocean, stirring up the froth in its wake like a bride trailing a train of white satin across the water. A border of sailors in their dress whites, standing at parade rest, each and every one of them looking tall and proud and handsome, flanked the sides of the ship as it pulled away from port.

It was only a few days after the shooting, and the Catholic school was still closed since it wasn't just a school anymore. It was a crime scene. Deeze had been interviewed countless times by the SDPD. He and everyone else in the city now knew the name of the young boy who started it all. Ramon Diaz. He was thirteen years old. The motive he gave for the shootings was that he hated Mondays.

He hated Mondays.

Later they would learn the boy was abused at home. When that knowledge became available, the whys of his murderous actions had a cause the pundits could point to. At least his motives were a little less ethereal now. What he did seemed less of a whim. In a dystopian sort of way, the boy's actions even made sense. His striking out. His asserting power over a world that let him suffer so at the hands of an abusive parent. Not that it mattered much to the victims why the boy chose to steal his father's rifle and start shooting at innocent people, at *babies* for Christ's sake. The deed was done and could never be undone. Everyone, including the boy, would have to live with the consequences.

Wyeth had decided to take a few days from work to help Deeze through the trauma of everything that had happened.

"How long are you taking off?" Deeze asked, worried.

Wyeth offered a gentle smile. "As long as I need to."

"Don't," Deeze pleaded. "You might lose your job."

Wyeth shrugged. "Some things are more important than jobs."

And that was that.

Deeze, with Wyeth at his side, attended two funerals that week. One for Mr. Biles, the transitional kindergarten teacher who had worked in the classroom next to Deeze and who died on the grass that day, and one for Father Mike, the priest who had helped Deeze acquire a teaching position at the school. Deeze had wept for both men, but only later. After the funerals were over. After he was home. For some reason, Deeze had developed an unreasonable aversion to showing emotion in public. He suspected his survivor's guilt had something to do with it, but he was in no mood to try to analyze himself. His feelings were still too raw to be picked over. He was still too emotional about it all. Too hurt. Too angry. Too *damaged*.

When the sorrow began to swoop in on him at odd times, Deeze turned to Wyeth to shield him from the pain. Gradually, the guilt diminished, even the nightmares lessened, but the horrific memories remained. Deeze suspected they would always be there, waiting to pounce from the shadows when they were least expected.

Yet in the midst of all this misery, happiness occasionally found a way to peek through too. And sometimes it did more than peek. It barreled right in like a Mack truck.

Case in point.

At Agnes's insistence, because she had heard it was going cheap, Wyeth and Deeze rented a two-bedroom apartment in Wyeth's building only four doors down from his old apartment. They began moving into their new digs three weeks after the shooting. With the school grounds released by the police, Deeze's kindergarten class was in session again, so with both men back to work, the move was scheduled for the weekend.

When word got out that Deeze was moving, six strong men, each and every one of them a total stranger, showed up outside the door of his apartment to help. They were the fathers of six of his students. When they told him this and Deeze tried to send them away, thanking them heartily but explaining he really didn't need their assistance, they wouldn't leave. Finally, since he couldn't very well toss them down the stairs, Deeze accepted their help.

He and Wyeth and all their belongings were moved into the new apartment in less than two hours.

They awoke the next morning in their new home, wrapped as always in each other's arms. After a brief respite of sunshine, the sky turned overcast again. Autumn was here. Wyeth tugged the covers up to their necks as they cuddled in the warm bed, both men hard, both men as much in love as they had ever been.

Apparently a truce had finally been reached between the other two members of the household. Napoleon purred at their feet while Chaucer pranced around in the other room, rattling his leash against the front door, pleading to be taken out. The apartment was a mass of unpacked boxes and jumbled stacks of furniture.

Wyeth had never been so happy in his life.

"I didn't have any nightmares last night," Deeze murmured around a yawn while he dragged Wyeth's warm, luscious body into his arms.

"That's good," Wyeth muttered, burrowing his face against Deeze's heavenly fuzzy chest.

A broad hand rested on Wyeth's ass. A gentle finger dipped languidly into the cleft there, making Wyeth purr.

"You're not off the hook, you know," Deeze said, nestling his nose into Wyeth's hair while his finger did all the work. "I still expect you to speak in front of my class."

Wyeth groaned. "Oh God. I hate public speaking."

"They're not the public. They're five-year-olds."

"That makes it even scarier. Five-year-olds can cut through bullshit far better and way faster than adults ever can."

Deeze laughed. "That's true enough. Do you like my finger?"

"Jesus, Deeze. I *love* your finger."

A comfortable silence settled over the two men. Hard cocks pressed to welcoming hips. Strong hands roamed lazily over accepting flesh while one exploring finger continued to send one man practically airborne in euphoria. The word "love" hovered in the air around them, unsaid because it didn't need to be.

Deeze's voice intruded on the lazy silence. "It's fading, Wy."

Wyeth lifted his head to gaze into Deeze's eyes. "What is?"

"That day," Deeze said. "It's not the first thing I see anymore when I wake up."

"What do you see?" Wyeth asked, his eyes kind.

Deeze slid a hand along Wyeth's flank and rested it to the side of his pale, freckled, upturned face. "I see you," he said softly.

Wyeth tried to joke. "That must be quite a jolt."

Deeze smiled, but there was no humor in it. Only contentment. "No. It's not a jolt at all. It's beautiful." He dipped his head and snuggled into the crook of Wyeth's neck, absorbing his heat, inhaling his scent. Never getting enough of either. "Thank you for letting me love you," Deeze whispered. "And thank you for loving me back."

Wyeth couldn't think of a thing to say. Not one thing. He lay in Deeze's arms and listened to their two hearts hammering a mellow morning song. The music was clearly meant to be a duet. Actually, since Napoleon was purring at their feet, it was a trio. Still, the melody was lovely. Both men enjoyed it thoroughly, and both men drew strength from it, just as they always did. Who knew what the hell the cat was thinking?

In the distance, Chaucer scratched impatiently at the front door. He was blithely ignored.

Wyeth burrowed deeper into the bed. His lips slid past a broad chest to a furry belly. There he also met a rope of turgid flesh that rose to meet the gust of warm breath slipping through Wyeth's lips. A drop of crystal liquid shimmered at its tip.

When Wyeth lapped the dewdrop away with the tip of his tongue, Deeze shuddered beneath him. When Deeze took him by the hips and eased him onto his stomach in the bed under a rain of kisses, Wyeth groaned in contentment and anticipation.

Seeing which way the wind was blowing, Wyeth reached for the nightstand drawer.

Chaucer would just have to wait.

DEEZE WAS unpacking a box of kitchen crap when he heard a soft rapping at the front door. Wyeth was out buying groceries, so setting a stack of plates aside, Deeze stepped to the door and yanked it open. Agnes stood there in a dirty housecoat, leaning heavily on her walker. She had a small pickle jar in her hand.

"Can you open this?" she asked, waving the jar under Deeze's nose.

Deeze laughed and twisted the lid open with no effort at all. In truth he was stunned by how much Agnes had failed in the past few weeks. The chemo was clearly killing her. She had lost weight, and she hadn't carried much extra poundage to begin with. Kindly, Deeze took her arm and led her into the apartment.

"I'm lonely," he lied. "Talk to me while I unpack boxes. I'll make you a cup of coffee."

He settled her at the kitchen table and placed a coffee cup and a scone in front of her. She sipped halfheartedly at the coffee and ignored the scone completely, plucking a gherkin from the jar instead. With rabbitlike nibbles, she gnawed on the gherkin and watched Deeze as he stacked dishes in the kitchen cupboard.

"You haven't heard," she said quietly.

Deeze stopped what he was doing and stared at her. "Heard what?"

Agnes's birdlike hand, speckled with age spots and sinewy with age, fluttered at the collar of her robe. Only then did Deeze see the sorrow in her eyes.

"What is it?" he asked. "What's happened?"

Agnes shifted her eyes to stare through the kitchen window. She heaved a great sigh and slumped a little more in the chair, listing to the left. Even sitting up seemed to be exhausting for her now.

"The boy," she said, her fingers still fiddling with the front of her robe. The coffee, the scone, and even the pickle were now clearly forgotten. A spasm of sadness crossed her age-lined face. Or was it pain? Deeze couldn't be sure. "Ramon Diaz," she said. "Just now on the news."

"The shooter?" Deeze asked. "What about him? He's in custody at juvenile detention. They're waiting to see what the judge will want to do with him while they wait for a trial."

Agnes turned from the window and studied Deeze's face. She reached out for his hand and he let her take it. Gently, she pulled him toward the table until he stood directly in front of her. She gazed up into his face with sorrowful eyes and cleared her throat. The moment she did, a spasm of discomfort tightened her lips. She shook her head, refocusing her gaze on Deeze's face. "There won't be a trial. The judge won't have to worry about what to do with him, honey."

"What do you mean?"

"He's dead," she said. "He committed suicide."

Deeze froze, staring down at the old woman.

"I'm sorry," Agnes said.

His legs grew suddenly weak. Deeze collapsed into a chair and sat staring at Agnes, his hand still trapped in hers. He was about to ask if she was sure, but he saw the truth of what she said in her eyes.

"It never stops," Deeze mumbled, turning away to stare at the wall.

Agnes tugged at his hand to get his attention. Her old eyes shimmered with tears. She gazed on him with pity. "It does though. The pain. It stops. Sometimes it just takes a while. Deeze, that boy's life was over anyway. He's away from his suffering. He's free of his guilt. He's in God's hands now, and God will take care of him. I'm sure of it."

Deeze could think of no argument to that, so he simply nodded and remained silent. Funny, but he couldn't seem to dredge up a tear. He was sorry for the kid, sorrier than he could ever have imagined. But he also knew Agnes was right. The boy's life was over the moment he started pulling the trigger back on that morning Deeze would never forget. If anyone was to blame for everything that had happened, it was the abusive father who tortured the boy, making Ramon feel he had no other way out than to do what he did. To strike out. To bring attention to himself in the only way he knew how. With his father's gun.

A glimmer of anger twisted Deeze's face. *Pity the boy didn't shoot his father instead.*

Deeze squeezed his eyes shut, forcing that thought to retreat. Enough people had been hurt. There was no point in wishing for more suffering to take place. The world was filled with enough pain already.

"I'm sorry," Agnes said again, patting Deeze's arm. Her fingers lingered there, tangled in the arm hair as if drawing comfort from it.

Abruptly dropping her hands to her lap, she stared at Deeze. "Are you all right?" she asked softly.

Deeze nodded. Businesslike. Brisk. "I'll be fine."

"Where is Wyeth? He should be here with you."

"He went to the store. He'll be right back." Deeze lifted his eyes and studied the old woman. His friend. He reached out and patted her cheek. "Don't worry," he said. "I promise. I'm fine. Life goes on, after all. Life always goes on."

"Only for some," she said. She had struggled to utter the words, and Deeze frowned at how weary she sounded. As she pushed herself feebly from the table and stood on wobbly legs, he took her arm.

"I'll walk you home," Deeze said.

A weak smile wafted briefly over Agnes's pinched face. "Thank you. Don't forget my pickles."

It was the last time Deeze would see her alive.

TWO DAYS later, Wyeth stood in the middle of their living room, admiring their new home. After a lot of wrangling as to what should go where, they had finally arranged the apartment to satisfy both their wishes. Deeze's sofa, lushly coated with cat hair, had been dumped on a street corner with a Free sign on it and had disappeared in ten minutes flat. Both beds went to the Salvation Army and were replaced with a new California king, which gave them plenty of room to roll around in. Their two desks sat side by side in the second bedroom, which now served as a den.

Wyeth jumped when Napoleon tore past, Chaucer hot on his heels. Lately the dog had begun fighting back, and Napoleon didn't like it at all.

"You started it!" he yelled at the cat. Chaucer barked in agreement as the two animals stampeded into the den.

"Help me pin this on," Deeze called out from the bedroom. "I can't get it straight."

It was the morning of the marathon Deeze had signed them up for months earlier. Deeze was dressed in bright yellow running shorts and a white tank top, newly purchased for the race. At Deeze's insistence, Wyeth wore the very same outfit.

Before Wyeth stepped forward to lend a hand, he stood at the bedroom door and admired Deeze.

"My God, you're beautiful."

Deeze had four safety pins cradled in the palm of one hand and a sheet of paper with his race number, which needed to be pinned to his chest, printed on it in the other. The handsomest smile in the world splattered across his beaming face. His wounds had healed, and little was left to mark that horrible day almost a month earlier but for a raw-looking scar still visible where the bullet had grazed his wrist. Deeze had taken to wearing his watch on that wrist, but Wyeth knew the scar would always be there, no matter how much Deeze tried to hide it. Fortunately, the other scars, the *internal* scars, were mending daily. But for occasional bouts of melancholy, Deeze was back to his usual happy self.

And Wyeth was more in love with him than ever.

They moved toward each other, stopping only inches apart, each set of eyes lost in the gaze of the other.

Wyeth reached out and trailed the back of his hand along Deeze's jawline. There was stubble there. They had awoken late, and Deeze hadn't had time to shave. Deeze's brown eyes, flecked with gold, simmered like molten lava in the morning sunlight streaming through the window.

"Remember what you told me once, Deeze? About how there is always one kid who doesn't know how to laugh. Doesn't know how to have fun. Remember?"

"I remember," Deeze said quietly, a gentle grin curving his mouth.

"I'm that kid, Deeze. I'm the kid who didn't know joy until you came along and shoved it under my nose. I'll never be able to properly thank you for that."

Deeze lifted his hand to stroke his fingertips over Wyeth's forearm. "You've already thanked me. You thank me every time I turn around and find you there beside me. You thank me every time I open my eyes in the morning and feel your warm, delicious body next to me in the bed. Don't say you never thank me, Wy. Everything you do is a thank-you." He stopped talking long enough to roll those simmering eyes over Wyeth's body.

"Wyeth Becker, you're beautiful too. It melts me every time I look at you."

No longer ashamed of his body, Wyeth stared down at himself. His pale arms and legs. The ginger hair everywhere. The freckles on his shoulders that he used to hate. Without a trace of self-mockery, he stared back at Deeze with a cocky grin, flexing his biceps. "Thanks. I've been working out."

When Deeze laughed, Wyeth snarled at him, then plucked the safety pins from his palm and carefully attached the race number to Deeze's shirt.

"Your first marathon," Deeze said proudly, watching Wyeth fiddle with the pins.

Wyeth swelled up like a bullfrog. "I'm going to beat your ass, you know. I've been practicing a lot. Just ask Chaucer. He hates my fucking guts."

Deeze snorted in what might very well have been derision. "It isn't all about speed, dipshit. It's about stamina, it's about pacing yourself. It's about trying not to make your lover look like a snail."

"My lover," Wyeth sighed. "I still like the sound of that. And don't worry. I'll try not to humiliate you too badly."

Deeze narrowed his eyes. "You're too kind."

Wyeth laid a hand to Deeze's chest, giving his race number a final pat before snatching his apartment keys off the top of the dresser. Locking the place up behind them, they headed for the elevator. At the last moment, Deeze stopped and stared back down the hall.

"What is it?" Wyeth asked. "Did you forget something?"

Deeze shook his head. His eyes were serious, his lips drawn back in a taut line, thin and bloodless. "I think we should check on Agnes. I haven't seen her for a while."

Surprised, Wyeth said, "Oh. Okay."

Side by side, they approached the old woman's door. Deeze tapped lightly at it. When no one answered and they didn't hear anyone moving around inside, he tapped a little louder.

Deeze tried the knob. To Wyeth's surprise, the door wasn't locked. Wondering if they would get their heads snapped off for walking in without an invitation, Wyeth held his breath as Deeze gently twisted the knob and stepped inside.

"Agnes?" Deeze called out. Wyeth heard nothing but soft music. She must have had her radio on.

"Oh God," he suddenly muttered, peering over Deeze's shoulder.

Agnes sat at the living room window, staring out at the city she loved to watch. It was from the same vantage point where she had witnessed a relationship blossom between the two young men who would later become her only friends. Maybe she had sat there for years, watching the world gradually slide by without her, knowing she could no longer keep up with it, knowing she was really no longer a part of the world at all.

She sat upright in her doilied chair, an untouched cup of tea, grown cold and scummed over, in front of her on the windowsill. The saucer holding the teacup had two cookies jutting over the edge. The cookies were covered with ants. A pair of binoculars lay on the floor at the old lady's feet, where they must have tumbled the moment her strength gave out. The moment death had claimed itself victor in Agnes's long-drawn-out war of life.

Wyeth shuddered at the sight of the ants. He laid his forehead to the back of Deeze's shirt so he wouldn't have to look.

Deeze's eyes were centered on the silent woman sitting in her favorite chair. "Agnes?" he said again, but Wyeth heard the resignation in his voice. Deeze knew. They both knew.

Agnes Mulroney—the irascible neighbor down the hall who in the end had turned out to be one of the most amazing women either man had ever met—was no longer listening.

CHAPTER FIFTEEN

DEEZE AND Wyeth stood over the casket, staring down at a stranger. Agnes was coifed and lipsticked and rouged until she was barely recognizable. No peach pits in her pockets. No hankies up her sleeve. The fact that her mouth was sewn shut and she wasn't railing about one thing or another or gossiping about anyone, made her seem even less familiar. At the foot of the casket stood a tall spray of roses and carnations. On the card, if one cared to read it, could be found two names. Deeze and Wyeth. All the other flowers present were supplied by the funeral home. Those bouquets held no cards at all. They were simply for show. Like stage props. In fact, they weren't even real. They were plastic.

Wyeth thought those artificial flowers were the saddest things he had ever seen in his life.

Deeze spotted the sadness on his lover's face and leaned in close. "Don't be glum about the race. I'll sign us up for another marathon, since we missed the last one. You can outrun me then. Okay?"

Wyeth pulled a handkerchief from his trouser pocket and blew his nose. "It isn't that. I'm just sorry is all. Sorry about Agnes, I mean."

Deeze stroked his cheek. "I know. So am I. But death isn't always a bad thing, Wy. It ended the woman's suffering, at least. That's a good thing, isn't it?"

Wyeth shrugged. "I suppose."

"You old softy," Deeze murmured, eyeing him fondly.

Deeze turned back to stare down at the body in the casket. His mind attempted to carry his thoughts to other recent deaths, to other recent losses, but he ground his teeth and refused to go there. Despite his best efforts, a screenshot of Father Mike wormed its way into his mind: the good man lying motionless in the grass, his empty eyes staring upward, unblinking, into the pelting rain. Blindly reaching out for Wyeth's hand, Deeze held on tight until the image faded. As if sensing Deeze's need for him, Wyeth sidled closer until their shoulders brushed. Deeze felt better immediately.

Agnes's funeral was scheduled for later in the day. Deeze and Wyatt, wearing their best suits, had attended viewing hours both this morning and the night before. In all that time, they were the only two mourners in attendance. No one else had shown up, even for the coffee and free cookies in the lounge in the back.

Agnes, it seemed, was as friendless in death as she had been in life. Not that Deeze was surprised. She had pissed off everybody she ever met, occasionally not excluding him and Wyeth, during her long decades of presiding over the planet with an acid wit and a conniving eye.

Still, it seemed mean-spirited for the world to ignore her death completely.

Mitchell's Mortuary was situated downtown, six blocks from their apartment building. Deeze turned his back on the corpse and stared around at the empty chairs, neatly aligned in endlessly vacant rows, all the while trying to ignore the piped-in hymns, which after two days were beginning to grate on his nerves. He would have preferred a little ABBA to lighten the mood.

Deeze jumped when a hand landed on his shoulder. He spun around to find the funeral director standing there. The man was so pale he looked like he had been spawned in a cave and periodically dipped in bleach. Everything about him was washed out. Skin, hair, eyes, demeanor.

"May I have a word?" the mortician asked, eyeing first Wyeth, then Deeze, and finally the dead woman in the casket as if, since it concerned her as well, he might as well include her in the conversation.

"Certainly," Deeze said. "What's up?"

The mortician cleared his throat, clearly embarrassed, then waved his hand toward the rows of vacant seats. "Aside from you two," he said, "as far as I know, only one other attendee plans to grace us with their presence at the funeral service."

Deeze perked up at that. "Well, good. At least that's one more. Who is it?"

The funeral guy had clearly lost the ability to smile long ago. It was like his lips had been slathered from a bucket of Deeze's school paste and set on a windowsill to dry. They were unbending. "The organist," he said. "And she works for me." He cleared his throat again but didn't say anything, as if the meaning should be crystal clear. Which of course it wasn't.

"What are you trying to say?" Wyeth asked.

The mortician gave a tiny jump, as if the question surprised him. "Pall bearers, of course. We need six. Even including myself, we only have three."

"What about the organist?"

"She's older than the corpse. Plus she'll be playing the organ. That's why we call her the organist." Unbending lips or not, apparently the funeral director could be sarcastic when the need arose.

"Oh," Deeze said.

He studied his shoe tops for a minute, then a grin crept across his face. He reached across and took a fistful of Wyeth's necktie, dragging him closer. "My friend and I will take care of it."

Wyeth's eyebrows rose. "We will?"

Deeze said, "We will," and shot him a wink.

While Wyeth stood there looking totally confused, the mortician, for some odd reason, decided to take Deeze at his word.

"Well, good then," he announced grandly. "I won't worry." And with that, he flicked an imaginary speck of dust off the edge of Agnes's casket and sauntered off to drain another corpse, or whatever it is morticians do when they have a little downtime.

Wyeth turned to Deeze. "Huh? What just happened? What did you just promise we would do?"

Deeze grinned. "We just committed ourselves to acquiring a few pall bearers for the service. No reason we shouldn't try filling a few seats while we're at it." With a maniacal glint in his eye, he rubbed his hands together. "Best get cracking. The funeral begins in two hours. Agnes is counting on us."

"Agnes is dead."

"Yes, well, maybe she's counting on us in spirit, Wy. Ever think of that? We wouldn't want to let her down, now would we?"

Wyeth opened his mouth, closed it, and then shook his head. "No, love of my life, I guess we wouldn't. So what do you have in mind?"

Deeze first patted his heart in response to the "love of my life" remark, then started dragging Wyeth through the funeral home doors and out onto the street. Once there, Deeze cornered him with his back to a palm tree and shared his plan.

When he finished, Wyeth said, "You're kidding."

"No, I'm not."

"Even for you, this is harebrained."

"No, it isn't."

"It won't work."

"Yes, it will."

Chewing on his cheek, Wyeth checked his watch and heaved a great sigh. When the sigh ran out of air like a leaky tire finally gone unquestionably flat, he looked at Deeze, pushed his glasses up his nose in a resigned manner, and said, "Best get started then, I guess."

Deeze chucked him on the arm. "Good man."

Pausing long enough to share a kiss, they headed off at a robust clip in separate directions.

Things to do. People to see.

WYETH STORMED through the front doors of the San Diego Public Library like he owned the place. Thank God it was a work day, and while Wyeth had taken the day off to attend poor Agnes's funeral, none of his homeless friends had.

He stopped by his locker in the employees' lounge to fill his pockets from the three boxes of energy bars he kept stored there for his lunchtime snacks. Thusly armed and loaded for bear, he set off in search of the library's merry band of homeless, aromatic readers. Luckily it was starting to look like rain outside, so they were scattered all over the library in abundance, ensconced for the day, as it were, with a good book, a nice cushy chair cradling their nasty, unwashed asses.

Wyeth found Crazy Bill first. He was sitting with an unlit half-smoked Pall Mall Light stuck over his right ear for safe storage while he scratched his armpit and skimmed through the pages of the *Wall Street Journal*. Apparently Crazy Bill was troubled by the viability of his portfolio. Not to mention fleas. Itty Bitty Bob sat at his side scanning the most recent copy of *Highlights*. It was the Halloween issue. He appeared to be testing himself by finding all the jack-o'-lanterns in a picture puzzle designed for six-year-olds. Bob was having trouble finding the last two "punkins."

Bill listened to Wyeth explain the circumstances, all the while eyeing the energy bar Wy was using for bait. Any fool in the world could have seen the man might have been bought and sold for far less than an energy bar, but since an energy bar was what was being offered, an energy bar was what he took. The same could be said for Itty Bitty Bob. He liked energy bars too.

For a *second* energy bar, which for any homeless person in the world was the gastronomical equivalent of striking the mother lode, Bill and Bob were easily coerced into the role of recruiting surrogates, and set off on their own search for more homeless to entice. And entice them they did. Big Lola. Frankie the Fridge. Betty Boop. Eleanor Roosevelt (no relation to the original). Stanley G. Peckerhead. Cheesy Chuck. And a score of others.

Between Wyeth, Crazy Bill, and Itty Bitty Bob, they emptied the public library of derelicts in no time, filling the street front outside with a motley collection of humanity, male, female, some an odd mixture of both or neither, and each and every one of them nibbling an energy bar while they milled around fouling the air and awaiting further instructions.

With Crazy Bill at his side, Wyeth gazed upon this horde of down-on-their-luck miscreants and thought, *Who says the work ethic is dead?* Plucking the final energy bar from his suitcoat pocket, he tore the wrapper away and joined his friends in a midmorning snack. While he ate, he did a quick head count and came up with thirty-two souls. A decent enough turnout for *anybody's* funeral.

Clapping his hands to get their attention, he stood on the street corner under a glowering sky that threatened rain at any second and explained the situation. He watched proudly as his audience began to get the picture, straightening the rags on their backs, trying to make themselves a little more presentable. An unfamiliar look of purpose lit the occasional tired, rheumy eye. A smile here and there displayed neglected teeth and offered a peek at an occasional wad of half-chewed Clif bar.

"Does everybody understand what we're doing?" Wyeth finished up after rambling on for three minutes, trying to get his point across.

"We figured it out two and a half minutes ago," Crazy Bill informed him, beginning to look bored. He was leaning with his arm atop Itty Bitty Bob's head like Bob was a newel post, but Bob didn't seem to mind.

Wyeth knew his limitations as far as public speaking went, so before he lost them completely, he raised his hand high like a trail boss preparing to move the herd. "Let's do it then!" he bellowed in his most commanding voice, and together, the whole crowd headed off up the street in Wyeth's wake, congenial, stinking to high heaven, chattering back and forth like magpies, and having the time of their lives.

What might be noted, although Wyeth didn't realize it, is that each and every one of his homeless friends were aware of the lounge area in the back of Mitchell's Mortuary where a generous spread of free cookies and an urn of hot coffee were offered up to visiting mourners. In fact, several of the homeless in Wyeth's little parade visited the funeral home almost as often as they visited the library. There might not be much to read at Mitchell's Mortuary but religious tracts and obituary print-outs, but the free cookies made up for it.

Crisply attired in his best black suit with his favorite power tie knotted neatly at his throat and his spit-shined Thom McAns glittering on his feet, Wyeth led this ragtag group of discarded humanity like a Pied Piper, clearing the city of unfortunates. To say that innocent pedestrians scattered when they saw them coming would be dabbling in reckless understatement. They positively *flew*.

WHILE WYETH emptied the library of the city's homeless, Deeze had not been idle either. He rounded up Laurie at the Tan Banana along with three of her clientele—two as pale as fish bellies who hadn't been spray painted yet, and one pudgy gentleman with an extremely small head who *had* been sprayed and who was now complaining that he'd turned out orange, which indeed he had. From the neck up he looked like a tangerine with ears.

Sending Laurie and her three customers on ahead, Deeze set off for the apartment building, where he started knocking on doors.

It was a workday after all, so it was amazing Deeze gathered together as many people as he did, or that he could find ones who could actually be made to feel guilty about not attending a lonely old woman's funeral. It was especially surprising since most of those he coerced into going were happy as clams to learn Agnes was at long last dead and made few bones about letting Deeze know it. In fact, Deeze suspected that some of those he convinced to attend were simply going to make sure the woman was truly deceased and out of their hair forever.

When his rounds were complete and Deeze had knocked on every single door, he ended up with three Mexican maids, a pest control technician with a spray tank of bug killer on his back, a babysitter with a screaming two-year-old in her arms, a couple of old men who looked like they would be laid out at the funeral home soon enough themselves, and a young woman and a man who, by the shimmer of nervous sweat on the man's brow and the hastily rearranged state of his attire, Deeze suspected wasn't the good woman's husband at all but had simply stopped by for a little hanky-panky while the real hubby was at the office. This impression was amplified when the woman actually forgot the man's name during introductions. Why those two chose to follow Deeze to the funeral home was anybody's guess. Maybe to assuage their own guilt. Or maybe after the illicit expenditure of body fluids, they were craving cookies too.

At any rate, by emptying the Tan Banana and the apartment building, and by grabbing at the last minute a couple of innocent bystanders off the street who didn't look like they had anything better to do, Deeze ended up with a respectable following.

DEEZE'S MOB and Wyeth's mob marched into the funeral home at precisely the same time, each group suspiciously eyeing the other. Wyeth half expected to see Agnes sit up in the casket and gawk when they entered. And while the mortician had probably seen it all in his many years of burying strangers, or thought he had, he most certainly had seen nothing like this. A couple of minutes later he was wandering up and down the aisle with a spray can of Glade, leaving a trail of evergreen-scented fog behind, trying to alleviate the reek of thirty-two homeless people and one dirty diaper, since the baby had taken the opportunity to fill the one he was wearing and the baby sitter had forgotten to bring an extra Pamper along for the ride.

The undertaker also kept an extra wary eye on the guy with the tank of bug spray on his back, all the while wondering what the hell *that* was all about. The *normal* people in attendance, of which there were actually very few, fidgeted about the room trying to decide what stroke of madness had led them there to begin with, half of them choking on the Glade and the other half, women mostly, peeking into the casket to see what Agnes was wearing. The *less* than normal audience members headed straight to the lounge in the back to fill their pockets with cookies, their priorities unclouded.

A few minutes later, over the rustle of settling bodies and the surreptitious crunch of countless Oreos and ginger snaps, the organist, looking a little shell-shocked by the odd assortment of humanity present, struck the opening chords of "In the Garden" and the crowd began to quiet down. While everyone claimed a seat, the normal people squirmed as far away from the homeless folks as they could get, and even the bug man considered letting loose with a barrage of bug killer if any stinky people came too close. Eventually a grudging truce was ironed out and the service at last began.

Before the opening hymn ended, Wyeth glanced over and spotted Crazy Bill and Itty Bitty Bob sitting side by side in the second row. Each man had a cookie sticking out of his mouth. Hands free, the cookies gradually shortened as they were quietly and tidily sucked inside and gnawed to oblivion. Before he could stop himself, Wyeth was trembling with mirth. When Wyeth indicated to Deeze what he was so amused about, Deeze started giggling and couldn't stop either. Before long they were both gasping and snorfling and trying not to pee their pants. When the pale mortician cast them an admonishing glare, they laughed all the harder.

"If Agnes was alive she'd kill us," Deeze sputtered under his breath.

Happy tears rolled down Wyeth's face. "At least she's got an audience for her big send-off."

Deeze wheezed in silent laughter. "They're only here for the cookies. We'll go to hell for this. I know we will."

"Worth it!" Wyeth snorted back, pulling a Fig Newton from his shirt pocket, then offering Deeze one as well.

"Thank you kindly," Deeze said, stuffing it in his mouth.

Twenty minutes later, after a minister no one had ever seen before gave a glowing eulogy to a woman he clearly had never met in his life or he wouldn't be offering such effusive praise, a motley collection of faux mourners dutifully filed past Agnes's casket to say their final goodbyes to a woman most of them never knew any better than the preacher did.

Wyeth and Deeze brought up the tail end of the procession. Deeze's face was properly serious now. He was all laughed out. He stood at the casket and laid his hand on Agnes's forehead, gently caressing her cold skin.

Wyeth was so touched by Deeze's gesture, he bit back a sob. He only smiled when Deeze pulled the day's newspaper from beneath his jacket and tucked it neatly under Agnes's folded arms. Atop the paper he placed a yellow pencil, Ticonderoga #2, purloined from his stack of school supplies back at the apartment.

Deeze bent low and whispered in the dead woman's ear. "Here's today's puzzle, Agnes. Just so you know, forty-two across is a bitch."

After Wyeth muttered his own goodbyes to the corpse, he and Deeze remained standing alongside the casket. Crazy Bill and three of his cohorts stepped forward to join them as previously arranged. They stood nervously fidgeting while the mortician closed the lid on Agnes's coffin, sealing her inside forever.

Directing the pall bearers to position themselves three to a side, the undertaker pointed to a door at the back of the hall. "Let's carry her to the hearse, gentlemen. This way if you please."

And so it was that Agnes Mulroney left the city she had spent every day of her life in. She left it cradled in the arms of two friends and four strangers.

Neither Deeze nor Wyeth noticed the gentleman in the herringbone suit standing on the steps outside the funeral home. They were too busy staring at the procession of sleek black mortuary limousines lined up at the curb waiting to carry the mourners to the graveside ceremony.

It seemed Agnes Mulroney had thoroughly planned this day in advance, leaving nothing to chance. She fully intended to be carted to her final resting place in style. Entourage and all.

AT HOLY Cross Cemetery, five miles out of the city, Deeze and Wyeth and all the other "mourners" traipsed up a hill in drizzling rain and gusting wind to Agnes's final resting spot, where a large tent had been erected. The funeral home supplied black umbrellas to everyone. And judging by the effusion of thanks the undertaker received from the homeless in attendance, who seemed to think the umbrellas were some sort of door prize, he was pretty sure most of those umbrellas would never be returned.

While the tent flapped over their heads in the rising storm and the preacher once again started blathering on about a total stranger and how happy God would be to see her arriving humbly at the Golden Gates, as if Agnes had ever arrived anywhere humbly in her life, Deeze and Wyeth were surprised to feel themselves being tugged into a corner, away from the benediction, by a pair of strong, well-manicured hands.

Once away from the crowd, they had no choice but to lay eyes on the man who dragged them there. The man in the herringbone suit.

He was perhaps fifty years old, exquisitely maintained, with a neat head of snow-white hair and a necktie Wyeth had seen at Macy's selling for $125. He carried a Gucci attaché case in one hand and a mortuary umbrella in the other. There was a diamond on his hand big enough to trip over if it ever slipped off his finger.

"Wyeth Becker and Darryl Long, I presume," the gentleman said with an ingratiating smile.

Deeze eyed the guy up and down. "If you're a cop, we didn't kill her, I swear. It was a natural death. Ask anybody."

Wyeth snickered at Deeze's dry humor while the man in the herringbone suit merely smiled regally. At that moment, the man's umbrella accidentally popped open with a *whoosh* and all three of them jumped in surprise. After that, they seemed to regard themselves as friends.

"My name is Lawrence Waverly. I'm Mrs. Mulroney's lawyer," he said. Stuffing the recalcitrant umbrella under his arm to keep it from flying open again, he stuck out a hand, first to Deeze, then to Wyeth. Both men obediently offered a handshake back, and their friendship was sealed.

Still, Wyeth appeared more surprised than Deeze at this sudden turn of events. "So. Agnes had a lawyer, huh?"

Again came that mellow, lawyerly smile. "She had several, in fact," he said merrily. "Mrs. Mulroney was quite the businesswoman."

This caught Deeze off guard. "She was?" All he could think of was her spitting peach pits and orange seeds into her housecoat pocket. "Are you sure?"

"Undoubtedly," the lawyer exclaimed as if his word were his bond and everyone damn well knew it. "I'm here because she left a few things in her will to various heirs. And by various, I mean you two."

"Us two?" Wyeth echoed rather brainlessly. He even knew he sounded brainless, although he didn't much care.

"Yes," Mr. Waverly said. "Her boys. That's what she called you. You two are the sole heirs to her estate."

Deeze blinked in vaudevillian amazement. "There's an estate?" He tried to snort back a laugh but didn't succeed very well. "What did she leave us? Her floppy slippers? Her collection of foam rubber hair rollers? I hate to be the one to tell you, but she didn't own anything. She couldn't even afford a newspaper."

"Yes, she mentioned that. You boys were generous enough to see that she received home delivery of the *San Diego Union-Tribune* so she could work her crossword puzzles on a regular basis which meant the world to her. Very fussy about her crossword puzzles was Mrs. Mulroney."

"Fussy about a lot of other stuff too," Deeze slipped into the conversation under his breath.

To which the lawyer appeared to agree. "Yes, indeed. A truly trying woman." He looked like he meant it. "Nevertheless, it was a very kind thing you did for her. She appreciated it deeply."

Deeze shook his head. "Actually we did it so she wouldn't steal everybody else's paper off their front step. She was so brazen about it the apartment building was on the verge of throwing her out on her ear."

Mr. Waverly offered up a doubting grimace in response. "I hardly think Mrs. Mulroney would need to steal newspapers from a newspaper company she owned fifty percent of the stock in. Nor would she be evicted from an apartment building she owned outright. Lock, stock, and barrel. Why do you think you received such a reduced price on the new two-bedroom apartment you recently leased?"

Deeze and Wyeth both looked like they'd just stepped into an electric fence. Numbed from the neck down. "I thought we got lucky," Wyeth stammered, while Deeze blankly nodded in agreement.

"And so you did," Mr. Waverly said. "And now you're about to get a whole lot luckier."

Wyeth and Deeze stood silently staring at each other. They were vaguely surprised to find themselves holding hands. Neither could quite remember when that happened, although the lawyer didn't seem to mind.

The graveside ceremony taking place behind them was all but forgotten. The drumming of raindrops on the canvas roof seemed to seal the two young men inside their own little bubble of astonishment while they stared at the really elegant lawyer with the really good suit and the really expensive tie and wondered just what the hell was really going on.

A sizzle of lightning shot across the sky, making them jump again. This time all three giggled nervously.

Giving himself a reality-inducing shake, Deeze inhaled a great gulp of ozone and asked the question he had been aching to ask for the last several minutes.

"So, Mr. Waverly. What exactly did she leave us, then?"

Mr. Waverly tucked the umbrella between his legs to get it out of the way and started digging through his attaché case. A moment later he plucked out a sheaf of legal papers. Extracting the first sheet from the bunch, Mr. Waverly dangled it in midair by his thumb and forefinger, inviting them to see for themselves.

"There you go, gentlemen. Agnes Mulroney specifically stipulated that everything she owned be divided equally between the two of you. It's all yours now, the entire Mulroney estate, minus a few percentage points going to me for my many years of loyal legal counsel and conscientious fiduciary guidance." With that, he had the good grace to blush.

Deeze and Wyeth leaned forward, perusing the paper. Clearly confused by what they were trying to read, their foreheads creased in unison.

"It's legal gobbledygook," Deeze said.

"No," Wyeth replied. "I think I'd recognize gobbledygook. This looks more like Martian."

Mr. Waverly sighed and brought a perfectly manicured index finger around to point to a number at the bottom of the page. It was a very large number with a freight train of zeros chugging along behind it.

"But, but, but…," Deeze stammered, still counting zeros.

"Holy cow!" Wyeth barked. "Look at all those fucking—" Before he could finish, his eyes rolled up into his head like Venetian blinds, and as stiff as a board, he keeled over backward and landed in the mud with a *splat*. Deeze and Mr. Waverly stared down at him in amazement.

"He's a little excitable," Deeze calmly said.

"So I see," Mr. Waverly blandly answered. "He'll never get that suit clean, you know."

Every tooth in Deeze's head appeared. If his smile had been any broader, the top of his head would have slid off. "I guess now he can buy a new one."

Mr. Waverly smiled right back. "Indeed he can."

While Wyeth snored peacefully in the mud and the preacher still rambled on from the other side of the tent, giving Agnes the longest send-off in history and boring his audience senseless, Deeze was shocked to see the lawyer step forward and pull him into an embrace.

The older man whispered in Deeze's ear, "Thank you for what you did, son."

Deeze tried to wiggle free, not only embarrassed, but wondering if the guy had slipped a cog. "I don't know what you mean, sir."

The lawyer gripped Deeze's shoulders and stared deep in his eyes. "My granddaughter is one of your students, Mr. Long. She was there that day in your classroom. She told us how you threw yourself on top of everyone to protect them from the bullets. Mrs. Mulroney knew about it too."

A flash of pain crossed Deeze's face. He hated being reminded of that day. Since the shooting, he had grown adept at disguising those searing flashes of memory when they came at him out of left field. Or like now, when they were flung in his face. For reasons of self-preservation, he buried the hurt behind a weary smile. "I-I never knew Agnes had a connection to any of my students. She never said."

"No, I don't suppose she did," Mr. Waverly sighed. "Still, she knew. She knew, and she appreciated all you did that day. As do I. As do a great many people. More than you will ever know, I expect."

Deeze stood silent, staring back at the man, his gaze hooded.

Sensing Deeze's discomfort, Mr. Waverly plucked a business card from his jacket pocket and slipped it into Deeze's hand. "But back to business," he said, clearing the emotion from his throat. "Come to my office tomorrow, son, and bring your unconscious friend along with you."

"I have to work tomorrow," Deeze said, rather dreamily, once again pondering all those zeros.

"Then come after work. I'll wait."

Deeze glanced down at Wyeth still snoozing in the mud. "And he's not my friend, Mr. Waverly. He's my lover."

Mr. Waverly gave him a congenial pat on the shoulder. When he studied Deeze's face, his eyes were kind. "I know that, son. I know. So will you come?"

"Yes, sir," Deeze said. "We'll be there." He inhaled a great gulp of air as if he was suddenly short of oxygen. Then he remembered his manners. "Thank you for everything. By the way, which student is your granddaughter?"

Mr. Waverly smiled. It was the first smile he had offered Deeze that contained true heart. It was a grandfather's smile, not a lawyer's. "Mary Lou," he said. "Mary Lou Jones."

Deeze nodded. "The one who never stops giggling."

"Yes," Mr. Waverly said with a flash of pride. "The one who never stops giggling."

Catching a blur of movement down around their feet, both men gazed at the ground to see Wyeth staring up at them from the mud. He looked remarkably confused.

"What the hell am I doing down here?" Wyeth asked, blinking himself awake.

"Ruining your suit," Deeze said.

Wyeth's eyes brightened as the memories flooded in. The last few minutes. The lawyer. The legal forms. The zeros.

From the other side of the tent, the preacher announced, "Amen!" and Agnes's send-off was complete—to the immense gratitude of everyone present. Sighs of relief filled the air. Cookies appeared from a dozen different pockets.

Wyeth rose from the mud, stood there dripping for a minute, then threw himself into Deeze's arms while the elegant lawyer looked patiently on.

Overhead, tears of either laughter or grief rained down from the sky. Later in the day, after thinking about it for a while, Deeze decided they were tears of laughter. After all, Wyeth *had* looked remarkably silly lying there in the mud.

EPILOGUE

"No WONDER we got this apartment so cheap."

"Yes, Wy, but you're missing the big picture. It won't be cheap anymore."

"It won't?"

"No. It'll be free. We own the building. That's assuming we deign to live here at all."

"Deign? Did you say deign?"

"I'm rich now. I can say snooty things like that."

"Oh yeah." A silent moment passed. "Deeze?"

"Hmm?"

"Does that mean I can say snooty things too?"

"You most certainly can. You're just as rich as I am."

"Then stop talking and kindly resume fucking. You've been inside me for the past three minutes and your dick hasn't moved except for an occasional twitch. Don't get me wrong. It feels great. But I'm about to come without you."

Deeze giggled and stuck his tongue in Wyeth's ear. "All right, my pet. If you insist. Let me share my end of the weary load. And when I say load…."

"Just shut up and do it."

"Ooh, so romantic."

On that note, Deeze took his long cock out of Park and got it moving again. Sliding deep. Sliding hard. Sounding Wyeth's luscious heated depths. He was rewarded by Wyeth shivering in ecstasy beneath him.

"Oh God," Wyeth gasped. "That's perfect." A heartbeat later, he said, "Oh no."

"Now what?"

"I'm going to come anyway."

"Well, some people are just *never* satisfied."

As if belying his own last statement, Deeze slipped his hand under Wyeth's trembling body and gave the lad's dick a gentle stroke. Before he could stroke it a second time, Wyeth cried out and filled Deeze's fist with steaming gouts of come.

Spurred on by Wyeth's spasms beneath him, Deeze thrust his hips forward and, buried as deep as he could get, exploded in his own orgasmic eruption. Both men clung to each other as they shuddered and gasped and drained themselves dry. While their hearts were still pounding like crazy, Wyeth craned his neck around to cover Deeze's mouth with his own. In the middle of the kiss, Wyeth's body started writhing in bliss all over again when Deeze inched his still erect cock a millimeter deeper.

"You like that," Deeze cooed.

"Oh God, yes," Wyeth murmured back.

Slowly, but not *too* slowly, it all quieted. Voices, breathing, heartbeats, lust. Deeze softened and slipped free of Wyeth's warm sheath, creating just enough friction to make them both happily convulse one last time.

Wyeth quickly turned and buried his face in Deeze's chest while Deeze gathered him close, cradling him in his arms.

It was two hours after the funeral. Rain still pounded the bedroom window. San Diego hadn't seen a rainstorm like this in months. Who knew Mother Nature would be so devastated by Agnes's demise that a biblical deluge would be sent to herald the woman's exit.

Among the sounds of rainwater sluicing through the gutters outside and the distant rumblings of receding storm clouds, Deeze's warm breath flowed over Wyeth's skin as he uttered lazy words. "That was the strangest, smelliest funeral I've ever attended. Usually it's the corpse that stinks, not the mourners. Agnes would have found all sorts of fault with it."

Wyeth snorted a tiny laugh. "Since it was *her own funeral*, I'm sure she would."

"If it weren't for the cookies, it would have been a complete flop."

"Crazy Bill and Itty Bitty Bob would probably agree. They're lovers, you know."

Deeze emitted a tortured moan. "Sweet Jesus, why do you tell me these things?"

Wyeth snickered.

Silence gradually reclaimed them as they lay listening to the rain. Heartbeats thudded in soft unison. Gentle fingers stroked well-traveled stretches of oh so familiar skin.

"No one knew she owned the building," Wyeth pondered, snuggling closer, his voice still fragile after his explosively exhausting orgasm and the fact that he had never been more comfortable in his life. "Not to mention half the Union-Tribune Publishing Company and God knows where else the woman had dipped her oar. How could that be? How could we not have known how rich she was?"

Deeze gave a contented grunt. He was comfortable too. "No one knew much of *anything* about her."

Wyeth tilted his head up to study Deeze's eyes. "You liked her though. Don't try to deny it. You liked her from the very beginning. Even when you thought she was poor."

Deeze stared back, his gaze softened by the nearness of the man he loved more than anyone else in the world. The man he would do anything for. He squeezed his eyes shut, sending a silent prayer skyward, thanking the unknown entities in charge of such things for the simple and astonishing fact that Wyeth loved him back.

In the silence of Deeze's prayer, Wyeth pressed his lips to the stubble already blossoming on Deeze's cheek. Only then did Deeze offer an answer.

"I did like her," he muttered softly. "She was one of a kind. And she was brave. She fought her battle with cancer on her own terms and never once complained about it. Well, not to me anyway." His mouth puckered into a mischievous grin. "Lord knows what hell she put her doctors through."

"I'm sorry she's gone," Wyeth said.

Deeze's arms tightened around him. "So am I, baby. So am I."

A moment of silence settled over them, then Wyeth rose up onto one elbow, lifting himself higher to get a panoramic view of Deeze's perfect face. A shimmer of light sparked in his eyes, a precursor to tears.

"I never knew living could be like this, Deeze. I never knew I could be this happy."

Deeze trailed a fingertip over Wyeth's moist lips. They were red and swollen from kissing his bristly face. "This happy or this rich," he whispered back.

Wyeth grinned. "Yeah. That too." He leaned into Deeze's touch, brushed his lips over Deeze's smile. "It's a rollercoaster, isn't it? Life, I mean. One minute you're up, the next minute you're down. Then you do it all over again."

"Laugh, cry, repeat," Deeze murmured. As always, with Wyeth in his arms, his voice was a contented purr.

Wyeth lowered himself back down to the bed and laid his cheek to Deeze's chest at the spot where he could best hear Deeze's heart pumping life beneath him.

As the rain pummeled the windows and Chaucer and Napoleon played quietly in the corner—friends at last, at least for the moment—Deeze and Wyeth cuddled their way to stillness.

"Sleep, baby," Wyeth gently coaxed, brushing his fingers through Deeze's curly hair.

Deeze gave a short happy sigh and closed his eyes. When sleep did find him, it was dreamless and sweet. Wyeth watched him until his own eyes closed.

When they awoke hours later, they made love. Just as they always did.

And with a little luck, just as they always *would*.

JOHN INMAN has been writing fiction since he was old enough to hold a pencil. He and his partner live in beautiful San Diego, California. Together, they share a passion for theater, books, hiking and biking along the trails and canyons of San Diego or, if the mood strikes, simply kicking back with a beer and a movie. John's advice for anyone who wishes to be a writer? "Set time aside to write every day and do it. Don't be afraid to share what you've written. Feedback is important. When a rejection slip comes in, just tear it up and try again. Keep mailing stuff out. Keep writing and rewriting and then rewrite one more time. Every minute of the struggle is worth it in the end, so don't give up. Ever. Remember that publishers are a lot like lovers. Sometimes you have to look a long time to find the one that's right for you."

You can contact John at john492@att.net, on Facebook: www.facebook.com/john.inman.79, or on his website: www.johninmanauthor.com

ACTING
JOHN INMAN
UP

It's not easy breaking into show biz. Especially when you aren't exactly loaded with talent. But Malcolm Fox won't let a little thing like that hold him back.

Actually, it isn't the show-business part of his life that bothers him as much as the romantic part—or the lack thereof. At twenty-six, Malcolm has never been in love. He lives in San Diego with his roommate, Beth, another struggling actor, and each of them is just as unsuccessful as the other. While Malcolm toddles off to this audition and that, he ponders the lack of excitement in his life. The lack of purpose. The lack of a man.

Then Beth's brother moves in.

Freshly imported from Missouri of all places, Cory Williams is a towering hunk of muscles and innocence, and Malcolm is gobsmacked by the sexiness of his new roomie from the start. When infatuation enters the picture, Malcolm knows he's *really* in trouble. After all, Cory is *straight*!

At least, that's the general consensus.

www.dreamspinnerpress.com

THE HIKE

JOHN INMAN

Ashley James and Tucker Lee have been friends for years. They are city boys but long for life on the open trail. During a three-hundred-mile hike from the Southern California desert to the mountains around Big Bear Lake, they make some pretty amazing discoveries.

One of those discoveries is love. A love that has been bubbling below the surface for a very long time.

But love isn't all they find. They also stumble upon a war—a war being waged by Mother Nature and fought tooth and claw around an epidemic of microbes and fury.

With every creature in sight turning against them, can they survive this battle and still hold on to each other? Or will the most horrifying virus known to man lay waste to more than just wildlife this time?

Will it destroy Ash and Tucker too?

www.dreamspinnerpress.com

Love

WANTED

JOHN INMAN

When it rains, it pours. Not only has Larry Walls been evicted from his apartment, but his hours have also been cut at the department store where he works, leaving him facing homelessness.

Meanwhile, Bo Lansing, a total stranger to Larry, toils at a dead-end job as a fry cook while attending night classes to become a certified chef. When the school closes its doors without warning, leaving Bo in the lurch for thousands of dollars in tuition, his dream of becoming a chef is shattered and his financial troubles spiral.

Desperate for a new beginning, each man answers an ad for live-in help posted by a wealthy recluse, and wonder of wonders, they are both hired! Just as their lives begin to improve, a young Kumeyaay Indian named Jimmy Blackstone joins the workforce at the Stanhope mansion.

When Mr. Stanhope's true reason for hiring the young men is discovered by one of the three, a fourth entity makes its presence known.

Greed.

With all these players vying for position in a game of intrigue orchestrated by one lonely old man and a mischievous ghost, can a simple thing like love ever hope to survive the fray?

www.dreamspinnerpress.com

MY BUSBOY

JOHN INMAN

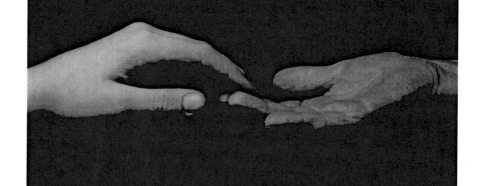

Robert Johnny just turned thirty, and his life is pretty much in the toilet. His writing career is on the skids. His love life is nonexistent. A stalker is driving him crazy. And his cat is a pain in the ass.

Then Robert orders a chimichanga platter at a neighborhood restaurant, and his life changes—just like that.

Dario Martinez isn't having such a great existence either. He needs money for college. His shoes are falling apart. His boyfriend's a dick. And he has a crap job as a busboy.

Then a stranger orders a chimichanga platter, and suddenly life isn't quite as depressing.

But it's the book in the busboy's back pocket that really gets the ball rolling. For both our heroes. That and the black eye and the forgotten bowl of guacamole. Who knew true love could be so easily ignited or that the flames would spread so quickly?

But when Robert's stalker gets dangerous, our two heroes find a lot more to occupy their time than falling in love. Staying alive might become the new game plan.

www.dreamspinnerpress.com

MY DRAGON, MY KNIGHT
John Inman

Danny Sims is in over his head, torn between his abusive lover, Joshua, and Jay Holtsclaw, the bartender up the street, who offers Danny the one thing he never gets at home: understanding.

When Joshua threatens to get rid of Danny's terrier, Danny knows he has to act fast. Afraid of what Joshua will do to the dog and afraid of what Joshua will do to *him* if he tries to leave, Danny does the only thing he can do.

He runs.

But Danny isn't a complete fool. He has enough sense to run into the arms of the man who actually cares for him—the man he's beginning to trust.

Just as their lives together are starting to fall into place, Danny and Jay learn how vengeful Joshua can be.

And how dangerous.

www.dreamspinnerpress.com

JOHN INMAN

TWO
PET
DICKS

Old friends and business partners, Maitland Carter and Lenny Fritz, may not be the two sharpest pickle forks in the picnic basket, but they have big hearts. And they are just now coming around to the fact that maybe their hearts are caught in a bit of turmoil.

Diving headfirst into a whirlwind of animal mayhem, these two self-proclaimed pet detectives strive to earn a living, reunite a few poor lost creatures with their lonely owners, and hopefully not make complete twits of themselves in the process.

When they stumble onto a confusing crime involving venomous reptiles, which is rather unnerving since they're more accustomed to dealing with misplaced puppy dogs and puddy tats, they take the plunge into becoming real-life crime stoppers.

While they're plunging into that, they're also plunging into love. They just haven't admitted it to each other yet.

www.dreamspinnerpress.com